praise for **CRIMSON ORGY** by Austin Williams

"An authentically seedy, almost charming tale of zero-budget horror moviemaking morphs cleverly into a genuine splatterfest in Williams' unnervingly enjoyable debut...wholly convincing, escalating crises and all...horror film buffs should be delighted and chilled in equal measure."
—*Publishers Weekly*

"A deftly written, exciting tale from first page to last."
—*Midwest Book Review*

"A mystery in which the fantasy and reality of madness, murder, and mayhem blur into a nightmare with one color: red."
—Douglas E. Winter, *Film Threat*

"A gruesome and enjoyable whodunnit...does a great job of evoking this period...highly recommended."
—William Smith, *Hang Fire Books*

"Extremely entertaining...mixes suspense with black humor and old fashioned gory horror to create a gripping read."
—*Book Buzz*

"Prose that invokes Jim Thompson's relentlessness, Elmore Leonard's offbeat humor, and Ramsey Campbell's atmosphere."
—Daniel R. Robichaud, *Horror Reader*

"Williams gradually ramps up the pace, tension, and suspense as the inevitable conclusion draws ever closer until it becomes almost unbearable."
—Brian Lindenmuth, *BSC Review*

"Fans of urban legends, splatter cinema, and sharp tools will want to get it on with *Crimson Orgy*. Austin Williams' debut novel pays respect to the cinematic trail blazed by H.G. Lewis—with sex, storms, and suspense."
—Rod Lott, *Bookgasm*

"A fascinating look at the exploitation film industry...the tension builds as we move toward the conclusion...it's a book that will leave you twitching uncomfortably when you finish."
—Don D'Ammassa, author of *Narcissus* and *Dead of Winter*

The Platinum Loop

Austin Williams

Upaya House

www.upayahouse.com
www.crimsonorgy.com

Library of Congress Cataloging-in-Publication Data

Williams, Austin [date]
The Platinum Loop by Austin Williams

p. cm.

ISBN 978-1-936965-00-7

1. Underground cinema—fiction. 2. Las Vegas,
United States—fiction. 3. Hollywood,
United States—fiction. 4. Tijuana, Mexico—fiction.
5. Crime—fiction. 6. Pop culture—fiction. I. Title

10 9 8 7 6 5 4 3 2 1

Manufactured in the United States of America
First Edition

THE PLATINUM LOOP

Dear S,

Never been much for writing letters, I'm just too nervous to sleep. Four people are dead and we'll be lucky to leave Mexico in one piece ourselves.

I don't blame Floyd, not really. Without my help he'd never have gotten out of Vegas alive. There's no point wondering how it might be different if I walked away from the wheel a little sooner. Or if I hadn't gone to Binion's in the first place, maybe thought of a smarter way to raise the option money.

Never complain, never explain. That's my motto. Always served me well, so I won't start complaining now. But I'd sure like to explain a thing or two. It's just too late for that, doll.

This letter is pointless, I haven't said any of the things you need to hear. I'm gonna stop now and tear it up. But maybe you'll get the message, somehow.

— Gene

PART I

VEGAS

1.

The rush of blood into Floyd's head was making him dizzy. A bad case of vertigo threatened to take hold. He'd really love to be standing on the balcony of his spacious room on the fourth floor of Binion's Horseshoe Hotel and Casino right now, instead of dangling over the rail like a worm on a hook.

Billy Bob was using both hands to clench Floyd's left ankle hard enough to leave bruises. Holding him aloft, upside down, so he could observe the grim possibilities awaiting him. Ten sinewy fingers were all that prevented a probably fatal, certainly crippling, plunge to the black asphalt below.

How much longer could Billy Bob hold on? Floyd Manning didn't weigh more than a buck fifty well fed and dripping wet, but he'd been suspended in midair for some time now. Might have been around five minutes but it felt like considerably more than that. At some point Billy Bob would either have to pull him back over the railing to safety or just let go. Calculating the odds, Floyd gave himself 50/50.

"Gentlemen, please," he said, inwardly impressed at how calm he sounded. "Let's handle this situation in a civilized way. I'm sure there's an agreeable resolution at our disposal."

No answer came. Not from Billy Bob or the other two men huddled on the balcony. Were they pondering the options for a quick getaway or just enjoying a bit of fun at Floyd's extreme discomfort?

He still didn't understand how the situation had degenerated to such a dire impasse. Things seemed to go fairly well at first. Upon meeting the trio of Texans downstairs at the lobby bar earlier tonight, the mental image he'd formed over the phone was verified: three oversized shitkickers with way too much oil money to burn, duded up in the obligatory snakeskin boots, ten-gallon hats, and bolo ties.

Crushing Floyd's hand with a beartrap shake, Randolph had introduced the other two in a loud, slightly slurred voice. Tommy was his brother-in-law (*"Call me T-Ray, gawldangit, ever'body does!"*) and Billy Bob was a business acquaintance from the pits. They'd just dropped five bills on a late dinner at Binion's Steakhouse on the 24th floor and were ready to do some business. Once the transaction was completed, they were going on a "honey hunt" at the Mesa Club and Floyd was coming along if they had anything to say about it.

Watching Randolph stick two bejeweled fingers in his mouth and whistle for the barmaid like he was competing in a hog-calling contest, Floyd had felt the first shimmer of concern. While alcohol could be an

11

effective lubricant to ensure a smooth transaction, consumed in excess it usually caused problems. He didn't like dealing with drunks, especially loud, obnoxious ones who acted like they owned the place. These good ole boys were already overserved, and their rambunctious manner indicated trouble.

He did nothing to show his unease. Floyd could keep a poker face in the tensest of situations, and he trusted himself to steer this one to a profitable conclusion. After three quick rounds of Wild Turkey, he determined the only way to close these fools was to get them away from the bar. As casually as possible, he suggested they repair to his suite where the merchandise could be privately appraised.

Now, less than twenty minutes after letting them into room 413, things had taken a decided turn for the worse. Floyd had anticipated some complications in completing the sale, but squirming in blind panic four stories above concrete was not among them.

"Come on, fellas. Just give me a chance to explain. I'm sure we can hash this out peacefully."

"Quiet, boy!" That came from Billy Bob, whose arms had started trembling slightly from the strain.

Floyd craned his neck, trying to establish visual contact with the man who clearly called the shots in this group. But Randolph's back was turned as he puffed a cigar and traded low murmurs with T-Ray.

"Hold your water there, pard," Randolph said over his shoulder. "I'm still deciding what to do with you."

"Might wanna hurry it up," Billy Bob rasped, the trembles increasing. "Pretty soon won't be no decision left to make."

All three men chuckled so Floyd figured it was a malicious joke designed to heighten his unease, rather than an actual threat. Or maybe not.

12

The ghostly image of a moss-covered tombstone materialized in his mind's eye:

Floyd Roland Manning
  b. April 1, 1944 - Mercy Hospital, Flushing, NY
  d. September 10, 1973 - Binion's Horseshoe
     Hotel and Casino, Las Vegas, NV

What a sorry life span to engrave in granite, and what a lousy place to end it.

Room 413 was located on the west-facing side of the hotel, which seemed like a blessing under the circumstances. At least he'd be able to die in privacy. If he got dropped from a room on the eastern side, his body would land directly on the bustling sidewalk of Fremont Street. No doubt spreading blood, bone, and viscera on the usual flow of tourists, whales, and low-rollers populating Glitter Gulch on a hot Saturday night.

This side of the building looked off into a decrepit part of Vegas few out-of-towners ever visited, at least not on purpose. Block after block of gas stations, liquor stores, rub joints, and cheapo housing units gradually diminishing into desert scrub. The same desert where thousands of holes had been dug and filled with the freshly deceased, if even a small fraction of Vegas Mob lore was to be believed.

Manning had to wonder if he was headed for a hole out in the sand. Or would these guys not even bother planting him before they skipped town on the first plane back to Houston?

Trying not to thrash, feeling a blackout gain momentum, he made one last stab at diplomacy.

"In light of this misunderstanding, I'd be willing to knock twenty percent off the asking price. Hell, let's make it twenty-five."

Randolph leaned over the rail to flick some cigar ash into his upturned face.

"Warned you fair and square not to fuck me, Floyd."

"Nobody's getting fucked here. The goods are legit, I can prove it beyond any reasonable suspicion."

"You said he'd be here. That's the only proof I'm interested in, got it?"

"Trust me, his absence is equally upsetting on my end."

"I'm starting to think you don't even know the man."

"I'm no liar, Randolph. When we talked on the phone, there was every reason to believe a meet and greet was possible. If you recall, I never gave a guarantee."

"He ain't even in town, probably."

Billy Bob's grip slackened in a way that did not feel intentional. Time was running out fast.

"Look there!" Floyd pointed frantically into the room. "On the bedside table. See that copy of the Entertainment Guide?"

"Yeah, what about it?" Randolph asked without turning.

"Check the schedule at the Dunes. Frank's got three gigs this week, with Joey Bishop opening up. It's a warm-up for his comeback run at Ceasar's in January."

"What's that supposed to prove? Any lying maggot could find that out. These are your own damn dice, for all I know."

"Oh, please. They're monogrammed, for Christ's sake!"

The indignant spike in his own voice surprised Floyd a bit. More surprising was the impact it had on Randolph, who stepped into the room and reemerged moments later with a pair of green dice in his hands.

"I don't see no monogram."

"Not on the surface, his initials are cut into the center of each die. Hold them up to the light, you'll see an 'F' and 'S' quite clearly."

Randolph paused, doubt written across his swarthy brow. Then he went back inside and held one of the green cubes against the glow of an ornate brass lamp. Squinting, he nodded slightly before examining the other.

"OK, so I see the letters. Don't prove a goddamn thing, any ol' novelty shop could make these."

"That's pure onyx, Randy. Showroom-grade rock only an ace jeweler knows how to cut."

"Enough!" T-Ray shouted. His first word since they'd entered the room, it took everyone a little off guard. "Drop this sack of shit. Wasted enough time on him already."

"Don't listen to him!"

Billy Bob was staring closely at Randolph for confirmation. None came, instead he just tossed his cigar nub over the railing.

"Floyd, we had an agreement. You said we'd meet the man. Said he'd confirm to us directly these are his property."

"So Frank can't cancel at the last minute, for any reason that might pop into his head? That's showbiz, my friend!"

Randolph shook his head slowly.

"No Sinatra, no deal."

He reached down and grabbed one of Floyd's hands. Pressing the dice into his palm, he closed the fingers around them tightly.

"You can keep 'em."

"He *said* he'd be here," Manning pleaded, now

15

hearing true fear invade his voice and unable to keep it out. "I'm just sorry as can be about all this."

"Nope," Randolph said with an almost wistful last glance. "Not yet you ain't."

Floyd couldn't see him nod to Billy Bob. There was no need. He knew he was falling a fraction of a second before it happened.

The plummet began at sickening speed, robbing him of the chance to scream. Flying headfirst straight down into the darkness, Floyd's eyes clouded at the wind rushing up against them. But they didn't close.

He'd traveled half the distance, time not freezing but assuming a syrupy slowness, when he first saw the dumpster. It was lodged against the wall, next to a door that probably led to the kitchen, in a narrow corner where the parking lot ended flush against the hotel. Directly beneath him, the dumpster grew wider, yawning like a filthy mouth in his vision as he accelerated toward it.

In the last moment before collision, he saw a pile of shiny black garbage bags stuffed into the opening, and knew he would not die. At least not on impact.

His shoulder caught the edge of the topmost bag, pushing his legs over his head in a summersault. Both knees slammed against the dumpster's metal side, sending flares of agony in a runaway trail across every nerve ending in his body.

The scream in his mouth got caught somewhere behind his tongue, unable to break free as anything louder than a whimper.

Even in the throes of mounting shock, one thought remained clear in Floyd's mind: he still had the dice! Both cubes were clenched in his right hand tightly enough to leave permanent indentations on his palm.

A second realization arrived with greater clarity. The Texans must have seen him survive the drop. They were either watching from the balcony right now or, more likely, racing down to finish the job.

No time to waste.

Unsure if he could stand, let alone run, Floyd reached up to grip the dumpster's rim with both hands. Knees still afire in pain that was throbbing towards numbness, he hoisted himself up.

Managing to lift one leaden leg over the rim and then the next, Manning gritted his teeth and hurled the rest of himself over. He folded onto the ground, trying to regain his breath. How long would it take them to get down here from room 413? The elevators at Binion's were torturously slow, but a stairway led directly to the rear entrance.

Rolling onto his stomach, he tried unsuccessfully to stand. Nausea took hold and he considered another plan. His car was parked in this same lot, only two rows from where he lay, a small bit of good fortune that might make all the difference. By habit, Floyd Manning parked in the back of whatever hotel he was staying at in Vegas, eschewing valet service in favor of a complimentary space that allowed for a swift escape if needed.

The Texans didn't know what kind of car Floyd drove. If he could get over to his champagne Cadillac Eldorado in time to pop the trunk and crawl inside, they'd never find him. Might have to spend a few hours in there to make sure the coast was clear, but that sounded like paradise right now considering the other immediate alternatives.

Using his elbows, Manning crawled crablike across the asphalt. His progress was far too slow. Biting down a howl of pain, he willed himself into a standing position and staggered forward.

The closest row of cars was less than twenty feet away. After that, probably another thirty paces to the Eldo. There was still a chance, if only his legs would operate at even half their normal capacity.

He reached the first row. Passed it. Reached the second row and turned left. His car, his salvation, came into view. Ten paces away, no more.

Then he heard their angry commingled voices, followed by a sixpack of cowboy boots pounding the asphalt. Trying not to turn around, he was unable to halt an instinctive swivel of the head.

Even as Floyd went into a low crouch behind a white Chevy van, Randolph's voice boomed out a shout of slurred recognition. The boots scuffled faster in his direction.

Fingers fumbling with his keys, madly and futilely trying to open the trunk, Floyd knew it was a lost cause even before the first crushing kick landed.

2.

Gene Hoffman pushed himself away from the roulette table, biting down a string of obscenities that wanted to fly from his mouth at elevated volume. Even in the grip of defeat, he respected the decorum a class joint like Binion's Horseshoe demanded of its patrons.

The little white ball sat snugly in a red slot marked 22, leering up at him in the neon glow. Red was the wrong color, the only color he could see in a mist of vaporous anger rising before his bloodshot eyes.

For his last bet, the one he placed just seconds ago, Hoffman let his entire chip stack ride on black. He'd been killing with black all night. Straight sucker's play, ignoring the numbers. But it worked, and it kept working until his winnings had quadrupled in size. More than enough for him to consider a success if he was in town to do some simple pleasure gambling. Not nearly enough to satisfy the urgent requirement that brought him here tonight.

He'd gotten so damn close. Just needed the luck to hold a little longer, for once, to see him through.

Now, with a single spin, it was all gone. Everything won over the past three hours, not to mention his stake money, claimed by the house.

The croupier, a faded redhead with killer curves barely hidden beneath her tuxedo shirt and rawhide cowgirl skirt, gave a sympathetic shrug. She'd shown enthusiasm over Gene's hot hand, seeming to share his pleasure every time the ball found its way to black. Now her face was stricken, sagging in a way that revealed her age for the first time.

"Not my night," Gene said, forcing a grin that actually hurt it was so false.

"Sometimes I'd like to take a hatchet to this ol' wheel," the croupier commiserated.

Hoffman liked the sound of her languid bedroom drawl. He'd heard the legend that Benny Binion staffed his casino exclusively with natives of the Lone Star State from which the impresario hailed, but that sounded unrealistic. Binion's Horseshoe was the most expertly managed joint in town and had to employ at least a thousand people. What were the odds of finding that many competent Texans in the gaming industry?

And what difference did it make to Gene, now that he'd pissed away his entire bankroll with a few bad spins?

Fucking imbecile! he silently lambasted himself, feeling a queasy tightness spread across his chest. Beads of sweat formed on his brow, and he forced himself to calm down. The only thing that could possibly make this night worse would be a paralyzing attack of angina here on the casino floor. Or even a full-tilt coronary of the kind Gene sometimes felt was stalking him with the tireless patience of a trained assassin. That might actually be preferable, if it happened fast enough to spare him further humiliation.

"I can't stand hearing a gambler whine," he said, flipping his last $5 chip to the croupier. "Especially if it's me."

"My shift ends in twenty," she replied, holding the chip between her fingers like a lewd invitation. "Buy you a drink?"

"Tempting offer. I gotta pass."

"You could buy me one instead, if that sounds better."

"You're too kind, Darlene. Wouldn't want my shit luck rubbing off on you."

"Maybe I can rub some good luck on you. Might be fun."

He mulled it for half a tick before shaking his head.

"Some other time."

"Does that mean you'll be back for another spin?"

"Masochist like me? Bank on it."

Shooting her a wink, Gene turned and walked away from the table, moving in long strides before he changed his mind. He almost couldn't believe he was turning down the offer. What better way to shake off his gloom than a few stiff drinks and some sympathetic cooze?

His mood wouldn't allow it. Hell, he didn't even want to feel better. Hoffman had lost a lot more at the tables than he did tonight, but it never mattered so much. He'd never come to Vegas with the intention of winning money he actually needed. Just the opposite; his previous trips had always been funded by a predetermined "entertainment roll" he was happily prepared to piss away. Losing never bothered him as long as he had a good time doing it.

Sheer desperation had steered his actions this time, and the results should have been all too predictable. What kind of fool tries to launch a serious professional endeavor with money taken from the roulette wheel?

Not like I had too many other choices, he thought, using all of his 360 pounds to cut an aggressive path toward the double glass doors at the back of the casino. *I need that damn script. And now I'm fresh out of ways to get it.*

Gene Hoffman hadn't produced a movie since last summer. August of '72, to be precise. He hadn't conducted so much as an audition in nine months, and the inactivity was killing him. For a guy who used to crank out three low-budget flicks per annum back in the salad days of his career, it felt like a kind of slow death.

Since relocating to Hollywood from Miami three years ago, Hoffman had not exactly floundered but neither had he flourished. It was largely a matter of lowering the expectations he'd brought with him.

Gene's producing experience in the most modest spectrums of cinema, consistently gainful track record at the box office, and imposing physicality acted in concert to secure a handful of promising contacts within his first month of hitting the West Coast. But the ceiling of potential success available to him in the big leagues of moviemaking became evident soon enough.

The two-bedroom apartment he'd rented in the "Yucca Flats" (so named for the main artery running through a ruinously crime-ridden slum beneath the

Hollywood foothills) wasn't likely to wow any potential backers. Still, it served well enough as both office and domicile. He's gotten into a king-hell argument with the manager about installing a four-foot brass plaque reading "G.H. Productions" outside the front door, but that got settled with a cash handoff.

The plaque proved to be a worthwhile investment. From his years making exploitation flicks in Florida, Gene had learned some well-chosen details can go a long way toward establishing a veneer of professionalism.

That first year in L.A. was not entirely fruitless. He cobbled together enough resources to produce a cheap softcore feature that picked up national distribution. *Cheerleaders In Jail* turned quite a nice little profit, running for months in dozens of well-trafficked theaters catering to the raincoat set. But Gene hadn't dragged his ass all the way across the country just to keep cranking out the same Z-grade dreck he'd mastered in Miami. Visions of ascending to the rarefied arena of mainstream movies had propelled him westward.

After barely scraping out a marginal profit with three more softcore numbers, he realized a surprising truth: the key to breaking through in the majors lay with the written word. Throughout his career, Gene never placed much value on story content. Packing the screen with titillating sex and/or violence generated ticket sales; the plot itself was largely interchangeable from one flick to the next.

In Hollywood, he learned the only way to shine was to own a script worthy of attracting some marquee talent. By pure chance, Gene found a way to gain possession of such a property just last week. Killing a smoggy afternoon over beers in the cozy darkness of the Formosa Cafe, he fell into conversation with a young screenwriter of some burgeoning renown.

Barely twenty-five, the kid had already penned two reasonably successful drive-in potboilers, a violent biker flick called *Hell Riders* and a collegiate sex romp with the supremely bankable title *Panty Raid*. Hoffman had seen both movies and was sufficiently impressed. A certain literary quality indicated real talent in the writing. That's exactly what he told the young scribe, signaling to the bartender for another round.

The kid was soused when they started talking and by the time they shook hands in the parking lot he could barely stand. But he remained coherent enough to pitch Gene on an unsold script he'd just completed, and it sounded like pure gold. Not some trashy piece of shlock, but a serious drama about the difficulties faced by a battle-scarred Vietnam vet upon returning home to his small Midwestern town.

It was a dynamite concept, dramatic and topical. Gene knew, even without seeing the pages, this was exactly the kind of project that could nudge him toward legitimacy. And the writer was just drunk enough to accept his proposal of a six-month option for a cool grand. Hoffman jotted the basic deal points on a cocktail napkin, which they both signed.

Beautiful, he'd thought with a grin, tucking the napkin into his wallet. *Maybe things are finally turning for me.*

There was just one snag: he didn't have the option cash. Didn't have anywhere near a grand to part with. The next few days were consumed by a frantic mental inventory of ways to raise some quick bread. At 11:59 P.M. Friday night, roughly twenty-eight hours ago, he landed on the unpalatable conclusion he'd been trying to avoid.

A single route lay open to him: the casino tables in L.V.

Not giving himself time to reconsider, Gene locked the door to his apartment on Yucca, walked half a block toward Ivar where his '67 Plymouth Valiant was parked, fired the engine and gunned it for the 101 South. He didn't plan to touch the brakes until the neon castles of the Vegas Strip loomed tall in his windshield.

Well, now he'd given the roulette wheel a shot. And the wheel had burned him good. Nothing to do but troop three blocks to the El Cortez, where he had a discounted room for the night, and grab a few hours of bitter sleep before driving back to L.A. to contemplate the full reality of his failure.

Weaving through a field of slot machines near Binion's rear doors, Gene was jostled to the side by three men who came barging out of the elevator like they'd heard a fire alarm. A trio of cowboys, drunk and obviously up to no good. Assholes didn't even stop to apologize, just kept running for the exit.

"Watch it!" Hoffman yelled after them, but they'd already burst through a pair of swinging glass doors and disappeared into the early morning darkness.

It looked like the aftermath of a bungled theft. Gene turned around, expecting to spot a pit boss or security guard in hot pursuit. Relishing the thought of seeing a nightstick swung with purpose against someone's head. But no one was behind him.

Redneck bastards.

Hoffman could feel the last vestiges of his composure disintegrating. Shoved aside like a damn vagrant by a bunch of overdressed hicks; it was just too much to bear peacefully.

He decided not to allow this slight to go unpunished. Someone was going to pay for the bad luck he'd endured, not just tonight but for as long as he could remember.

Hoffman pushed through the double doors and stepped out into the parking lot. Only half filled with cars, it was dark and quiet except for a flurry of activity off to the left by some trash dumpsters.

He heard them before he saw them. Curses rendered with a conjoined Texas twang, just barely restrained. Another voice babbling incoherent pleas for mercy. And the unmistakable sound of blunt objects pummeling flesh.

Breaking into a jog, the closest thing to a run he could muster these days, Gene closed the gap after thirty paces and got a clear view.

A full blown stomping was in progress. The three cowboys were taking turns kicking a scrawny figure that lay curled in a fetal ball on the pavement between two rows of vehicles.

"Hell's going on here?" Gene growled, his level of irritation spiking to thermal.

One of the cowboys turned without pausing the attack.

"Mind your own bidness, fat man."

Good, an insult. Provocation aplenty.

Laying both hands on the suede-cloaked shoulders of the closest man, Hoffman swiveled to the right and hurled T-Ray face-first into the side of a white Chevy van. A dull metallic thud and the acute pop of liberated teeth announced the mustachioed Texan's entry to oblivion.

With barely a second to spare, Gene saw the switchblade arcing toward him. Clenched in Billy Bob's grip, it flashed in the reflection of an overhead lamp. Hoffman's left arm flew up in an instinctive motion and blocked the knife before it could slash his face. Locking both hands on the wrist of his would-be assailant, Gene twisted clockwise with enough force to loosen a fire hydrant.

The scream came fast on the heels of a crisp snapping of bone and tendon. Billy Bob dropped the blade and fell to a crouch, babbling in pain.

Randolph froze, sizing up his chances against this massive new presence. The two men were actually just about the same size, with maybe two inches and twenty pounds in Gene's favor.

Floyd didn't seem worth the trouble, after all. With one of his pals squirming in agony and the other out cold, Randolph chose a prudent course.

"OK, pard. You made your point."

He stepped slowly over to where T-Ray lay and called out to Billy Bob. "Lend a hand here."

"My fuckin' wrist's broke!"

"So lend the other one."

Hoffman watched them awkwardly pull T-Ray upright, wrapping an arm around each shoulder to support his deadweight. A few guttural groans escaped the hombre's bloody mouth, indicating to Gene's profound relief he'd survived.

Randolph shot one last look of rheumy-eyed venom at Floyd.

"This ain't over, you lyin' sumbitch."

"It is for now," Hoffman answered, stepping forward. "Start moving."

3.

When Floyd Manning first caught a blurred glimpse of Gene Hoffman lumbering across the lot in his direction, his bowels constricted with dread. Despite being recently launched from a fourth-floor balcony, he still harbored some hope of talking his way out of a *really* bad night. But if this hulk was part of the assault squad, he was a goner.

So when he watched Hoffman launch T-Bone's callow face into a parked van, then snap Billy Bob's wrist like a wad of taffy, Manning was perplexed. It hardly seemed possible to believe the stranger was intervening on his behalf.

Even now, as he heard the Texans' footsteps staggering in retreat and felt himself being pulled upright, he couldn't process what was happening.

"You OK?"

Floyd nodded mutely, too short of breath to speak. Running a hand through his curly mop of black pomaded hair and smoothing his well-groomed mustache, he took a moment to appraise this unexpected savior. A Sherman Tank decked out in a Hawaiian shirt and sharply creased chinos, that's what the guy looked like. But a tank that clearly had a few miles on the odometer, as evidenced by Gene's wheezing breath and the streams of sweat pouring down his wide red face.

"My friend," Floyd sputtered after they introduced themselves. "I just can't express sufficient gratitude for this act of kindness."

"Ah, don't mention it. Gut reflex more than anything else, those punks made the mistake of shoving me inside."

"Don't downplay the significance of what you've done here. You've salvaged a fellow human being's sense of optimism from the proverbial gutter of despair. Just when I thought there's no empathy left in this world for a stranger in dire straits, a man of your caliber steps in and blows that sorry outlook to smithereens."

"Like I said, no problem."

Hoffman started to turn away, already regretting he'd gotten involved. This skinny kid, decked out in a perfectly tailored sharkskin suit and wingtips, seemed harmless enough but his motormouthed drone was a little hard to take.

"Allow me to buy you a drink!" Floyd urged, reading his mind. "Hardly adequate compensation for the great assistance you've offered, I admit. But a token no less."

"Skip it," Gene replied, thinking he must look like a real charity case since this was the second free drink he'd been offered in ten minutes. "Already downed my share tonight."

"At least give me the distinct pleasure of shaking the hand that smote my enemies. Do me that small courtesy, I beg you."

Gene reluctantly offered his hand for a terse shake and when he retracted it found a laminated business card flattened against his palm.

Printed on the shiny black surface in silver calligraphic letters:

Floyd Manning
Procurer of Dreams

On the back side, above a Los Angeles address with a zip code only one digit different than that of the Yucca Flats, were the words:

Specializes in the rarest movieland memorabilia

"You found me in a moment of temporary disadvantage, but don't let that fool you. When it comes to one-of-a-kind gems from Hollywood's golden era, there's no equal to yours truly. Alas, sometimes I encounter a buyer who doesn't respect a good faith transaction previously agreed upon."

Hoffman caught a glimpse of two teeth with bloody roots on the pavement by his feet. He took a step away from them.

"That what this was about? Business deal gone sour?"

"No moss on you, Gene. I drove in from L.A. this very morning for the purpose of selling a highly valuable item."

"Long way to go to get your ass kicked." Even as he was saying the words, Gene realized with a sour inward smile they applied pretty well to himself.

"No big whoop, I make the drive all the time. I'd say a third of my best customers are in Vegas."

Floyd punched a cigarette out of his pack, offering one. Knowing he should refuse, Hoffman decided to worry about his heart some other time. Both men lit up and dragged deeply.

"Did you know there's a booming interest in Hollywood arcana out in this desert?"

"Didn't know that, Floyd."

"Gotta go where the money is, right?"

"So what happened?"

"Don't ask. Should've been so sweet, my biggest score of the year."

Reaching into his pocket, he offered the emerald cubes. Gene took them in hand and whistled.

"Fancy rocks."

"Mr. Sinatra's personal set. Used to call them his lucky *stugots* till they went cold last year and stayed that way for him."

Hoffman cocked a skeptical brow and passed the dice back. He tucked the card in his breast pocket, planning to drop it in the first trash can he saw.

"Pleasure meeting you, Floyd."

"The pleasure was all mine, Gene. Believe me when I tell you that."

Hoffman took three steps and had every intention to keep moving. But some weird impulse kicked his usually disciplined tongue into gear and he heard himself say, "I'm in pictures myself."

"I knew it!" Manning almost shouted. "The moment my vision came into focus and I got a good look at you, I said to myself: Floyd, here we have a bona fide captain of the dream factory."

"Relax. I produced a few flicks, that's all. Nothing you'd have heard of, grindhouse stuff mainly."

"Lay some credits on me, big daddy. I'm no stranger to the balcony seats."

"Ah, shit. Maybe you caught my last one, *Cheerleaders In Jail.*"

Floyd shook his head, wearing a look of intense concentration. Gene pressed on with his more recent titles, strangely unable to stop himself.

"*Eager Beavers? The Mile High Club?*"

Manning made a vaguely affirmative noise that lacked conviction. Gene could have rattled off some others but saw no reason to bother with it. He felt embarrassed to have mentioned those movies at all, as if the pathetic string of cheapies produced under his supervision constituted a body of work in which a man could take some kind of pride.

"Say, how about an early breakfast?" Floyd asked, mercifully changing the subject. "I know a little gem of a diner. Flapjacks fluffy as a showgirl's tit, best coffee in Vegas. It's my treat."

Hoffman wanted to decline, but he was just about starving and could barely afford gas money for the dismal five-hour drive awaiting him.

"Guess I could stand a meal, not that I miss too many."

"That's the ticket. Let's take my ride."

Hearing his stomach growl in anticipation, Gene flicked away the cigarette. His watch told him it was coming up on 5:30 A.M. but he wasn't tired. The violence had acted like a shot of speed, snapping him out of the gloomy fog that descended at the roulette table. He didn't even feel like beating himself up about losing the roll anymore. There's always a way to raise a buck, and he could probably stall the alkie screenwriter long enough to think of one.

Watching as Floyd sauntered to a gleaming champagne Cadillac Eldorado, it occurred to Gene he'd rarely been awake in Vegas at this hour. The artificial rainbow skyline of the Strip looked different in the dim illumination just before dawn. It seemed almost pure in a strange kind of way. Abstract shapes of looming color and light, strung together like a massive jeweled band across the desert floor. A damn beautiful sight, even considering the bottomless pits of depravity neatly concealed underneath all that neon and glitter.

"Why don't you give me the keys," Hoffman said as the kid fumbled with the driver's door. "You're probably still a little shook up."

Floyd started to protest, then shrugged.

"Guess it would be the acme of ingratitude not to trust you," he said, tossing over a sterling key ring. Hoffman caught it, fingers closing on the soft fur of the largest rabbit's foot he'd ever seen.

Gene had the driver's door halfway open when he saw the headlights. Turning left from the far corner of the parking lot, they fell over him in a blinding wash, highbeams burning into his retinas.

Floyd flinched like he'd been goosed with a cattle prod, jumping to the conclusion that Randolph and company had come back to finish the job.

"Oh, dear Lord."

As the car crept closer, Hoffman's intuition told him something he didn't want to believe. The knowledge produced a bodily reaction similar to Manning's but for an entirely different reason.

Gene *recognized* the vehicle slowly bearing down on them, blocking the only lane out. Standing his ground, refusing to take refuge inside Floyd's Eldo, it was not stoicism but irrational shock that rooted him in place.

"Unlock it, for God's sake!" Floyd yelled, tugging furiously at the passenger door's handle.

The car nosed to a stop about twenty feet away, highbeams erasing all visibility. Hoffman didn't need the use of his eyes to know it was a Dodge Dart with a nauseating lime green paint job. The same one he'd spotted three times over the past thirty-six hours:

First as he'd accelerated up the 101 ramp late Friday night on the way out of Hollywood, when the Dodge almost cut in front of him only to hit the brakes barely quick enough to prevent a collision. A second time at the gas station in Barstow where Gene stopped for a cup of coffee and some Twinkies before making the final push to Vegas. And then again yesterday afternoon, idling at a red light by the driveway of the El Cortez Hotel.

The same goddamned car. It had to be. There just weren't that many Darts painted such an obnoxious color on the road. Yet this one had somehow pursued him like a phantom for 300 miles across the wasteland of the Mojave Desert.

"What are you waiting for? They're probably armed!"

"Relax, kid. It's not who you think it is."

As if hearing those words, the driver of the Dodge slammed it in reverse and backed away. Fishtailing around the nearest row of cars, it peeled out of the lot onto 6th Street.

Exhaling for the first time in a minute, Gene got in Floyd's Cadillac and unlocked the passenger door.

4.

"The thing felt off from the beginning," Floyd said, using a fork to mop up some syrup with his last pancake wedge. "My instincts have yet to fail me when it comes to a sour deal, but what's the use of instincts if you ignore them?"

"Good question."

They were in a corner window booth at the Hash House diner on Sahara Drive, near the northern edge of the Strip. The sun was just cracking over the craggy horizon of low mountains to the East. In a few minutes their booth would be awash in the glare of dawn, but Gene didn't plan to be here long enough for it to bother his weary eyes.

He'd insisted on this spot, facing the entrance and only a few footsteps from the back door. They'd parked behind the diner, though there were ample free spaces up front. Since sitting down, Gene's gaze had searched the window every other minute, peering through smudged glass at the parking lot for any sign of that green Dodge. If necessary, he'd be out the back door and burning the Eldo's rubber onto Sahara in a heartbeat.

With that potentiality in mind, he made Floyd settle the check as soon as their food arrived. Gene wasn't about to stiff a waitress even if saving his own ass called for a hasty getaway.

As he worked his way through a plate of scrambled eggs, listening to Floyd prattle on at a clip most seasoned stenographers would have a hard time matching, he started to relax.

"Should've amscrayed the second I got a bad whiff. Desperate, I guess, which is a sad thing to admit. Trying to process that alien sensation obviously fragged my judgment, otherwise I would've been a vapor trail long before the situation spiraled out of control."

"Risky business, fencing bogus merchandize," Hoffman said to interrupt the flow. "Especially in this town. Locals tend to resent getting fleeced by outsiders."

"Those creeps weren't local. Flew in from East Cowpie, Texas for a weekend of whores and comped drinks. Represented themselves as close personal friends of Benny Binion and maybe they are, I could care less. Anyway, what makes you so sure the goods are bogus?"

Gene shook his head. "Frank's dice? How could you prove a claim like that?"

"I've received verbal confirmation from two croupiers at the Desert Inn and a third at the Dunes. Veteran guys, all."

36

Hoffman expressed his disbelief with a snort.

"Sounds airtight, kid. Show me statements from a cocktail waitress or two and I'm sold."

"Fine, don't believe me."

"I don't, Floyd. And you'll drop these chickenshit scams if you got any sense."

"Tread lightly there, Gene. I'm very grateful, but don't lecture me on doing business, OK? I've raked in more cash from top-line memorabilia in a single month than you've seen in your most profitable year, probably."

Hoffman chuckled, then let loose with a belly laugh that shook the formica. The balls on this scrawny dude. An hour ago he was face down in a dumpster about to get carved and now he's cracking tough on the guy who stepped in to save him.

Laughter expended, Hoffman took an appraising glance across the table. Floyd was unmistakably a low-rent clip artist, incompetent and quite possibly nuts to boot. He was exactly the kind of cheap hustler Vegas collects like so much bellybutton lint, the kind Hoffman couldn't stand to be around for more than a few minutes at a time.

So how come I'm sitting here?

Gene didn't know the answer to that question. Despite the cardboard-thin bluster, there was a strange quality to this guy making him hard to brush off. The faintest trace of something like fallen royalty. He could almost pass for a matinee idol, with a slightly straighter nose and a little more height. The clipped mustache made him look like Errol Flynn's less handsome brother.

"Truth is," Floyd said, reverting to a calmer tone, "I've got a piece of gold sitting in a safe deposit box back in L.A. You know *The Maltese Falcon*, Bogie's line about 'the stuff that dreams are made of?' That's what I'm talking about here. An item that can fetch life changing money. Kiss my ass money, the kind that means never having to sully myself with lowlifes of the ilk you put such a righteous hurt on in that parking lot."

Instead of asking for details, Gene said, "Why haven't you sold this treasure, if it's so valuable?"

"It's not the kind of thing you can advertise in the Penny Saver. I'm talking about a totally unique historical artifact, one of only six in existence."

"Offer it to a museum."

"No soap. Gotta be a private collector with discrete tastes, at least for any transaction with my fingerprints on it."

Gene didn't follow and didn't feel too interested in seeking clarification. His breakfast was finished and the sun was starting to blind him in one eye.

"There are potential legalities involved with the merchandise, OK? Copyright issues, of a sort. I don't know what kind of sanctions could be brought against the holder, and I'd rather not find out. My plan is to move it for a lump cash payment and vanish. I got a buyer lined up but I don't relish doing the deal on his turf, not alone. I'd feel a whole lot better walking in with some muscle to back my play."

Gene shook his head quickly.

"Not interested."

"Sure you are, you just don't know it yet. I'm talking an even split. Bring in more than enough to set up two enterprising individuals for whatever their next venture may be. Financing a motion picture, for example."

Floyd dumped another packet of sugar in his coffee. Jesus, the guy had a monster sweet tooth, or maybe was just looking for any kind of jolt to keep the patter going full-tilt.

"It's a stag flick," he said, leaning forward over his plate. "Not a professional job, more like a home movie. A little over three minutes long. Black & white, no sound. Looks like it could've been shot on 16 but it's just a regular 8mm loop, as your expert eye will easily discern."

"Sounds like box office dynamite," Gene said, irritably noting he'd already been insinuated into the plan.

"Just one scene," Floyd continued. "Very basic. Gorgeous blonde with lethal curves down on her knees, putting her mouth to the right kind of work on some guy's tallywhacker. He's standing, back against a doorway. His face stays out of frame the whole time. Looks like it was shot in a swank hotel room somewhere. There's an armoire with a decanter of booze on a sterling tray next to them. Two different angles, all the camera really shows is her. And it shows plenty."

"I'm still hoping this gets interesting at some point."

Floyd shook a Lucky Strike from the pack and sparked it with pronounced languor.

"It's Marilyn Monroe."

Forming an expert smoke ring, he settled back in the booth, looking calm for the first time since Hoffman laid eyes on him. Like a guilty man who'd finally gotten something of the greatest import off his chest. Smoking casually, he seemed content to wait for a reply.

"That's about the dumbest thing anyone's ever said to me."

"An understandable reaction, but a false one. Put your skepticism aside for a minute, Gene. This item is one hundred percent legit. I got my hands on it directly from an FBI operative in the L.A. Office."

"Look, I've heard that rumor about Marilyn before. Who hasn't by now? I just never believed it."

"So give me a chance to prove you wrong. What have you got to lose?"

"I think storytime's just about over. Thanks for breakfast."

"I should mention I have the paperwork to back it up."

Hoffman paused. Then found himself asking, "What kind of paperwork?"

"Photocopies of confidential Bureau documents, proving the film's authenticity."

"I've seen forged documents before."

"Stay with me," Manning said with some impatience. "This piece of celluloid has been floating around the Agency for over a decade. Only a handful of operatives have ever seen the thing, they call it The Platinum Loop. The original negative occupies a sealed vault somewhere in Virginia. It was J. Edgar Hoover's personal property until the old queen croaked last year. Precisely five prints were made under the Bureau's authority. One of them is now secured in a safe in my home in L.A."

Gene reached into the pack without asking and lit up.

"If I was interested enough to inquire, which I'm not, I'd wonder how something like this ever came into existence."

Floyd shrugged.

"Hoover kept a network of showbiz informants for decades, including some names that might surprise you. They fed him dirt, he stockpiled it. Ostensibly for leverage, but I suspect he just had a hard-on for movie star smut."

Whatever impulse of curiosity had kept Hoffman in his seat instantly evaporated under a heavy wave

40

of fatigue. He stubbed out the cigarette after barely two drags.

"Keep your nose clean, kid. No need to pretend we know each other if our paths cross again, OK?"

"Come on, slow down. You don't want to miss out on this action."

Taking a last glance out the window in search of the Dodge, Gene determined the coast was clear and stood.

"I'll be at the Golden Nugget," Floyd pressed on. "Call me if you change your mind."

Gene gave him a look, then nodded. "Guess you can't go back to Binion's, huh?"

"No need. I paid in advance. I've found it's wise to keep multiple accommodations in this town, just to allow for any unforeseen contingencies."

"How come that doesn't surprise me? Goodbye, Floyd."

Hoffman stalked through the diner's back door and began a weary walk back to the El Cortez. It was at least five blocks away. He could have hitched a ride from this Manning character, but somehow that didn't seem like a good idea.

5.

Not all that long ago, for much of the '50s and '60s, the El Cortez Hotel had rightly called itself the undisputed jewel of Glitter Gulch. It couldn't keep pace with the monuments to excess being rapidly erected along the Strip, but was without debate the traveler's most luxurious option on the north side of town.

These days it was a powerfully depressing dump, pulling in only the lower end of the out-of-town trade. Semi-desperate men and women who still had enough scratch to stay out of the truly dangerous roach traps on Paradise Road, at least for one more night. Hoffman could barely afford a room at the El Cortez, and that sorry fact bit his pride pretty hard.

Gene slid his key into the door of #206 and stepped

inside. The musty staleness of the room sapped him in an instant, draining the last vestiges of adrenaline he'd been using to stay on his feet.

The bed, a queen, was lumpy and barely large enough to support his rhino frame. Gene was a California King man by nature and considered anything smaller a gross imposition on his sleeping needs. But right now he was so tired the ratty little bed looked like a slice of heaven. Despite the semi-recurrent nightmares that had plagued him of late, Gene felt confident he'd be comatose within thirty seconds of hitting the pillow.

Wrong. Twenty minutes later he was still wide awake, staring at a thin ribbon of sunlight seeping through a gap between the drapes. His body was dog-tired but his mind was still whirling. Momentarily fun as the violent run-in with the cowboys had been, Gene's visceral satisfaction had evaporated in the glare of that Dodge's headlamps. In its place, waves of paranoia bloomed.

Could he actually believe the same green Dart had materialized in the parking lot of Binion's? Its appearance rendered all logic useless.

Makes no damn sense. How could it have followed me all the way from L.A. without my noticing?

Mulling that question, trying to find a comfortable position on the mattress, it began to seem less implausible. He'd been in such a manic state when departing Hollywood, focused solely on visualizing how he was going to come back at least a grand healthier than he left, that it was eminently possible for a long-distance trace to go unnoticed. Route 15 from Barstow to Vegas was sparsely trafficked that late in the evening, and a pursuing car could easily hang back far enough to keep Gene's taillights in view without getting close enough to draw notice.

Even so, the fact that Gene failed to spot a vehicle following him clear across the desert was unsettling to consider. All his life, from the tenements of Chicago's south side to the roughneck midways of the carney world and into the anything-goes grindhouse of exploitation filmmaking, Hoffman had remained bodily intact and two steps ahead of innumerable antagonists by virtue of the invisible eyes located on the back of his head. Clearly, those eyes had failed him.

His ears were working fine, though. They pricked up instantly at the sounds of footsteps outside room 206.

Turning toward the door, he saw the outline of two shoes silhouetted by the hallway light. Someone was standing right outside, motionless and silent.

Gene bolted upright, heart racing. He felt suddenly short of breath and a band of fresh sweat seeped across his hairline. For a fleeting moment he thought he might be having a heart attack.

A thin metallic scratching came from the opposite side of the door. Whoever stood out there was picking the lock. Not very proficiently, by the sounds of it. The operation was being performed with such a haphazard array of jabs and scrapes Gene had to conclude it was the work of an amateur.

Bounding from the bed, his feet barely hit the carpet. In two broad steps he was inside the bathroom, which stood directly to the door's left.

With a soft click, the lock turned. Gene's head swiveled in the darkness, looking for something solid to grab. The bathroom held nothing that could be used as a weapon. The flashlight in his overnight bag was on the other side of the bed, no time to make it. It would have to be a bare hands job.

The door opened an inch, stopping on a squeak.

44

Gene had neglected to attach the chain, for which he was grateful. Removing it by force would cause too much racket. He wanted the intruder to enter the room as easily as possible.

The door swung wide in a single brisk motion and a man stepped in. Both of Gene's hammock fists were clenched high above his shoulders like someone getting ready to split a log with an ax. His plan was to wait until the door closed again, but there was no time. Seeing the empty bed, the intruder's head instinctively rotated toward the bathroom.

Gene brought down both fists like a thunderclap, striking the base of the neck. The intruder fell to his knees and Gene got right on top of him with another bash to the head.

The guy was out cold. His ratty madras jacket hung open, revealing a leather shoulder holster. Hoffman extracted a snub nose .38 and confirmed a full load of five rounds in the chamber. Reaching into the man's hip pocket, he pulled out an alligator skin wallet.

Gene sat on the bed and turned on a lamp. Flipping open the wallet, he found a thin wad of bills and crumpled receipts. Not much else of interest, other than a Class "C" Private Investigator's License. Gene didn't even have to look before knowing where it was issued.

Florida.

Of course. Was it ever reasonable, or even sane, to think he'd effected some kind of lasting escape from his legacy in that godforsaken state? Sooner or later, Florida was bound to catch up with him. And now, in the form of the unconscious man at his feet, it had.

The guy's name was Ben Malton, if the ID was legit. Home address listed on his Driver's License was in Miami, 418 Collins Avenue. Not too far from where Gene used to live.

Dumping out the rest of the wallet's contents on the bed, he made a quick appraisal of the receipts. They covered mainly gas and food purchases from the last few days, all California and Nevada vendors. Didn't tell him anything he hadn't already figured out.

Though he never laid eyes on Ben Malton before, Gene didn't have to guess why he'd broken into the room. Almost been expecting something like this to happen from the moment he spotted that green Dodge Dart idling by the El Cortez's entrance yesterday. Seeing that car for the third time brought to mind one of his favorite literary quotations, taken from Ian Fleming's classic Bond opus *Goldfinger*: "Once is happenstance, twice is coincidence, three times is enemy action."

So Ben Malton was a private detective. A pretty cheap one, based on his clothes and the paltry $39 he was carrying. It was now beyond the point of debate that he'd taken enemy action. The only question was why, and Gene had a hunch. All that remained was to flesh out some details.

Hoffman pocketed the cash and tucked the wallet back into Malton's jacket.

Almost a relief, he thought as he stood and walked to the bathroom. *At least now I can stop looking over my shoulder all the time, waiting for this moment to come.*

Removing a plastic cup from its crinkly cellophane wrapper, Gene filled it with cloudy water from the tap and walked over to where the KO'd gumshoe lay. He emptied the cup into Malton's face, and when that failed to revive him offered a few measured kicks to the ribcage.

Before Ben Malton's eyes had completely fluttered open, a size-13 Florsheim settled on his chest, keeping him pinned to the carpet.

"Start talking, shitbird."

"Holy hell, mister," the prone man gasped. "Did I make a mistake!"

"Who hired you?"

"Nah, nah, you got it all wrong!"

"Don't test me," Gene said, pressing down with a less casual application of force.

"I got the wrong room, that's all. Thought my girl was shacked up in here with some filthy taco bender. I'm sorry as all hell."

"Don't rate me too bright, do you, Benny? Think I don't know you've been on my ass the last three days? Trying to corner me behind Binion's, that was your mistake. I'd almost forgotten about you since I got here, had my mind on other things. If you'd played it a little closer to the vest you might've gotten the drop on me."

"Look, friend. I got absolutely no idea what you're talking about."

Gene exhaled wearily. All he wanted to do was sleep but that wasn't an option until some questions got answered.

"I have a pretty good idea why you're tailing me, but you're gonna fill in a few blanks. Like who's paying you, for starters."

Malton tried to look nonchalant as his left hand made a surreptitious advance toward his shoulder holster. Hoffman had to smile.

"I'll kick it out of you if need be, but that sounds like a lot of work. I'm tired and my patience is limited, so please make this easy for both of us."

Malton nodded in false acquiescence, fingers still inching across his chest.

"Standard missing persons case," he explained calmly. "Nothing personal. I earn a few bucks to find out where you are."

"Bangup job. Leave me your card in case I ever want to hire Florida's worst private dick."

Figuring it was now or never, Malton grabbed wildly for the gun. His eyes went saucer when he felt nothing but air under his arm.

Hoffman laughed out loud, then waved the .38 to remove the mystery of its location.

"Why the heater, Benny? That's a little heavy for a standard tail. And why break in if you're just interested in my whereabouts? You've known that for three days."

The look of disappointment on Malton's face almost induced sympathy in Gene.

"Yeah, I spotted you in Hollywood. Didn't think much of it till the third time. So why follow me here?"

"Client's orders. When I called from the coast to say I'd tracked down your address, she... um, they said to stay on you for a few days. Wasn't expecting a midnight dash across the Mojave, you really caught me off guard there."

"Next time I'll send a memo. You haven't answered my question."

"Come on, be reasonable. Client confidentiality's the cornerstone of repeat business in my racket. Word gets back I blabbed, I can kiss that account goodbye."

"You'll be kissing a lot more goodbye if you don't start cooperating," Gene said, his foot stomping harder on the man's trachea and producing a wheeze.

Ben Malton started babbling, but nothing more than a rehash of the same partial facts and complete lies. It became pretty obvious he wouldn't part with any key information without the kind of harsh motivation Gene was really not equipped to provide. Not right now, anyway.

He felt no pressing urge to hurt this man. Far more important was a chance to mull things over without any distractions. Unwilling to let the P.I. walk just yet, Hoffman figured a long forced nap was the next best option.

"Sorry about this," he said, retracting his right leg into a prime kicking position. "Nothing personal."

Before Malton could utter a sound, Gene's foot swung like a wrecking ball into the side of his jaw. There was no need for another kick. The private detective had been knocked clean out for the second time in less than five minutes.

Sitting back on the bed, Gene tried to think clearly. A premonition was making itself known in the form of a noticeable churning in his gut. He'd learned to trust these intuitive clues over many years, and this one was loud and clear:

Malton's just the first wave of attack. Anyone willing to send him all the way across the country to find me isn't fucking around. If he fails, they'll just send someone heavier to do the job right.

That logic was inescapable. And with it came the suspicion that whenever the next threat appeared, Gene would not be able to deal with it as easily as he'd dispatched this one.

Looking down at Ben Malton's sprawled form, an idea came to him. It was rash, but the details fell into place with crystal clarity. He could conjure no other course of action that made sense.

Gene needed two things right now, time and money. The best way to buy a little time was to throw his pursuer off the scent using the most visible piece of bait available. His car.

Just like that, he decided to vacate the El Cortez pronto while Malton slept it off. Hoffman would drive his Plymouth Valiant three blocks south and park in the free lot directly behind the Four Queens. It wouldn't get towed for at least a week, maybe more, but it would be easy enough to spot for anyone who might be canvassing Glitter Gulch in search of it. With a bit of luck Malton would deduce he was still holed up in Vegas, and pass that false lead along to whoever was paying for it.

As for money, Gene had an option to explore on that end as well. He'd much prefer another way, but the roulette wheel had already proved a dead end.

Quickly packing his bag and sweeping the room for any incriminating traces before Malton came to, Gene tried to quell a host of purely rational concerns that nothing good could possibly come from this plan. There was no sense in worrying about it, because he really wasn't able to see any other choice.

Almost as an afterthought, Gene emptied out the five rounds from the .38, wiped his prints with a towel and dropped the gun on the floor. Its owner was too stupid to be walking around with a loaded weapon, but Hoffman had no use for it. If Ben Malton was possessed of any sense, he'd wake up from this encounter with the notion to drop the pursuit regardless of who was paying for his services.

* * * * * * *

Sitting in a poolside room at the Golden Nugget, smoking one last cigarette before going to bed just as people in locales more sane than Las Vegas were starting their day, Floyd Manning wasn't exactly waiting for the phone to ring. But neither was he all that surprised when it did.

"Figured I'd be hearing from you, Gene. Maybe not so soon, but then again why wait? A man of your acumen understands the importance of acting fast on an opportunity of this magnitu..."

"Pipe down, for Christ's sake!" Hoffman barked loud enough to make Floyd jerk the phone away. "Just listen."

"All ears, *amigo*."

"I want to see the loop, the paperwork too. And I want to know everything about the buyer. The whole story, every detail. Got it?"

"You bet."

"No promises, understand? Let's just go to L.A. and check out the goods. Then I'll let you know if I'm in."

"Sounds more than fair. I can head back any time. When are you planning to leave town?"

"Right now. Come pick me up, I'm at a phone booth in front of the Four Queens."

"Um... I thought you drove out. You're leaving your car?"

"No questions, Floyd. If you want me to consider the offer, get your ass over here. On the hop."

Floyd didn't try to ask any more questions. All he did was confirm that he'd be there in fifteen minutes. But Gene didn't hear the words because he'd already hung up.

PART II

HOLLYWOOD

6.

She looked good. She looked better than good, at least from fifty paces in a light drizzle at twilight. Standing tall in a cream colored dress and high heels, she was a beacon of stubborn glamour highlighted in sharp contrast by her decrepit surroundings. The grime and desperation of the Boulevard on a Sunday night made her look like a mirage, a silver screen goddess alive and breathing in three dimensions. She deserved a red carpet under her feet, instead of a smudged brass star emblazoned with some silent film actor's name long forgotten by the masses.

A persistent haze of smoggy heat was finally lifting under the influence of some freakish late summer rainclouds. The denizens of Hollywood Boulevard awoke, following a silent circadian rhythm at direct odds with what most citizens of this fair city looked upon as normalcy.

They were making a show of force tonight. The pimps and hookers. Wastrels and washed up wannabes. Junk hawkers and pickpockets with a predatory eye for unusually careless tourists. Street dwellers of every stripe were crawling out of whatever holes they used to hide from sunlight and the Boulevard was starting to hum. In timed response, a roaming host of prowl cars canvassed each block, ready to do whatever was needed to maintain something like order.

Hoffman lit a cigarette and just watched her. He'd been watching her for almost ten minutes but saw no rush to move closer. It was pleasant enough to just stand here and maintain this low-key surveillance.

He leaned against a lamppost on the southeast corner of Hollywood and Highland, oblivious to the river of bodies navigating around him to access the crosswalk. Put on a bit of weight over the past few years, stretching into something that was starting to look unrecognizable in the mirror. Worse, his episodes of mild chest pain and shortness of breath were starting to come even in moments free of stress or exertion.

Troubling signs to be sure, but Gene wasn't thinking about his health or the throngs of camera-wielding saps clustered about him on this damp evening at the epicenter of Tinsel Town. His entire attention was focused on the woman four traffic lanes away, pacing the "walk of fame" in front of Grauman's Chinese like genuine Hollywood royalty instead of a cheap knockoff.

She didn't look like Marilyn. She *was* Marilyn, right down to the mole. The only thing missing was an open grate for her to straddle and halfheartedly keep her dress from blowing up so the crowd could enjoy a free peep show. It was the same dress from that iconic scene, Hoffman noted. Or a near-perfect facsimile of it. Just as she herself was a near-perfect facsimile, at least from this distance.

Flicking his smoke into the gutter, Gene figured it was time to take a closer look.

He crossed Hollywood at a mellow pace, then over Highland toward the theater. Even on an inclement Sunday night this scene was just one shove short of pandemonium. Early September brought in more busloads of gawkers from around the country than usual. Weaving among the hoi polloi were walking recreations of at least a dozen icons of filmdom.

There's the Little Tramp doing his waddle with the bowed cane and derby. Check out Jimmy Dean signing autographs for a gaggle of squealing teeny-boppers. The accuracy of these impersonators ran the gamut from pretty good (Laurel and Hardy clones packing the right match of corpulence and emaciation) to laughably bad (a sadsack John Wayne who couldn't carry the real Duke's jockstrap, let alone his six shooter.)

Then there was Marilyn, in a different league altogether. Standing under the marquee with her back to Hoffman, a cool breeze snaking down from the canyons ruffled her hair and dress. Gene caught himself holding his breath, waiting for her to turn around and ruin the mirage with a gap between her front teeth or a misshapen schnoz. He was less than ten paces away now, casually pretending to groove on Bing Crosby's pint-sized footprints in the cement below.

When he glanced up she was looking right at him, close enough to touch. A shiver ran down his spine.

She was uncanny. Eerie. Perfect.

Then she ruined everything with a few words.

"Fifty cents for a Polaroid, mister. No wandering hands."

This curt admonition, delivered in a flat Midwestern twang that was both bored and semi-hostile, shook Hoffman from his trance. The voice was so out of place with the vision, he experienced an odd blend of relief and disappointment.

"Sounds like a bargain to me."

He fished in his pants for a half-dollar and she waved to a mangy street urchin in faded black leathers hovering nearby.

"Pay the cameraman," she said, a small grin melting the frosty guard just slightly. "No pockets on this dress."

"Doesn't need pockets. You're not likely to spend any money looking that good."

"Sweet talker, aren't ya?"

Gene got lost in her eyes for another moment and almost forgot about the photographer. Dude looked like he was riding out the bitter end of a three-day speed jag. Dropping two coins into a sweaty palm that trembled visibly, Hoffman stepped back to escape a monstrous waft of b.o.

Marilyn pressed up against him, wrapping a downy arm around his shoulders and flashing two rows of flawless pearlies in a robotic fixed smile. The photographer grappled with the Polaroid like it was a futuristic piece of machinery he'd never seen before.

"None of my business," Gene whispered, "but you deserve a more competent shooter."

"He's a backup," Marilyn said, leaning close enough for her hair to brush against Hoffman's neck. He inhaled some kind of vanilla shampoo and felt movement below the belt. "My regular's laid up with the flu."

Before Gene could reply, a flash popped in their eyes.

"I'd almost swear you were the real item, may she rest in peace. Except I'm not sure she ever looked this good up close."

"I'd rather be Jane Russell," the impersonator murmured, lowering her voice as if in a confessional booth.

"Jane was red hot in her day," Hoffman conceded with a fond nod of remembrance. "Ever see her in *The Outlaw*? Howard Hughes damn near got busted for obscenity, all the cleavage he made her show in that one."

"She was even prettier in *Montana Belle*. I always wanted to be a brunette. Not from the bottle, the real kind. Brunettes are mysterious, don't you think?"

"I'm not all that choosy."

"Anyway," she sighed wistfully, still leaning into Gene, "no one remembers Jane Russell anymore. Probably wouldn't get me much business out here."

Detaching herself quickly, she blew him a kiss before spinning on one heel and strolling away. The sudden departure almost made him wince with an absurdly sad sense of longing.

"Toodle-loo, big fella."

The cameraman was shaking the Polaroid, either intentionally to hurry the emulsion process or because he was undergoing a withdrawal spasm. Gene grabbed it from him and strode off in the opposite direction, taking one last look at the ersatz Marilyn.

He moved slowly east along the Boulevard. No rush, he wanted a few minutes to enjoy the night air. Besides, Floyd wasn't going anywhere.

They'd pulled into L.A. three hours ago. Their drive across the desert, which should've taken no longer than four and a half hours, consumed most of the day, thanks to a prolonged stop at a greasy spoon in Barstow. Manning struck up a conversation with the proprietress, a wide-hipped brunette named Shirley, upon noticing a framed photo of Tom Jones nailed above the counter. Hoffman saw a predatory gleam light the kid's eyes, followed by a barrage of hypnotizing words.

In less than ten minutes Floyd had sold a "one of a kind" piece of merchandise he just happened to have in the Eldo's trunk: a handheld microphone T.J. himself had used onstage at the Hollywood Bowl, its black plastic grip autographed by the great crooner in sliver ink. Watching him retrieve the item from a large duffel bag, Hoffman noticed at least a dozen similar mics jumbled together inside. He didn't bother looking to see whose signatures adorned them. Floyd quoted a fair asking price of $250, but said he'd be willing to give it to a devoted fan like Shirley for one crisp c-note. Done deal.

Orgasmically thrilled with her acquisition, she gave them multiple coffee refills and a bag of donuts on the house. Watching Floyd stroll out of the diner into the desert sun whistling "It's Not Unusual," Gene had to admire the smoothness of his sales craft. He also suspected the whole scene was designed to impress him more than anything else.

When they finally hit L.A., Floyd suggested they stop at the Pig & Whistle for a quick one. It was his favorite Hollywood watering hole, and a short hop from his home where The Platinum Loop waited. Gene expressed his desire to go straight there and take a look. Manning demurred, insisting he needed to quench his thirst after the hot dusty drive. Besides, there was this absolute knockout of a Marilyn impersonator he thought Gene should see. She worked the same stretch of the Boulevard four nights a week.

When Hoffman asked why it was so important to see her, Floyd just said, "Indulge me."

So he did. And had been suitably impressed, while trying to dispel a nagging suspicion this whole scheme he'd been sold was a pile of bunk. Stepping into the darkness of the Pig & Whistle, Hoffman determined not to waste any more time finding out.

Floyd was nursing a rum & coke at the bar. Gene took the stool next to him, waving off the bartender.

"So what do you think, big daddy?"

"You were right. Dead ringer."

"Amazing, isn't it?"

"At first glimpse I wondered why she hasn't parlayed those looks into a sweeter gig than trolling for tourists outside Grauman's."

"Did you talk to her?"

"Just enough to stop wondering."

"Don't judge too quick. She's a tough cookie, and smarter than you might guess."

"What's her name again?"

"Stella. Stella Chomsky. Did I mention how we met? It's a fairly amusing anecdote, actually."

Manning started to repeat a story he'd already related about meeting the girl on Zuma Beach last summer and being responsible for encouraging her to pursue the Marilyn gig. She'd always wanted to use her God-given resemblance to some life-enhancing effect but never figured out how until Floyd pointed her in the right direction. At least that's the narrative Gene was hearing now, for the second time today.

"Floyd, what the fuck. Do you intend to show me the loop or not?"

"Absolutely. I just figured you'd get a kick out of Stella, in light of the project we're partnering on."

"I haven't agreed to anything yet, and my patience is running out fast. Time to put up or shut up, pal."

"No dinner first? Kitchen makes a mean French Dip, it's on me."

Gene grabbed one leg of Floyd's barstool and jerked it sideways, hard enough to get his attention.

"I'm serious. No more stalling."

Manning took a slow sip off his drink, refusing to look even slightly pressured.

"Whatever you say. Let's hit it."

7.

The house was unbelievable. As Floyd's car nosed into a leafy, winding driveway that sloped sharply upward, Gene thought it must be a gag. Either that or his sleep-deprived eyes were failing him. This was one of the most stunning residential structures he'd ever seen.

"Not exactly my dream home," Manning said, hitting the brake. "I'm a beachfront man myself, but it's fine for now."

As they parked in front of a barn-shaped garage, the top floors of the house disappeared from view into a cluster of tall elms. Hoffman craned his neck until it hurt, spotting a massive gothic turret emerging from the foliage against a darkened sky with a few stars peeking through the smog. This place wasn't just the size of a castle, it was actually built to look like one.

Gene had taken some exploratory drives into this section of the Hollywood Hills before, just mapping the area in case he ever hit it big and could afford to move out of the Yucca Flats. He'd noticed that many of the residences up here were designed in ostentatious motifs, some of them bordering on cartoonish. Back in the silent film boom of the Roaring Twenties, a bunch of nutty movie folk blew their wads on domiciles made to order for whatever fantasy or fetish they could invent. Crammed together on steep twisting lanes were Spanish villas, French chateaux, Moorish palaces, Tudor cottages, Chinese pagodas, and more than a few storybook castles.

The last of these was the style chosen by whoever built this gargantuan crib nestled high in the heart of Beachwood Canyon, within spitting distance of the dilapidated Hollywood sign. Stretching his legs as Floyd popped the trunk, Gene just couldn't believe the person he met last night in the parking lot of Binion's Horseshoe was the owner of this place.

But how could he argue? Bag in hand, Floyd walked across a path of embedded flagstones to the front step, fished in his pockets for a key and swung the door wide for Hoffman to enter.

"My home is your home, pal. I hope you'll think of it that way."

After a detailed tour of the grounds that lasted a lot longer than Gene thought it had to, they ended up in the cavernous basement which was appointed with everything needed to qualify as a world-class recreation room. Professional-size billiards with a red felt, darts, backgammon, shuffleboard, and a casino style poker table. Maroon shag carpet three inches deep, wall to wall. Plus a wet bar, jukebox, projection

TV, and ample seating for at least two dozen.

Sensing his guest's impatience, Floyd begged a few more minutes of indulgence to show off the crown jewels of his memorabilia collection. Directed to a large trophy case, Hoffman tried to look impressed at what was on display within. A fairly bizarre collection of oddities, each of which Floyd boasted was imbued with historical merit that warranted a hefty sale price to the discerning collector:

Gig Young's ten-gallon hat from *Only the Valiant*. LAPD-sanctioned brass knuckles used in Bob Mitchum's 1948 reefer bust. A set of enamel fangs worn by Bela Lugosi in *Mark of the Vampire* floating in a glass of murky water. A brass chamber pot used by John Barrymore in his dipsomaniacal dotage. A pair of lace panties signed in lipstick by Mamie Van Doren, flattened beneath a half-inch pane of glass like some odd prized butterfly to preserve her wobbly penmanship.

Were the items authentic? Who knew. If so, were they actually worth anything? Who cared. Gene was at least halfway convinced Manning was sandbagging him.

At the same time, the guy's encyclopedic breadth of detail, delivered with the zeal of a true fetishist, made it hard to dismiss his claims outright. Being a lifelong movie fanatic himself, who'd never made it beyond the most obscure fringes of the filmmaking world in his own career, Gene couldn't help being reluctantly entranced by this miniature world of curiosities.

"I know you're anxious to see the item in question," Floyd finally said, opening a cabinet hidden in the wall. "Take a look at the documents first, for context."

Hoffman accepted a stack of about ten sheets

of paper, stapled together at the top, and sat in the nearest chair.

"Photocopies," Floyd added, taking the adjacent sofa. "Obviously."

"Where are the originals?"

"Probably some filing cabinet in D.C. I have no idea."

Gene's eyes rapidly scanned the top page. The outline of a stamp's circular indentations were visible on the upper right corner, its marking too faint to read. Typed below:

4/17/61. Classified & Confidential 2-A: Restricted Agent Access / Pertinent Facts & Observations on File Film Ref. #A-4761K. Subject: MONROE, MARILYN (born MORTENSON, NORMA JEANE; baptized, BAKER, NORMA JEANE) (female Caucasian / DOB: 6/1/26, Los Angeles, CA.)

Information pertaining to Film Ref. #A-4761K (Item) outlined as follows. Item first brought to Bureau's attention 4/17/61. (Note: Initially logged at Los Angeles Office on same date.)

Special Agent Charles Raymer, assigned to Los Angeles Office, first contacted on 4/13/61 via telephone by Harry Dolitz (male Caucasian / DOB 9/13/20, South Bend, IA.)

Dolitz proposed transfer to S.A. Raymer of an 8mm filmstrip containing images of Monroe that would merit Bureau's interest. S.A. Raymer arranged to meet Dolitz at Trader Vic's Restaurant in the Beverly Hilton Hotel at 8:00 P.M. PST on 4/17/61 under proviso that Dolitz deliver said Item at that time.

Dolitz had produced for Agents in Los Angeles Office numerous confirmations on activities related to noted Hollywood personalities for some time. Information has proved both accurate and useful on a consistent basis. See accompanying file (ref: DOLITZ, H.) for reference.

During interview on 4/17/61, Dolitz claimed no participation in Item's manufacture, nor any precise knowledge of the date. Dolitz claimed Item came into his possession directly from an Unidentified Source who "owed me a favor for certain indiscretions I helped to make disappear." Dolitz refused to offer more details regarding Unidentified Source or said indiscretions.

Upon transferring Item (1 single 8mm reel of approximately 5,040 frames, contained in aluminum canister) Dolitz claimed to have received the following data from Unidentified Source: The location of the film's manufacture was the Hollywood Roosevelt Hotel (7000 Hollywood Blvd. Los Angeles, CA 90028). Date of manufacture estimated by Dolitz to be approximately three years previous.

S.A. Raymer left Trader Vic's and brought Item directly to Los Angeles Office where it was filed and viewed by Head of Special Hollywood Investigations Department for verification.

With a running time of 3 minutes 21 seconds, Item comprises two separate camera angles spliced together. First angle is a medium-wide shot showing Monroe kneeling on the floor performing an unnatural act (oral copulation) on unidentified Caucasian Male, standing.

Angle favors Monroe's right side. Camera appears to be operated by unidentified Third Party. Use of tripod is likely as camera does not wobble throughout duration of this angle.

Monroe wears what appears to be a gold or silver lamé dress or evening gown, pulled down to her waist. No brassiere. Male's face remains out of view for duration, shown from midsection down only. Shirtless, dark trousers lowered to below the knees. Dark socks with "clip" garters. No visible marks or tattoos evident. Approximate height 5'10" - 6'.

At 2 minutes 07 seconds, Male strokes Monroe's hair with left hand for roughly 4 seconds. Otherwise motionless for duration. At 2 minutes 20 seconds film cuts to second angle.

Second camera angle taken from above, looking down at <u>Monroe</u> as unnatural act continues. Angle seemingly intended to mimic <u>Male</u>'s point of view but obviously shot by <u>Third Party</u> as both of <u>Male</u>'s arms visibly held at sides for duration. Some detectible camera wobbling suggests handheld operation by <u>Third Party</u> rather than tripod for this angle.

<u>Monroe</u> kneels on what appears to be a white bath towel, clearly differentiated from the darker carpet beneath. Visible along towel's edge is a "fleur-de-lis" insignia with the letters HR stitched into the fabric. Insignia matches trademarked logo used by the Hollywood Roosevelt Hotel (on towels, stationary, and exterior signage) and would seem to verify claim from <u>Dolitz</u> regarding the location of film's manufacture. Second angle runs exactly 1 minute, 2 seconds.

Reading on, Hoffman could feel a flush of excitement he tried to conceal. If the loop really showed what was described in these documents, it could be worth a goddamned fortune. The most famous woman of the 20th century, her memory branded on the world's imagination as a tragic martyr to her own beauty, caught on film doing *that*? Years of salacious innuendo verified by the unblinking eye of an 8mm camera? It was almost too good to be true, unless it wasn't.

A separate sheaf of papers contained Xeroxes of various photographs. A half-dozen unposed of Marilyn, seemingly taken without her knowledge. A mug shot of Harry Dolitz, dated October 31, 1959. Exterior shots of the Roosevelt, with examples of the two-letter logo highlighted.

"Well," Gene said, setting the documents aside. "Looks official, I guess. Not that these would be too hard to fake."

"They're real, believe me."

"Show me the loop and I'll make up my own mind."

Floyd just sat on the sofa, drumming his fingers on its fine brown leather. His mouth appeared to be welded shut as if he'd been stricken with an instantaneous case of lockjaw.

"Hey," Hoffman said, snapping his fingers. "Let's go, chop chop."

After another long pause, Manning replied very softly:

"This is the hard part, Gene. I hope you'll bear with me."

The defeated tone erased any last vestiges of self-delusion Hoffman had been sustaining since they got to L.A. Hands starting to twitch, Gene's heart rate accelerated to a level primed for confrontation.

"I'm not playing with you, kid. Load a reel on that projector and show me what I've been hearing about for the last twelve hours, or we're going to have a real situation."

"I promise, if you can keep a lid on your temper for a few more minutes I'll explain everything."

"Wrong. No more double-talk. Show me the fucking film!"

"There is no film, Gene. I mean, there is, just not in my possession."

"Then go get it."

"I'm saying it never was in my possession. The guy who sold me those documents turned out to be less than one hundred percent reliable. He was a former agent with the L.A. Office, no longer active as he first described himself. Exactly why he was removed from duty I'll never know, but the upshot is he was shown the door before he could procure the film. With him cut off from the Bureau, I have no way of getting it."

Gene Hoffman was not often at a loss for words, but no immediate response came to him. He really didn't anticipate such an honest admission, and it caught him off guard. More blather, more stalling, some laughably transparent ruse to buy a little more time... these were the tactics he expected Floyd to employ. Anything to dodge or at least push back a truth that was so obvious Gene had known it in his gut from the beginning.

"I didn't bring you here to waste your time," Manning continued. "If you'll just let me explain a few things I swear..."

A wave of blind fury blotted out Hoffman's momentary state of inaction. With two broad strides he'd crossed the room, backing Floyd up against an oak-paneled wall. His hands locked around that scrawny neck, thumbs pressing the adam's apple in a constrictive vice on the windpipe. Floyd's eyes bulged in panic and his tongue protruded madly, transforming his face into a livid jester's mask.

Gene was yelling things that were barely sensible. Then his fingers unclenched and he stepped back, feeling suddenly nauseous. Floyd slumped down to a crouch on the carpet, hacking and sputtering and still trying to speak.

"Shut up for a second," Hoffman said, moving to the sideboard to grab a bottle of brandy. Helping himself to a bolt, he handed it over.

"Have some, it'll help."

Hands trembling almost too hard to bring the

bottle to his lips, Floyd forced down a swallow and winced at the burn.

Hoffman leaned in to grab the crook of his arm and hoisted him upright. Floyd staggered over to the couch and set the bottle down.

"Why, kid? What the hell did you hope to accomplish from this?"

"Everything I told you is true, except that part about actually having the loop."

"Christ. I can't believe I left a discounted room at the El Cortez for this bullshit!"

"Don't con me, Gene. You practically dragged me out of Vegas. Someone was on your tail. Still is, for all I know."

Hoffman didn't reply, waiting to see what Manning would say next.

"Oh yes, I saw your face when that car pinned us in behind Binion's. I was worried myself, but you looked like you saw a damn ghost. Don't deny it. So you give me the high hat when I offer to cut you in on this deal, then an hour later you experience a sudden change of heart. I ask you, who's the bullshitter?"

"You're tap dancing, Floyd. Just come out and say your piece."

"You were *desperate* to get out of Vegas. I gave you a reason, not to mention a ride."

"So I should be thanking you, is that it?"

"Better than attacking me," Manning said, a bit of confidence retuning to his cadence. "And you could at least come up with a decent cover story. Leaving your car at the Four Queens because they do better detailing work than you can find in L.A.? Why insult my intelligence like that?"

Gene knew he had every right to throttle this little bastard, but felt no desire to do so. For some reason, even now the kid inspired an indefinable measure

71

of sympathy. He'd probably been trading on that his whole life, which might explain how he'd made it this far without getting killed.

Floyd stood, grabbing the manila folder and slapping it down on the bar.

"These documents are real. My contact in the Bureau is real, or he was, and so is the buyer. Everything is lined up, I'm telling you. There's only one missing link in the chain separating us from a massive payday."

"Yeah, the only link that means jackshit. How do you expect to close a sale without the loop? No one's stupid enough to pay for some paperwork any half-skilled scam artist could forge."

"Exactly," Floyd said, massaging his throat with one hand. "Finally starting to figure how you fit in, Gene?"

"You said you needed muscle."

"That counts for something, but it's not your most important asset. Strong-arm talent's cheap and plentiful, filmmaking expertise not so much."

Hoffman was already shaking his head. He knew with near certainty what was about to come next, and he didn't want to hear it.

"So we don't have the loop," Floyd said, reaching slowly for the brandy. "No big deal. We just make it ourselves."

He poured two snifters and slid one across the bar. Both men drank, neither of them yet sure whether or not a bloody stomping was about to take place.

"Stella?" Hoffman finally said after draining the glass.

Floyd nodded, careful not to smile.

"Stella."

8.

Ben Malton fed a few more dimes into the pay phone. He'd been on hold for at least five minutes and the delay was starting to chafe. These were long distance charges he was paying. Not that the call was really coming out of his pocket. Malton's daily expense budget for this case ($25, plus any itemized overages such as gas, bail money, etc.) would cover the cost, but he still didn't feel like wasting any more time than necessary.

Frankly, the old woman gave him the creeps. Malton had never met her in person, for which he was grateful. There was a high-strung quiver to her voice that came out at unexpected intervals, discernible over the phone during each of their several conversations so far. It suggested, at least to his layman's ear, some partially embedded neurosis that might only require the right small push to come blasting to the surface.

Well, he was no shrink. Nor did he have the luxury of being too picky when it came to clients. Ms. Cheston paid cash, and had proven her commitment when she'd wired a month's advance to the Western Union near his home address in Miami.

Malton could barely believe almost three weeks had passed from the day that first payment arrived. Since then, he'd been bodily transported over 3,000 miles via airplane, taxi cab, and rented automobile in pursuit of his quarry. Only to end up here in the grimy confines of a phone booth in downtown Las Vegas, waiting for his aged benefactor to come back on the line.

What the hell was keeping her so long? Had she misplaced her teeth?

Malton idly watched the bustle of Fremont Street roar by in two chaotic directions. It was a little past 8:00 P.M. and the foot traffic was heavier than usual for a Monday. Obviously a big convention week, based on the drunken clusters of fez-clad Shriners he'd seen staggering around all day.

They didn't bother Malton nearly as much as the long-haired trash idling on damn near every corner. Do-nothing kids with no respect, not for themselves or their fellow citizens in the U.S. of A. Draft dodgers all, no doubt. Counting himself as a proud member of Dick Nixon's silent majority, few things yanked Ben Malton's chain more than that massive media-generated fraud known as the *counterculture*. What a crock. Why not just call these kids cowardly free-loaders and be straight about it?

Ben's neck was starting to stiffen from cradling the phone in the same position for so long. He had to hold it to his left ear, as the right side of his face was still way too tender for any direct contact. The swelling had started to subside, and amazingly all his teeth were still intact. But he wouldn't be forgetting that mule kick any time soon.

Just as he was muttering a few obscenities under his breath, he heard someone lift the receiver on the other end.

"Mr. Malton? Are you still there?"

"Yes, ma'am. I'm not going anywhere."

"My apologies for the wait. There seems to be some commotion in the front court. Could I ask you to hold for another moment while I see what it is?"

"I can call later, Ms. Cheston. We just need to clarify..."

"Thank you, Mr. Malton. This won't be a minute, I'll be right back."

Hearing the receiver drop again, Malton shouted "Fuck!" at the top of his lungs. He figured the elderly woman's auditory faculties were too dim to catch it over the long distance lines. But a couple of willowy young hippie broads walking past the booth heard it loud and clear. They pointed at him through the glass as if watching a zoo ape play with its own leavings, then pranced away emitting peals of laughter.

Nice. Another small indignity in pursuit of a career Ben Malton was feeling less and less confident he had the capacity to handle. The sound of those girls mocking him was just one more insult added to the injury he suffered courtesy of Gene Hoffman's black leather Florsheim early Sunday morning.

Malton could still see that beefy leg retracting from view, then coming back in a khaki blur that ended in stars. He never felt the actual blow, not until groggily regaining consciousness two hours later.

Then he felt it plenty.

Opening his eyes to find himself on the floor of

that shitbox room in the El Cortez, Malton almost wished the kick had killed him. The physical pain rocketing around his cranium was intolerable, but even worse was the infuriating knowledge of utter failure. He'd allowed an unarmed man to take his gun away and knock him out. Of course, a quick wallet check revealed all his cash was gone too.

Christ, what a fiasco.

The one positive shred Malton clung to from the whole sorry mess was that he'd refused to give up any information on who hired him. That might not be much, but it indicated maybe he had a little more grit than expected.

Picking the lock of room 206 was an incredibly dumb idea. That much was clear, in retrospect. He'd never have tried it if he thought Hoffman was inside. After almost running the man down (and inadvertently blowing his own cover) in the parking lot behind Binion's, Malton figured the last place Gene would go was back to the hotel.

All he'd hoped to accomplish was a quick scan of the room which might yield some piece of evidence Hoffman had stayed there. Something small he could mail back to Ms. Cheston, motivating her to forward another hefty advance.

As for the .38, it was cosmetic more than anything else. He never intended to fire it. Thanks to Hoffman's size-13 foot, that never even became a possibility.

After managing to rise from the floor without vomiting, Ben had pulled himself together and shuffled down to the lobby. The geek at the front desk told him Hoffman checked out around 7:00 A.M.

Malton spent the next few hours grimly canvassing downtown Vegas in his rented Dodge Dart, cursing himself for not demanding a less visible ride from the Hertz counter at the airport in Los Angeles. He should have been more insistent, made a scene right there at the counter until they offered him something better. The Dart's green paint job practically glowed in the dark, making it less than ideal as a tail car.

His elderly client didn't need to know any of those details. Ben decided not to share them when she came back on the line.

"Mr. Malton? Are you there?"

"Still here, Ms. Cheston."

"My apologies again. It appears a carpet cleaner parked in one of the tenant's spaces and it's causing quite a fracas."

"That's alright. This call comes out of my per diem."

"Your what?"

Ben rolled his eyes. "The money you're paying to cover my daily expenses. Now, as I was saying..."

"Do you know where the man is right now?"

"As I was saying, his car's still here at the Four Queens. In the same spot, hasn't moved since yesterday. I'm starting to think he's no longer in the area."

"Why would he leave his car? You told me he drove it out from Los Angeles."

"That's correct. Could be an attempt to throw me off. Kind of a decoy, so I'll think he's still in Vegas."

"I see. What do you suggest as a next step?"

"That really depends on your appetite, ma'am."

She didn't reply and Malton knew it was an inartful way of asking for more money. He tried again with, "I'm happy to stay on the case, assuming you still think it's worth the expense."

"I've already told you money is not my concern. Finding this man is all I care about."

"Well, I found him four days ago."

"And now you've lost him, if I understand you correctly."

Ben held back a salty rejoinder. This was one tough biddy, and a lot sharper than he initially gave her credit for. A native Bostonian, Malton had an innate reaction to lop off 50 IQ points from anyone who spoke with a Southern accent. Snobbish and counterproductive, especially for someone who'd recently made a home in Florida, but old habits are hard to shake. During a routine Q & A conducted over the long distance lines, Ben had learned Scarlett Cheston resided in an upscale South Alabama retirement community. Despite her hothouse drawl and obviously advanced years, she was certainly nobody's fool.

Scarlett was also about as unlikely a client as Ben Malton ever imagined would pay for his services. Rather than seek out a detective in her home town of Mobile, she'd chosen to engage someone sight unseen from the iniquitous city on Florida's Atlantic Coast that had been the locus of a ghastly personal tragedy defining the last decade of her life.

The old woman wasted no time outlining the situation during their initial phone chat. In the summer of 1965, her granddaughter Barbara died of mysterious and almost unimaginably gruesome circumstances in Miami. Nothing had been done in the intervening years to rectify this appalling injustice. Seeing no other alternative, Ms. Cheston said she would pay Ben Malton any fee required to track down whoever was responsible.

The only lead information she could offer came from an article she'd saved from the Miami *Ledger*, dated August 13th, 1965. In mercilessly brief wording, it stated that a 22-year-old amateur actress named Barbara Cheston had died as the result of a "freak accident" during the production of a low-budget movie in a small town ninety miles north of the city limits.

According to the *Ledger*, two men identifying themselves as principals in the motion picture company were questioned in association with the girl's death. After an examination of the crime scene, investigating officers determined there was scant evidence of foul play. In the end, no charges were filed. Over the next several months as she begged for more robust action from the Miami Sheriff's Department, Ms. Cheston encountered indifference at every turn. The police continued to inform her with dwindling patience that Barbara's death was, as reported, nothing more than a tragic accident.

That wasn't good enough for the bereaved grandmother, as Ben Malton had recently come to learn. She'd lived with the sour taste of unrequited outrage for eight painful years, and she couldn't live with it any longer. Those two movie men had to be held accountable somehow, no matter how slim the chances of finding them after so much time.

She'd instructed the private eye to spare no effort in his search. He cautioned it could get expensive, especially if travel was necessary. Scarlett wired him a month's advance and stated in very direct language that financial concerns would not be an impediment in her pursuit of redress.

Leaning against the glass of the phone booth, Ben decided now was a good time to test that claim.

"I think the thing for me to do," he said amicably, "is head back to L.A. The apartment building on Yucca Street is a long-term residence. I braced the super and he was vague but that's the impression I got."

A long pause. Malton thought he could hear the old woman working her jaw in contemplation, producing a dry smacking sound from her lips.

"Are we absolutely sure you've found the right man?"

"Yes, ma'am." Malton flipped open his notebook to the pages containing a brief biographical sketch he'd pieced together. "As I told you, Gene Hoffman is without question the person you're looking for. He's one of the two men who hired your granddaughter back in '65, rest her soul."

"And the other one?"

"Sheldon Meyer. He seems to have disappeared completely. These two men used to be business partners in Miami. They made movies together. Hoffman appears to have been the primary player and he's continued his filmmaking career solo out west. He might be able to provide some info about Meyer's whereabouts, given the proper motivation."

"You mean... you'd *beat* it out of him?"

There it was, that semi-psychotic flutter at the edges of her voice. Malton couldn't tell if she was repulsed or turned on by the prospect of violence. Maybe both.

"As I've told you, strong-arm work isn't my forte. I could maybe point you in the right direction, make a few phone calls. But that's something to be discussed once I reestablish steady surveillance on Hoffman. I can keep poking around Vegas till Christmas with no better chances than I have now. It's kind of a dead end here."

"You want to drop the case?"

"Definitely not. I just get the sense you don't really know what you're paying me for."

"I suppose that's true," she said after a long pause. "I haven't really decided yet, I just felt the need to do *something*."

Her voice trailed off. Malton thought he could

hear her choking down a sob.

"Look, I'll pick up Hoffman's trail soon enough, if you want me to stay on it."

He paused, cruelly letting her wallow for a protracted moment. Then dug the needle in deeper: "Might be cheaper to call it quits for now. Your granddaughter, if you'll pardon my saying... she's not going anywhere, right?"

An empty silence followed those words, causing him to think he might have overplayed his hand.

Then Scarlett Cheston spoke, her voice again clear and firm.

"I want you to stay on it, Mr. Malton. Go back to California if you think that's the right thing to do. Call me when you find that evil man again."

Ben hung up the phone, but not before telling his aggrieved client he'd do exactly as she requested.

9.

Gene ducked just in time. Sixteen ounces of freshly brewed coffee flew past his head, a few brown drops scalding his right earlobe.

Floyd never saw it coming and had no chance. An entire mug's worth of piping hot java caught him flush in the kisser.

The heavy pewter mug, once owned by Steve Mc-Queen and monogrammed on one side with his initials, sailed by Manning's head seconds later. Might easily have knocked out all his front teeth if Stella Chomsky had thrown it with a little more accuracy.

Yelping like a cat with its tail caught under a rocking chair, Floyd elevated off the couch in a spasm of shock and pain. Both hands clutched over his steaming face, he blindly staggered towards the bathroom while unleashing a volcanic string of high-pitched obscenities.

Off to a promising start, Gene thought, wiping his ear dry and suppressing a delirious laugh.

It was his own fault, and he knew it. Never should have agreed to let Floyd do the talking. This was a delicate pitch, to say the least. It called for just the kind of deft hand Gene had employed countless times over the course of his exploitation filmmaking career, the ability to present reluctant "actresses" with a proposition their better judgment instinctively warned them against accepting.

Watching with semi-disbelief as Floyd made a wounded retreat from the basement recreation room where this meeting had begun just minutes before, Gene knew he had to promptly reclaim order or lose the opportunity for good.

Stella was already rising from the couch, lacquered nails splayed like talons ready to finish the job on Manning's scorched visage. Yelling oaths almost as loud and profane as his.

Gene intercepted her by the jukebox. Careful to keep his own face out of clawing range, he guided her back to the couch with a soft but firm grip on her elbow. A few minutes passed, and in retrospect Gene couldn't even remember what words he used to tamp down the girl's indignant fury. He was a little distracted at seeing her without the full Marilyn facade. If anything, she looked even sexier *au naturelle*, with lush strawberry blonde tresses framing that perfect face. No sign of the mole, which Gene could live without. In or out of costume, she was a stunner.

Manning's call to invite her up to the Beachwood Canyon house was flawed from the start. Hoffman thought a public venue offered a more desirable, less threatening environment. Stella would be far less likely to feel cornered in an open setting. And the presence of onlookers diminished the likelihood of a heated confrontation of exactly the kind unspooling right now.

With those concerns in mind, Gene had argued to set the meeting at Musso & Frank. They could sip a few martinis at the bar and loosen the mood before describing what they had in mind. In the worst case scenario—if her response proved vehemently negative—they could always laugh it off as a dumb joke and maybe try again a few drinks later.

Floyd didn't buy that plan. He said the top priority was to implant in her mind the notion they were at least semiprofessional filmmakers, not a pair of hustlers pulling some cheap scam. His mansion was sure to wow a girl like Stella, he knew it.

In the end, Gene yielded. And was now kicking himself for it.

By the time Floyd crept back into the rec room wearing a new shirt and freshly combed hair, Stella had more or less composed herself. Gene hastily assumed control of the discussion.

"Take a seat," he said to Manning, pointing to the furthest chair from the couch where she sat.

"Now let's just start over, shall we? There's no reason not to act like adults."

Stella said nothing, crossing her arms to convey the thinnest veneer of patience.

"It pains me to say this," Floyd began, "but I'm not sure there's much left for us to discuss. This girl's clearly unbalanced, we can't trust her with such a delicate project."

"Don't worry about it, creep. I'm leaving anyway."

"Try not to suck any more intelligence from the room on your way out."

"Screw you!"

"Calm down," Hoffman intoned, "the both of you. No one's leaving, not till I say so."

Stella looked at him, slightly agape. She obviously didn't care to take orders from some guy she'd just met yesterday. But Gene's manner was so smooth, almost fatherly, it was hard to rebuke.

"Look, I've heard plenty already. The answer's no, got it?"

"Could've just said so," Floyd muttered. "You almost blinded me, and that shirt's ready for the Salvation Army."

"What'd you expect, Floyd? I can't believe you'd ask me to do something like that. You're supposed to be my friend."

"Who's dying to make it in pictures, Stell? How many times have I heard you complain about never catching a break, being stuck on the Boulevard like something that walked out of a wax museum? I come to you with a chance for some highly specialized film work, and what thanks do I get? A mugful of second degree burns, that's what."

"Stop bellyaching," Gene said with a peek in his direction. "You look fine."

He had to turn away after those words because in truth Floyd's entire face was lobster red. Some blistering seemed likely, but they had bigger concerns to deal with now.

"Specialized work, that's what you call it?" Stella's voice was rising again. "What do you think I am, some kind of *whore*?!"

"No, I thought you were a little more broadminded. My mistake. Your head's still in Iowa, baby. These kinds of arty pictures play to sellout crowds in the fanciest movie palaces in Europe. But go ahead, turn down a golden opportunity."

"Save the smooth talk for your moron girlfriends. I've got a college degree, jerk."

"We're not getting anywhere," Gene broke in. "This whole meeting started on the wrong foot, there's no denying that. Floyd's already admitted he made a hash of it."

"I never said that."

A dagger look from Hoffman. "Floyd botched it, we all agree. But if we can forget that little misstep, I think there's plenty for us to discuss."

Stella did not look convinced, but was at least still in the room.

"It's a good thing my boyfriend isn't here."

"You're still with that guy?" Floyd asked in a tone of astonishment. "I thought you'd had enough of his macho b.s."

"He's making a real effort to be a more sensitive individual, OK? Not like you care, anyway."

"You were free to bring anyone you wanted," Hoffman said solicitously. "We should have made that clear as well."

"Just be glad I didn't. He's a Marine with two Silver Stars earned the hard way in Da Nang. He'd twist off both your heads in about five seconds if he heard this conversation."

A silence took hold of the room. Floyd cast a reflexive glance over his shoulder, half expecting some kind of vengeful Sgt. Rock to come kicking in the door.

"Well," Hoffman said quietly with a shake of the head, "there's unfortunately been a breakdown in communication. Your boyfriend..."

"Lenny," Stella snapped. "Corporal Leonard B. Hart to the likes of you."

"God bless his patriotic courage. Corporal Hart should have been present from the start, so our intentions would not be misconstrued."

"Can't you use normal words, for Pete's sake?"

"Young lady, who do you suppose we envision as your costar in this unique entertainment?"

It took a moment for the suggestion to sink in.

"You want *Lenny* to do the porno with me?"

"Naturally. You don't think we'd ask you to involve yourself on such an intimate level with a stranger, do you?"

"How was I to know, you never said. And what difference does it make?"

"I'd say it makes a world of difference. If I wasn't partially responsible for the confusion I might take offense myself."

Listening intently, Manning felt a stab of envy for Hoffman's facile command of language. Where'd the big ox learn to lay it on like that? Gene was supposed to be the muscle in this team, Floyd the silver-tongued front man. It distressed him to see Hoffman reveal an entirely new skill set he'd thus far kept hidden, one that veered alarmingly into Floyd's wheel house.

"Exactly right, Stell," he said in an attempt to regain some influence in the conversation. "I guess we blew it by not making that clear from the outset. This isn't a dirty movie, it's a cinematic portrayal of love. We're artists, for Christ's sake. Not pimps."

"Well," she muttered, her voice slowly ramping back down to a calmer level, "I don't even know where to begin. There's no way Lenny would take part in something like this. He's a twice-decorated veteran..."

"And the last thing we'd dream of is embarrassing a national hero," Hoffman jumped in. "To reiterate, this entire film consists of only two shots. His face won't be visible at any time."

"Not even for a frame," Floyd continued. "Your soldier boy will never be recognized, at least not by anyone who isn't extremely well acquainted with him."

"What's that supposed to mean?" Stella hissed, eyes narrowing to a squint. "He's a one-woman man."

"Of course he is," Gene said quickly, using his heel to crush Floyd's foot under the table.

Stella lit a cigarette and gazed into the exhaled smoke as if it contained some coded message.

"OK, fine," she uttered. "So no one will know it's him. What about me? I'd still like to have a shot at legitimate work someday. What are my chances if I'm on film doing *that* for the world to see?"

Hoffman smiled, knowing she was already halfway there.

"Two critical points to emphasize. First, the world's not going to see this. We're making one print for a private collector who will sign a contract agreeing never to show the film in a commercial arena, nor sell it to another buyer."

Floyd nodded briskly, feeling his corns throb.

"That's right, Stell. You can watch us burn the damn negative, so there's no possibility of it ever being duplicated."

"Well, I don't know," she replied, a new spirit of something not far from acceptance creeping into her voice. "What's the other point?"

Gene settled back in a relaxed pose, displaying through body language there was no longer a need to hustle anyone.

"You're not going to do anything on camera, sweetheart. Marilyn will."

10.

The nightmare was always the same. A series of overlapping images and sounds echoing from the depths of his unconsciousness, seemingly more real and alive than anything experienced when he was awake.

That crumbling warehouse on the edge of the beach, one of the most remote areas on the entire Eastern coast of Florida... huge hands closing around his throat, choking his breath away one second at a time... screams of terror and madness... that monstrous buzzsaw, rattling in a mindless blur of rust and steel... and the girl's sweet body disintegrating into a spray of blood and bone fragments.

Say her name. Say it.
Barbara.

Hoffman always woke up with her name on his lips, feeling quite sure he'd uttered it aloud in his sleep.

The dreams began stalking him in the summer of 1971, six full years after the bloodstained events that fueled them. It was his own fault, his own doing. If only he'd never agreed to make that fucking movie! Most days he could barely even bring himself to recall the title, but it came to him just the same.

Crimson Orgy.

The one picture of his entire career Gene had sunk good money into that never turned a profit. Never played before an audience, for that matter.

Base greed propelled him to make the damn thing, overriding every other impulse. Gene was so convinced it would be a box office monster, he ignored countless indications the project had been conceived under a bad sign.

After a half dozen profitable years producing racy drive-in fare in Miami, a hubristic sense of infallibility had overtaken his better judgment. The thought of losing an investment, much less losing control of the production itself, seemed ludicrous at the time. If he'd been a little less consumed by runaway ambition, he might have backed out before it was too late. Hoffman never bought into any kind of fatalistic crap, but a blind man could've seen that there was something seriously wrong with *Crimson Orgy* from day one.

Still, even after what happened to the movie and to Barbara, he'd persisted. Too much time and money had been spent for him to give up without a fight. Ultimately it wasn't his choice to shelve the aborted project after months of futile effort to salvage something from the wreckage. In the end, circumstances dictated no other alternative. When his business partner Shel Meyer suffered a nervous breakdown and disappeared with the original 16mm negative, there was nothing to do but write off the whole disastrous enterprise and try to move on.

For a long while, Gene believed he *had* moved on. Three thousand miles used to feel like plenty of distance. He only spoke publicly of the movie one time, to an interviewer for some obscure French film magazine, a decision made out of sheer desperation to generate some publicity in Hollywood. Despite that small lapse of judgment, Gene felt he'd relegated *Crimson Orgy* to the past.

Then, as if waiting in the back of his mind for the right time to strike, the nightmares began. And didn't cease.

On the rare nights he could doze off without the aid of alcohol, they came roaring to full horrific life, erasing any traces of self-delusion that he'd truly left the ghosts of Florida behind. Every time he'd lurch upright in tangled sheets with a scream at the back of his throat, Gene grew increasingly wary of lying back down. At the moment his mind dipped back into repose, the dream continued full-stop.

It hit him again early this morning at the Yucca Flats. Caused him to thrash so wildly he rolled clear out of bed, landing face-first on the floor, pulse pounding and soaked with perspiration.

A delightful way to start the day.

Lumbering to the bathroom, Gene wondered what he could do to dispel the nightmares that wouldn't require the use of a time machine. Fortunately, he was too busy to brood on the past. A laundry list of very concrete pre-production details occupied his full attention.

At the top of today's task list: wardrobe. He'd already swung by Adele's Costumers to pick up a faux lamé gown Stella would wear for the shoot. In order to get the right fit, Gene now had to drive over to her pad so she could try it on. Floyd had loaned him the Eldo, urging him to use it as long as he pleased.

It would've made a lot more sense for Stella to meet him at the costumers, since some alterations would almost certainly be required. But Gene knew every small step he could take to create a sense of deference to his hesitant starlet was a worthwhile investment of energy. The more coddled and appreciated she felt, the less likely her chance of bolting before the camera rolled.

And so, loyal and attentive producer that he was, Hoffman would deliver the dress right to Miss Chomsky's doorstep. He'd do his best to note where any hemming needed to be made to the garment, and then drive it back to Adele's for the necessary stitch work.

In all truth, he was grateful for the assignment, as it gave him something specific on which to focus his attention. Stepping into the shower, he tried to persuade himself the past was dead and buried, and all the mistakes he might have made along with it. Nothing from Florida could hurt him now.

Oh yeah? What about that private eye you left KO'd in Vegas?

Gene turned the shower's heat all the way up to scald away any nagging inner voices. It almost worked.

About ninety minutes later, he parked on a shady block of Sierra Bonita south of Melrose. Stella's building was the third from the corner, and a surprisingly nice one. Considerably more attractive than his place in the Yucca Flats, not that that was any great accomplishment. Gene surmised with an amused smirk that trolling for tourists in front of

Grauman's must pay pretty well. Either that or the girl had some sugar daddy lurking in the shadows, a possibility that could only create trouble.

With the gown in a garment bag slung over his shoulder, he scanned the list of names on the call box. There it was: S. Chomsky, #212.

The phone rang four times and Hoffman started to grumble with frustration about her inability to be home at the time they'd agreed to meet. She picked up on the fifth ring, and he knew right away something was wrong.

"Gene, is that..."

The sound of a man yelling in the background drowned her out, a hoarse baritone rumble that fairly well shook the call box.

"Yeah, it's me. You OK up there?"

For a moment there was only the commingled screaming of two voices, individual words impossible to decipher. Then she came back on.

"You'd better leave, Gene. This isn't a good time."

"Leave? I'm here with the dress. We gotta see how it fits."

"I know, I'm sorry. Trust me, it's just can't happen right now."

More insensible cries from the unseen man. Hoffman thought he picked up a Southern accent amidst the ranting.

"Is that Lenny I hear?"

"Yeah, and he's super pissed right now. Can you just leave? I'll call you guys when things calm down."

He paused, unsure of his next move. Rescheduling the wardrobe prep would be a hassle. It could push everything back a day, at least.

"Let me in, doll. I want to talk to him."

93

"Trust me, that's a very bad idea."

"Is it the flick? Is that what he's steamed about?"

"Yeah," she answered with what could have been a giggle or a moan. "I told him about it and he went totally ape. Even worse than I thought he would."

Gene's jaw clenched silently as he wondered why nobody was able to follow the simplest instructions.

"I thought we agreed that was a discussion we'd all have together. If you'd let me describe the project in the right way, he might have reacted differently."

"So sue me. We're having a bad day. There's other problems too."

"Try to relax," Hoffman said. "I'm pretty good at cooling people down. Give me a few minutes, OK? If we can't get anything done about the dress today, that's fine."

He could hear her breaths through the intercom, each exhalation seeming to come at a price. He wondered if she'd been knocked around, and how he'd react if he saw any bruises. Christ, he hoped not. On a practical basis, Gene figured it would cause a major delay in shooting. But that's not what concerned him the most. He didn't trust himself to stay calm if confronted with evidence that some coward had raised a hand to that gorgeous face.

Just as he was asking again to be let in, the gate buzzed open. Gene stepped into the foyer, telling himself to keep cool. He'd played the role of mediator in any number of conflicts during the course of his career, from fidgety actresses to unruly crew members to overbearing law enforcement figures. The key was to remain detached from the fracas. No matter what was waiting in that apartment upstairs, he couldn't get emotionally involved.

That resolution got put to the test the instant

he stepped into #212, which was open. A hardback chair flew straight at him, summersaulting end over end.

Hoffman didn't have time to duck. One of the wooden legs clipped his shoulder and sent the chair splintering against the front door.

"Y'all just turn around and walk outta here now. Assumin' you got the least sense in that fat head o' yorn."

Those words of admonition, delivered in an easy backwoods brogue that would not sound out of place singing a lullaby to a sick child, came from a man whose powerful arms had launched the heavy projectile just seconds before.

He was leaning casually against the kitchen nook, barefoot and shirtless in a pair of fatigues, wearing a genial smirk above a bald American eagle tattooed in spread-winged formation across his wide pectorals.

Damn, Gene thought, despite himself. *Gonna need a lot of pancake to cover up all the ink.* Then he brushed that thought aside.

"Just about took my fat head off," he said, careful to keep any trace of confrontation from his voice. "An inch to the right and you'd have brained me good."

The chair-thrower scratched the back of his own buzzcut melon, looking vaguely bored. Any sign of fury audible on the intercom had dissipated. Stella was nowhere to be seen.

The only clue of domestic disturbance in this unit was an incessant pounding from an unseen room down the hallway. Gene figured the tattooed imbecile must have locked her in somewhere.

"Tell me this, cousin. What's a fella supposed to do when an intruder decides to enter his domicile unlawfully?"

"Your name's not on the call box, and I was invited in by the person who lives here. But you know that, don't you, Lenny?"

A slight stiffening of the man's posture motivated Gene to quickly say, "Corporal Hart, that is."

This formal address seemed to placate the barefoot cracker. Feeling some measure of calm return, Gene took a moment to appraise the apartment. Standard one-bedroom furnished rental most likely built in the '30s. Crown molding, faded floral wallpaper, furniture that looked like it belonged to someone's dotty old aunt. Gene smiled at the framed poster of *Montana Belle* hung over the sofa, Jane Russell's natural assets shown to full Technicolor advantage.

"You're still here," Hart said, taking a step forward. "Now that don't make a whole lotta sense."

Hoffman stood his ground, working to suppress a rush of anger. He'd almost been decapitated by this hick, and Stella's muffled but insistent demands to be let out were starting to infuriate him.

"I'm surprised your aims sucks so bad, Lenny. Guess it's better when you're pointing an M-16 at women and babies." Clocking the look of irritation, he added, "Yeah, I heard all about them medals you brought back from Nam."

"Wasn't trying to hit you flush with that chair." Two more steps toward Hoffman. "Just lookin' to get your attention."

"Mission accomplished, dickhead."

The two men were standing nose to nose. Despite an advantage of at least a hundred pounds, Gene knew he couldn't take this guy. The muscled torso, scarred knuckles, and crazy eyes articulated quite clearly that Corporal Hart was a dirty fighter as well as a skilled one. Probably carrying a blade somewhere in those filthy fatigues.

The best move was to just keep him talking as

long as possible, until an opportunity for action presented itself.

"Where is she?" Hoffman asked quietly.

"Who?"

"You know I'm here to see Stella."

"Now that's my woman you're talkin' about. An' I understand you wanna put her in a dirty movie."

"Both of you, actually. Why don't you let her out so we can talk it over."

"I ain't tellin' you to leave again."

"This is stupid. What'd you do, lock her in the crapper?"

As if in answer came the sound of a door jamb creaking open by force. A few seconds later Stella stormed into the room, swearing a blue streak at her boyfriend. He wheeled on her hard, fists clenched.

Moving briskly to position himself between them, Gene felt a weary sense of *deja vu* from playing peacemaker with Floyd and Stella just two days before. Yet he was pleasantly surprised at how easy it was to restore calm on this occasion. Lenny agreed with a terse nod to sit on the sofa and listen without interrupting, at least for a few minutes. Stella perched herself on the arm of a La-Z-Boy, sulkily lighting a cigarette.

OK, champ, Hoffman thought grimly. *Time to earn your share of the cut.*

Speaking in his deepest, most solicitous voice, he started to lay out the numerous benefits available to anyone smart enough to recognize what a great opportunity The Platinum Loop represented. Both "performers" stood to collect handsomely for their participation, and both would remain totally anonymous throughout. It was a win/win if ever such a thing existed.

His pitch seemed to go over pretty well, at first.

Corporal Hart was content to sit quietly, arms folded over his chest in a way Gene knew was intended to show off a pair of rippling biceps Popeye would covet. Stella listlessly killed her smoke, but the alertness of her gaze indicated she was hanging on every word.

Alternating his attention from one to the other, Gene concluded the spiel with a few lofty catch phrases about the satisfaction gained when a group of people pool their resources in pursuit of a common objective. The words felt stale and hollow leaving his mouth, and he ended more abruptly than he'd planned.

Now all he needed was some sign of cooperation from the other two people in the room, and then they could proceed with trying on the goddamned dress.

Lenny was plainly more interested in studying his physique than offering a response. Failing to read anything clear in the Corporal's walleyed stare, Gene couldn't tell how much of what he'd just said had sunken in to whatever passed for a brain inside that cropped skull. Thinking maybe Stella could translate his words into hick-speak, he turned his back on Lenny for a brief moment.

It wasn't brief enough.

Startled by the sound of an Appalachian battle cry, Gene caught a jolting vision in the corner of one eye: Corporal Hart launching from the sofa like a human missile, straight at him.

With barely enough time to pivot, he managed to avoid a direct hit but the impact was still powerful enough to disrupt his balance. The airborne soldier's body weight and velocity came down on him like a load of cinderblocks.

The carpet rose up to smack the back of Hoffman's head. Lenny was right on top of him and it was no contest. Before Gene could make any defensive moves, a pair of muscled hands converged in a skilled chokehold. The two men thrashed on the floor, smashing into a tall bamboo lamp. A shower of sparks and broken glass fell to the carpet, which Lenny used to his quick advantage by grinding Gene's face into the glittering pile.

Vision strobing, Hoffman barely saw Stella's shapely ankles moving in his direction. He didn't hear the thump of a ceramic vase against Corporal Hart's skull, but the grip on his own throat eased instantly. Lenny drooped forward on his back and Gene pushed him off roughly.

"Oh, Jesus Christ," Stella wailed, clutching the vase in her hands. "Are you OK?"

Yeah, just barely, Hoffman wanted to reply in an unruffled tone. *Thanks to you, doll.*

The words wouldn't come. He felt like he'd just gargled a pint's worth of battery acid mixed with rock salt. Stella gingerly set down the vase, which must have been pretty thick as it was still in one piece.

Gene stood, using the sofa for support. She tried to help but he waved her off, attempting to maintain some miniscule shred of dignity. His left arm was on fire, throbbing with waves of angina harder than any he'd felt before.

"I'm so sorry, Gene," she said. "I had no idea he'd do that. Usually he only gets physical with guys smaller than him. Or with me."

"Can I have some water please?" The wheezy sound of Hoffman's voice disturbed him more than the febrile pain radiating through his torso.

"Sure, of course."

She hustled into the kitchen. From the floor, Lenny groaned quietly but seemed nowhere near regaining consciousness. Gene stood ready to swing that vase right into his ugly map at the first provocation.

Stella reappeared with a glass of tap water. Hoffman downed it, wincing at the chlorine sting.

"So you're OK?" she asked, her eyes widening in an expression of real concern that surprised Gene. She hadn't so much as glanced in Lenny's direction, not all that worried about how her psychotic beau was doing down there.

"I'll live. If you weren't so quick on your feet I'd probably be ready for a slab right about now."

"It's my fault. Never should have let you in, not with him acting so crazy. He can be sweet as a kitten but he has a nasty jealous streak. It's only gotten worse lately, I must've been nuts to tell him about the movie."

"Well, can't really blame a guy for taking offense at the suggestion. Especially if he doesn't know all the particulars."

Hoffman chugged the rest of his water and set down the glass. He noticed it was covered with sunflowers that looked hand-painted, and found himself wondering if Stella had wielded the brush herself. That notion made him feel stupidly happy for about half a second.

The pain in his chest and arm had receded to a mild tightness. Each breath was coming easier.

Stella picked up the garment bag and unzipped it halfway. A small smile crept onto her face.

"I can still try this on if you want. It's beautiful."

"No," Gene said, reaching to take the gown from her. "Today's obviously not a good time, I should've listened to you."

She zipped the bag up slowly, plainly reluctant to let it go.

"Too bad. I was really looking forward to seeing myself in it."

"Maybe we can reschedule, I don't know."

100

Hoffman didn't have the slightest inclination to talk or even think about the loop right now. Meeting Corporal Hart had rapidly drained his interest in the project. How could they proceed as planned with this lunatic chawbacon on the team?

"You want my advice," he said with a turn for the door, "any guy who'll smack you for good reason will probably do the same for no reason at all. Maybe not today or tomorrow, but soon enough."

She was again looking at him intently, and there was even something else behind her eyes. A trace of desperation for him not to leave, certainly. But another emotion as well, one that promised nothing but headaches and made Hoffman flush slightly.

"I want to believe he can change," she said, taking a step closer. "At least I used to. He always says it'll never happen again, and I always give him another chance. Sad, huh?"

Two more steps and her body was pressed right against Hoffman's, the closest they'd been since that first meeting on the Boulevard. His discomfort shot up in prefect harmony with his arousal. He needed to leave, now.

"I'll be in touch."

Gene was halfway out the door when she stopped him with a word:

"Wait."

He paused, knowing on a very rational level the smartest thing he could do was walk out of the apartment, go home, and forget all about The Platinum Loop.

And knowing on a deeper level he wasn't going to do anything of the kind.

"I'm coming with you," Stella said, grabbing her purse and a set of keys.

"Hold on. What about him?"

"He'll wake up eventually, and I don't want to be here when that happens. Besides, he'll need some time to think about what a jackass he's been."

She slipped an arm though the crook of Gene's and they assumed the conjoined pose of two lovers ready to take a stroll. He stood in place, still fighting the situation without resisting all that hard.

"I'm serious," Stella said, speaking with more command. "I want to see what that gown looks like."

11.

Parked at the northwest corner of Hollywood and Mariposa, Ben Malton kept a keen eye on the front door of Adele's Costumers. The shabby little rental house stood directly across the street, its entrance partially concealed from view by several clotheshorses planted on the sidewalk. A sampling of outfits wilted in the furnace-like heat: canary yellow zoot suits, cracked leather cowboy regalia, glittery flapper skirts, two shiny spaceman getups complete with fishbowl helmets, several Roman togas, a Catwoman leotard, and a bunch of other disguises Malton couldn't see from his vantage point.

It was just past noon and the private eye was perspiring with abandon. He didn't dare turn on the Dodge Dart's AC unit for relief. It worked alright when the car was in gear but seemed likely to induce engine burnout if engaged while idling.

Malton had been maintaining a steady tail on his quarry since Hoffman left the apartment on Yucca this morning. Reestablishing a bead on him was even easier than anticipated. The fat man had run right back home from Vegas, just as Ben surmised.

Hoffman's decision to dump his Plymouth behind the Four Queens remained a mystery, though now an irrelevant one. Malton suspected his initial notion was right, that it was a half-cocked bid at misdirection. The simple fact that his instinct about returning to L.A. had proven sound gave the P.I. a tangible and welcome jolt of confidence.

When Hoffman left the apartment this morning in a champagne Cadillac, his first stop was a side street in the Melrose district where he'd entered a residential building and emerged shortly afterward with a blonde knockout on his arm. From there, a straight shot to this costume shop on the somewhat seedy eastern lip of Hollywood.

He and the girl entered Adele's with their arms linked and a long garment bag in tow. They'd been in there now for the better part of a half hour.

Malton considered cutting bait and going back to lie down in his rented room for a while. This heat was punishing, a man couldn't accomplish anything worthwhile under such conditions. The temperature in Miami rarely bothered him even at summer's peak, so he figured it must be the smog that depleted him so badly today. Why anyone would choose to live in a city covered by a permanent canopy of shit-brown pollution escaped him.

He decided to hang tight for a few more minutes, for the hell of it. There was really no need to follow Hoffman's every step, not any more. Malton knew where the man lived and could make his move at any time.

Except he wasn't ready yet. Despite committing himself to an irrevocable course of action over the phone eighteen hours ago, Malton wasn't a hundred percent sure he'd *ever* be ready. A certain prudent sliver of his brain struggled to believe he was capable of premeditated murder.

Calling his answering service from the motel he'd checked into upon arriving back in Hollywood, the private dick felt almost gleeful to hear he had eight messages waiting. Perhaps business was starting to pick up. That hopeful assumption was quashed when he learned all eight were from his only client, Scarlett Cheston. The service said some old woman had grown increasingly frantic, demanding he call her immediately without regard for the time.

So he dialed her home number, even though it was past ten o'clock in Mobile. Scarlett answered on the second ring, sounding just slightly closer to hysteria than usual. She hadn't said more than a dozen words before Malton picked up her intent. It didn't surprise him all that much.

He'd been anticipating this shift in the equation as one of two equally likely developments. After almost a week of pointless surveillance, Ben Malton's gut told him Ms. Cheston would either drop the case or take it to another level.

And now he had his answer. The grieving oldster had decided nothing less than freshly spilled blood could atone for the evil inflicted upon her granddaughter. Gene Hoffman's blood, to be precise, along with irrefutable evidence the man would never draw another breath. Scarlett promised Malton ten grand for performing that service, and promptly wired him five hundred as a carrot.

He could have refused. Even gone so far as to report the crazy old bat to the proper authorities in Mobile. Or he could have followed through on his implied promise from their last phone conversation, to act as a middle man by finding someone willing to pull the trigger for a percentage of the fee.

Based on the street trash he'd seen loitering outside his flop, Ben didn't figure he'd face much of a challenge in scaring up a suitably desperate candidate. He'd have his pick in selecting some shambling lowlife willing to play rubout man for the price of a quick fix. Each corner within a five-block radius offered an assortment of down-and-outers of every stripe. Street level pushers, shellshocked vets, wetback day laborers flagging down cars for construction work, any of them might fit the bill.

He quickly rejected the idea. Why reduce his own payday, and risk a botched job that could be traced back to him? Made no sense, assuming he could actually do the deed himself.

Hoffman and the stacked blonde reemerged from the costumers, snapping Ben out of his reverie. He noticed the garment bag was no longer with them.

The big man opened the passenger door for his companion, then got behind the wheel of the Cadillac and pulled into eastbound traffic on Hollywood Boulevard.

Ben's foot froze on the accelerator. More valuable than pursuit at this moment was getting a handle on the man's daily business, to better map out a smart time to make the hit. Of paramount importance was cornering the target alone. Malton had no intention of plugging any innocent bystanders, definitely not any as gorgeous as that blonde. Perhaps learning the purpose of their visit to the costume shop might shed some light on Hoffman's comings and goings.

106

Entering Adele's and feeling a wave of gratitude for its cool darkness, Ben approached a rather zaftig woman of maybe forty seated on a comically tiny stool behind the counter. She appeared to be the only person in the store, which was good.

"Afternoon," he said, pantomiming an interest in the innumerable wigs, hats, and makeup appliances on display above the counter. "You Adele?"

"That's what the sign says."

"I've heard a lot about this place." That inane remark, intended as a compliment, attracted no reply whatsoever. She didn't even bother glancing up from her copy of the L.A. *Free Press*.

Malton pressed on with, "Hot enough for you?"

Looking at him askance, she almost managed a smile. "What can I help you with today? We have a wide selection of elevator shoes, all styles."

Ben felt himself stiffen involuntarily. The nerve on this tubby bitch. How dare she insult someone who for all she knew was an honest paying customer?

"Actually," he said, no longer trying to sound friendly, "I'm here for some information."

"I figured that much."

"Oh? How's that?

"Doesn't seem likely you'd sit in your car all this time for the sheer pleasure of it. Not in this heat."

Another jolt. She'd made him! How was that possible? Maybe she was still busy setting up the clotheshorses out front when he parked at the curb. Regardless of how, what he really needed to know was if she'd said anything about it to Hoffman.

"So you're the owner of this establishment?"

"Who's asking?"

"Me," he said, flipping open his wallet. "I'm a licensed private investigator looking for a wanted man."

Adele raised her plucked eyebrows for a brief perusal of his proffered Class "C" License.

"You're a long way from home."

"That large individual who was just in here, with the girl. What did he want?"

"Nothing. Not that I'd be inclined to tell you if he did."

"Now see, Adele, your attitude's all wrong. I saw him walk inside carrying a garment."

"Of course you did, Ellery Queen. This is a rental house."

"OK, we're getting somewhere. Mind if I take a look at the receipt?"

"I do."

"How about telling me what name he gave you?"

Finally looking up from the paper as if deigning to take a serious appraisal of something stuck to the bottom of her shoe, Adele spoke in a patient voice.

"I really don't appreciate this harassment, Mr..."

"Malton. Ben Malton."

"Every customer of mine is entitled to privacy, and if you actually did see some of their names you'd understand that. So unless you're interested in any of the items currently in stock, I have nothing to say to you, Mr. Malton."

Her gaze returned to the paper in an unmistakably final descent.

Fair enough. This painted cow didn't want to be helpful. Time to provide her with a little rough encouragement.

Ben Malton did not normally respond well to confrontation, one of many tendencies that made him a poor private detective. He knew this, but that knowledge hadn't persuaded him to seek an alternate line of work. He simply managed to keep hanging on, absorbing the hatreds and frustrations of his bargain basement clients. Convinced that one big payday might elevate him to a higher stratum of his profession or just get him out for good.

That payday now hovered within reach. But it would not arrive without some effort that required Ben to overcome any number of personal barriers.

"Have it your way, Adele."

Reaching across the counter to grab a turquoise wide-brim ladies' hat of the type favored at the Kentucky Derby, he ripped it in half. A starburst of ivory down feathers fluttered to the floor.

Adele was off the stool in the blink of an eye, *Free Press* tossed aside.

"You rotten little creep! That cost a hundred dollars, I'll have you arrested!"

"You've got much bigger problems than the hat right now, believe me."

"Pay up and get out of my store! This instant!"

Ignoring her, he walked over to a shiny leopard skin bodysuit.

"My, this looks very expensive. Be a shame if it got torn."

Adele was already halfway around the counter, broad hips pumping. Malton ripped the bodysuit down from the neck, its thin fabric coming apart easily in his hands.

"I'll call the police! You'll be in a cell so fast your head will spin!"

Ben rotated on his heel to face her. His right hand knocked over a rack of dresses, causing it to clang noisily onto the floor.

These aggressive movements were enough to halt her progress abruptly.

Turning back toward the counter, she made for the phone in frantic strides. Malton beat her to it, yanking the cord from its jack.

For the first time since he came in, the plump woman looked at him with something other than naked scorn in her eyes. Malton saw fear in his ovoid double reflection, and it felt good. He knew this encounter had just taken a turn in his favor.

"Adele, we need to understand each other. I won't be leaving without some information, so let's make this as painless as possible, shall we?"

12.

To place the call or not? That was the question sniping at Floyd's peace of mind as daylight crept away over the rolling peaks above Hollywood. He'd neglected to turn on any lights and the Beachwood mansion was transforming itself into a lair of reaching shadows. For the past hour he'd been lounging on the Elizabethan four-poster in the master bedroom, trying to devise some kind of mental game that would distract him from the familiar nagging urge to pick up the phone and make the call.

He knew it was not a wise idea. No imaginable good could result from dialing those twelve digits connecting him to that gargantuan house seething with ill intent more than thirty miles across the Mexican border.

Floyd had already promised himself, almost a year ago, never to attempt contact with her until he was able to do so in person. To walk through those grandly sinister colonnades and show his face with no hesitation for the outcome of that action, however disastrous to his personal wellbeing.

It had been a long time coming, but the wait was almost over. When the loop was in his possession, he would see her again. Even if she spat in his face or just ran from the sight of him, he would be laying eyes on Celia very soon.

That dizzying prospect did nothing to lessen his desire to hear her voice right now.

Manning reached for the bedside table. Instead of picking up the phone, he grabbed his wallet from the dresser and extracted the small photograph carefully preserved within its side pocket.

He never got tired of looking at the photo. Didn't matter how wrinkled and faded it had grown over time. The colors still sprang vivid in his mind as he allowed his eyes to wander across every detail. He remembered snapping the picture, telling her to hold still, an instruction she'd had some difficulty follow-ing given her rush of excitement at posing beneath the Hollywood sign.

As she'd stood on that patch of ground not too far from where he now lay, long black hair fanning slightly with the aid of a canyon breeze, Floyd care-fully framed the shot so that the entirety of the sign was visible in the hilly background behind her left shoulder.

It had been a beacon, calling her across the bor-der into a new land. Not that Celia harbored any as-pirations of fame and fortune. The Hollywood sign had a very different meaning for her. That uneven line of blocky letters, stretching 450 feet across the scrub-covered hillside of the Cahuenga Peak, represented a more basic promise that no circumstances are insurmountable.

He'd insisted on snapping almost an entire roll, knowing she'd keep the best shots or take them back to Tijuana to show her little sister. Floyd saved this one for himself, just in case. As if even back then he recognized the possibility that things might go wrong and a future would arrive in which the closest he could come to touching her was by tracing a finger along the rumpled surface of a photo.

Screw it, he thought, carefully tucking the picture back into his wallet. What harm was there in placing a simple call?

Manning grabbed the phone and dialed. The international connection always took forever. Three rings, slightly fuzzy from the poor quality of phone lines in that remote part of the country. Four. He was ready to hang up on five, then someone answered.

"*Casa de Prewett. Diga.*"

Floyd swallowed dryly. Her voice was the last thing he actually expected to hear; much more likely that Rodrigo or Jaime would answer. But it was her, beyond doubt. Just those few words of greeting left no question in his mind who'd spoken them.

"It's me, Celia."

The pause that followed was difficult to gauge. Right as he was sure she'd broken the connection, she spoke again.

"What do you want?"

"Just to know you're alive and well."

"*Bueno.* Now you know, not that it's any of your business."

"Obviously I don't blame you for feeling that way. It still does me no end of good to hear your voice, just as clear and robust as in my memory."

"Floyd, I'm hanging up now. Don't call back."

"Wait," he said hastily. "Just wait a second, please."

"*Qué quiere?*"

"*Para hablar contigo.* Just for a minute or two. I'm guessing he's not within earshot?"

A pause.

"He's outside," she said. "With the others."

"Henry Prewett never changes, does he? Playing the gracious host to a collection of well-heeled degenerates again?"

"All summer long. One group leaves, two or three days later another arrives. European, American, Latin American... they're all the same. They eat, drink, scream and dance all night, watch dirty movies, probably screw each other silly. *No quiero verla,* I try to stay as far away as possible. It's not easy, even in a place this big."

"What are they all doing now?"

"Henry took them down to the kennel. They're betting on the dog fights."

"You weren't interested in placing a wager?" he asked, risking a joke.

"Please," she said, and he almost heard a sliver of wary amusement creep into her voice. "You know I refuse to watch that. Henry made me once and I told him never again. It's the worst thing I've ever seen. *Es muy bárbaro.* And you *gringos* say cock fights are bad."

"Abusing any animal for sport is purely atavistic brutality. I'd certainly never condone such a vile abomination."

A small exhale came as reply, one he dared to hope was akin to a laugh.

"Ah, Floyd. You probably think I miss hearing those fancy words of yours."

114

"Well, I don't know. Maybe *un poco*?"

"*Sí, solo un poquito.* And now I don't need to hear any more. Goodbye."

"There's one more thing you should know," he almost stuttered, racking his brain for a phrase that would convey he had something serious to say. "*No es... no es ninguna broma.*"

That didn't sound correct to his ear, but apparently it was close enough to the mark.

"I remember all your little tricks to keep me on the phone. They don't work anymore."

"No tricks. I really do have something to tell you."

"*Escuchando*, for another two seconds."

"I'm coming down, *chica*."

"Coming down where, *cabron*?"

"Mexico. The Plantation, a few days from now. Saturday at the latest."

"How come it's so easy to tell when you're lying? Didn't used to be."

"No lie. I've already spoken to Henry about it. I'm bringing something for him to look at, something I know he's interested in seeing."

"Don't!" she said, a new tone of urgency coming through the line. "I mean it. Whatever you're thinking, Floyd, do not come here. *Es definitivo.*"

As he combed his mustache with his fingers and tried to think of a persuasive reply, a loud sonic disturbance started emanating from the mansion's first floor. Someone was pounding on the front door. With a sledgehammer, from the sound of it.

Christ, the worst possible timing.

"Can you hang on, Celia? *A sólo un minuto*?"

He sat there holding the phone like a dolt, knowing she was already gone. And the pounding just kept getting louder.

Lurching to his feet, Floyd told himself to keep cool. There was no way the person he most feared might be knocking at the door was actually here. That just was not possible for at least another two weeks. And besides, the old man could never generate that much noise with his own feeble arm strength.

Running down the hallway to a large bay window that overlooked the mansion's front entrance, Floyd mashed his face against the glass in a futile effort to see who was standing outside three floors below. The angle was too sharp, so he walked downstairs at a brisk clip and opened the door.

Occupying almost the entire stoop was a burly gentleman of maybe forty in soiled dungarees and muddy boots. A large toolbox sat at his feet. The garden hoe slung over his shoulder was not held at a particularly threatening angle, but it sent a clear message nonetheless.

"Arthur, what brings you here?" Floyd said, trying to sound pleasantly surprised. "I didn't expect to see you till Thursday. Have you shifted your schedule for watering the eucalyptus trees?"

"Mr. Swanson calls me," the man said in a slow rumble indicating a delayed transmission from one synapse to the next. "He calls me at home, in the middle of the night."

"Quite rude, even for such a generous employer. Goes with the territory, I suppose."

Floyd's strained attempt at establishing a chummy mood was falling flat. It didn't seem to register with the box-framed handyman.

"Mr. Swanson says he's been calling all week, can't get you to answer the telephone. He knows the telephone is working because it rings but you don't answer."

"Well, I don't spend too much time lingering here

116

at his beck and call. That's not to be expected of a loyal tenant, is it? A man's got to stay active, I don't need to tell you that."

The handyman just blinked a few times. He'd heard Floyd's high-wire verbal locomotion before, and had either decided to ignore it today or never understood more than a fraction to begin with.

"Mr. Swanson calls me last night," he repeated as if the last ninety seconds never occurred. "Calls me at home when I'm sleeping!"

"Unconscionably rude," Floyd attempted to commiserate. "Of course, he may have been confused about the time difference. It must have been around lunchtime in Paris when he dialed. Can't you just picture the old boy strolling along the Seine, going pie-eyed at the medieval majesty of Notre..."

"Stop talking!"

Floyd recoiled slightly at these words, delivered as almost a shout, and the realization that there may be no easy escape began to set in.

"Mr. Swanson says you are to leave. Today. He says I am to make sure you leave. He says I am to stay here until he gets home from Europe to make sure you don't come back."

Deep breath, Manning told himself. Keep the mood light and agreeable.

"Arthur, I have no doubt you're carrying out his instructions to the letter. But the wisest thing would be to allow me to speak to our mutual benefactor myself. I have no doubt this misunderstanding can be cleared up in a matter of minutes."

"Mr. Swanson says you haven't paid rent in three months. He says I should call the police. I tell him I don't need the police to make you leave."

The hoe tilted a few inches in his direction. Floyd knew the movement was not accidental.

There would be no negotiating with this green-thumbed troglodyte. A regrettable turn of events, to say the least. Floyd had every reason to believe he could float the rent for another few weeks without this kind of rude eviction. With old man Swanson not scheduled to return stateside from his recuperative European holiday until the end of September, there seemed little reason to worry.

It was nothing short of a bald injustice. Hadn't Floyd been an ideal tenant, keeping the house in immaculate order while its doddering owner gallivanted across the continent in a haze of partial senility? So what if he'd failed to write out a check for a few months running? It galled him to realize Mr. Swanson showed so little faith in his promises to make good on a rather large balance of unpaid rent. The last time he'd spoken with the grizzled septuagenarian on the phone, roughly two weeks ago, he'd gleaned no indication such a dire move was in the wind.

And now he was to be replaced as the guardian of this domain by a Neanderthal groundskeeper who by any measure of common sense shouldn't be allowed to set foot inside a house containing such a multitude of rare antiques.

Unbelievable.

Well, there was no point in arguing the matter any further. Floyd got a sense that Arthur was itching to move this encounter to a physical plane, had perhaps even been encouraged by Mr. Swanson to do so at the first sign of resistance.

"I'll need about fifteen minutes to pack my things."

Without waiting for a reply, Manning turned and headed for the stairway. Hearing heavy footsteps behind him, he knew Arthur was following to closely supervise his egress from the property. Caught up in

the furious humiliation of the moment, Floyd didn't have time to consider how this untimely development would impact his plans with Gene Hoffman. They'd already decided to shoot the loop in one of the bedrooms here, an intention suddenly rendered hopeless.

But Floyd wasn't thinking about that right now. He was too concerned with trying to figure the best way to carry out his entire memorabilia collection. Not to mention where the hell he was going to sleep tonight.

13.

"Ready for another?" Gene asked, swirling the cubes in his freshly drained glass.

Stella murmured something into the creased flesh of his neck. It sounded vaguely affirmative.

"What was that?"

"I said," she replied, raising her head to give him a look of drowsy satisfaction, "let's split one."

"Sounds good to me."

He lifted his arm to slide out from beneath her. It felt good to get out of bed, at least for a moment. Hoffman was plenty thirsty for another glass but was also glad just to stand up. She'd been dozing in the same position for the past twenty minutes and his arm was starting to go to sleep.

Reaching to the floor to slip on his XXL boxers,

Gene grabbed the bottle from his desk. Decided to only pour a small one, out of deference to his next hard-on. He had at least one more good toss in him tonight, assuming Stella was game.

Game? The girl practically put me in traction.

Returning to the bed with a refill, he offered her the glass.

"So," she said, sitting up, "were you surprised to see me today?"

Gene paused before answering, remembering how he felt this afternoon when he came back from a three-hot dog lunch at Pink's to find Stella waiting on his stoop in front of the Yucca Flats. In truth, he wasn't surprised, not after the events of yesterday. Once the fitting at Adele's was done he'd driven her straight back home, overriding her pleas to stop at the Tiki-Ti for a few drinks first. Hoffman's willpower had proved strong enough to avoid any unwise dalliance, but he knew it would never hold up in the face of more overt temptation.

So her appearance today hardly qualified as a shock. He'd almost been waiting for her to show up. Knowing it was foolish to get mixed up with this broad and her maniac lover, even if any realistic chance of fabricating The Platinum Loop was now gone. And knowing damn well he'd never be able to stop himself if she made the first move.

Gene didn't give voice to any of those thoughts, just enjoyed a sip and smiled.

"Yeah, I was surprised."

"In a good way?"

"What other? Not every day I come home to find a movie star at my door."

She rolled her eyes in mock disdain at that comment, but he could tell it pleased her.

"So poor Marilyn gets to keep her dignity, huh?"

"Looks like it," he said. "I hardly see how we can proceed as planned. Not after what happened with the guy who was supposed to be your costar."

Stella wrinkled her brow. "We could always find someone else to do it with me."

"No. Floyd may have been kidding when he said we're not pimps, but it's true for me. I wouldn't let you go on film doing that with some stranger."

"I was thinking about you," she said, scratching his chest with kittenish amusement.

"Sorry, doll. I work strictly behind the camera."

"What?" she asked, reaching down to grab his goods. "Worried you might get stage fright? I'll take care of that."

"Some firecracker you are. Two days ago you almost ripped Floyd's face off for suggesting the thing, now you're all gung-ho."

She shrugged, disappointing Gene by releasing her grip.

"It's tough waving goodbye to all that money, assuming it was ever real to begin with. What were you going to do with your cut?"

He looked at her, reaching over to brush a golden lock from her damp forehead.

"That, my dear, is an interesting question. My plan was to sink some of it into a screenplay I think has real potential. Probably fork out some more for development expenses, whatever it takes to get the thing off the ground with me attached as producer."

"What's this one about? Marlene Deitrich's muff-diving adventures?"

Hoffman's barrel chest rolled with laughter.

"Nothing of the kind, it's a legit drama. Very topical, about this kid who comes home from Vietnam all screwed up, can't adjust to life in the States. It's the type of story that could draw name talent, I think."

"You don't sound all that enthused."

"Got no way to afford the property now. I'm starting to wonder if I'm cut out to make it in this town."

"Something will turn up. It has to."

"Oh yeah? Why's that?

"Because I'm counting on you to make a star out of me. A real one, not a fake."

"You're plenty real."

He leaned in for a smooch. Her response was warm, ready. She climbed on top, wrapping her legs around his broad waist. A kiss on the nose and a nimble swivel of her hips brought him inside her. Gene's hands each grabbed a supple cheek to offer balance as she began rocking in place, arching her back with a soft hiss.

A shadow passed across the bedroom window. Gene caught just a glimpse of it over her shoulder, the hairs on his neck rising in response.

"Hold on," he said in whisper, gently pulling her up and off of him.

"What's up?"

Raising a finger to his lips, he rose from the bed. Opened the closet door and pulled a Louisville slugger from inside.

Stella sat up, looking alarmed.

"What's going on, Gene?"

"Any chance soldier boy followed you here?"

"No. He's drinking in Long Beach with his Marine buddies all day."

"All right. Give me a minute."

"Tell me what's happening."

"Just sit tight. It's probably nothing."

He wanted to believe that as he stepped out of the bedroom, bat held high. But a queasy intuition told him another tale. Ben Malton, the grubby P.I. he'd almost managed to forget about for the last day or so, was back. After the beating he took in Vegas, the schmuck was probably playing for keeps this time.

Stepping across the darkened living room, Hoffman saw a man's figure silhouetted in the window next to the front door. Just standing there, face pressed close to the glass in an attempt to peer through the gauzy curtains.

I'm not letting him break in twice. Gonna take this asshole by storm.

Turning the bolt as quietly as possible, he yanked open the door, ready to decapitate whoever was on the other side.

Which turned out to be Floyd.

"Jesus," Hoffman exhaled, lowering the bat and willing his heart rate back to normal. "Trying to get your skull bashed in?"

"Fairly aggressive approach to home security you're adopting, Gene. A bit much, maybe?"

"We've had a lot of break-ins around here. Why the hell didn't you knock?"

"I wasn't sure you were home."

"Very dumb idea to go snooping into windows in this neighborhood."

"Noted. Are you going to invite me in?"

Gene stepped aside to let Floyd enter the apartment. He planned to get rid of him fast, but knew any move to telegraph that intention would only arouse Floyd's curiosity.

There was no need to hide the fact that Stella was in his bed. Manning had no claim on the girl, and other than the fact that Gene usually maintained a rule about not sleeping with his leading ladies until after filming, he didn't see anything wrong with tonight's energetic coupling.

Still, a gut sense told him Floyd would not react favorably. It could only cause complications, more

124

possible tension when that's the last thing they needed. Gene decided the wise move would be to offer him a drink and then show him the door.

"Scotch? It's all I got."

"Nah, I'm OK."

"So what's on your mind?"

"Been thinking about our location. Obviously you're the experienced filmmaker here, but it seems to me we need a real hotel room for authenticity."

"What's wrong with the mansion? Plenty of rooms we can shoot in there."

Manning sighed. He pulled a cigarette from his pocket but didn't light it.

"The mansion's off limits. We, uh, no longer have access to the property. Let's leave it at that."

Something clicked in Gene's head. A realization so conspicuous he almost couldn't believe it had survived his innate skepticism this long.

"That's not your place, is it?"

"What difference does it make? I was living there for a while. I no longer am."

"Jesus, have you been straight with me about *anything*?"

"Don't get carried away. I thought my lease would last a little longer than it did. The reasons why don't add up to much, what matters is finding a suitable alternative for the purposes of filming."

Hoffman felt halfway tempted to dig for some details, if only to cause Floyd the embarrassment of explaining the situation. But he couldn't muster much interest in that right now. Not with Stella lying nude in the next room.

And besides, he wasn't sure Manning ever said he actually owned the mansion, though the implication had been clear enough.

Gene also didn't have the stomach to tell Floyd

about his disastrous encounter with Lenny, or that the whole twisted scheme was more or less dead in the water.

So he just said, "Well, we could shoot here in a pinch."

Floyd pulled a frown. "No offense, Gene, but your pad struggles hard to pass itself off as a suite at the Roosevelt."

That was true enough. How could they expect to dress this dingy little apartment to make it believable as a penthouse suite in a luxury hotel? Even keeping the action framed as tightly as possible, which they intended to do with both shots, would the crumbling stucco walls and rat-chewed carpet pass the test of anything more than a casual screening?

All those concerns were probably moot, but Hoffman didn't feel like opening up that can of worms right now.

"Fine, I think it's a fair point."

This quick agreement seemed to catch Floyd off guard, as if he'd anticipated some resistance.

"Great, we concur. I'm thinking of a cheap little hotel over on Wilcox. The Mark Twain it's called, don't ask me why. I know the manager, a pockmarked old cretin named Angelo. Pretty sure we could swing a room for an hour or two, if we let him watch."

"Forget it," Gene said bluntly, realizing the stupidity of arguing. "It'll be touchy enough, the last thing we need is another body in the room."

Floyd started pacing the carpet. He didn't feel like mentioning that he'd already offered the manager a chance to peep on the shoot in return for a few free nights at the Twain. It was a desperation move, but one more attractive than bunking with the rest of Hollywood's homeless at the Catholic mission.

"Angelo could loiter back somewhere, out of sight.

I'd impress upon him the need for total silence."

"It's a bad idea, Floyd. If you think my apartment won't work and you can find a better replacement on the cheap, fine. But we're not inviting any gawkers. You gotta trust me on this, I know talent."

Manning took him aback by abruptly switching gears:

"All clear in Vegas?"

"Come again?"

"Just wondering if whoever or whatever ran you out of town is still a problem. None of my concern really, but since I've come clean with you about a few things I thought maybe you'd want to get square with me."

"You're right, kid. It's none of your fucking concern."

Hoffman's voice telegraphed a latent violence. Neither man had forgotten that disturbing moment when Gene's fingers locked around Floyd's throat in the Beachwood mansion. They hadn't mentioned it since, but the memory was still raw.

"Know what?" Floyd said, casually taking a seat on the couch. "I wouldn't object to a quick one. Two fingers, tops."

Hoffman paused a beat, then got up and lumbered to the sideboard. He was grateful for the momentary distraction.

"Whatever happened in Vegas doesn't impact our business, Floyd. Don't make me repeat that too many times."

Manning reached over and picked up the baseball bat. He tapped the fat end against his upturned palm, chuckling.

"Lot of break-ins around here, huh? You really should learn not to shit a shitter, my friend."

Hoffman splashed some Scotch into two glasses,

127

waiting for Floyd to say whatever he'd really come here to say.

"I recognized the look on your face when you opened the door. The same look you had at Binion's when that green car closed in on us. I figure whatever it is you're running from, it has a hell of a lot to do with your involvement in this endeavor."

"Let's just say we've both been less than candid with each other and leave it at that."

"So why not tell me what it's all about? I might be able to help."

"Some beef I left unresolved back in Florida," Gene said, handing him a glass. "No big deal."

"Financial in nature, by any chance?"

"A little more serious than that."

Floyd gave a look of incomprehension.

"We had some problems on this one flick. The last one I made in Miami. There was an accident, someone got hurt."

"Hurt physically, you mean."

"You could say that."

Gene bolted his drink in one long pull.

"Like I said, it was an accident. But some people probably don't see it that way."

"What kind of accident?"

"One of our crew guys went apeshit, just completely snapped. There was a struggle, he attacked me. Barbara tried to intervene and..."

The words stopped there. Manning sensed it would cost Hoffman too much to offer any further details. He didn't press for more.

"Anyway," Gene continued after a long pause. "The girl who... got hurt. I think her people hired a shamus to tail me. That's just a hunch, but I'm sure it's the right one."

Floyd didn't evince any readable reaction. If he

128

felt relief upon learning that Hoffman might harbor even greater cause for past regrets than he did, he made no sign of it.

"Since this was an accident," Floyd said, making sure he sounded like he believed it, "maybe you can buy the problem off. Make restitution somehow."

Gene almost spoke to negate that idea, but stopped himself. It actually made sense.

Why not? Even if he never fully expunged his role in the events of that week in Florida eight years ago, never did anything to bring Barbara Cheston back to life, he could still make some measure of amends with a cash payoff.

Isn't that what happened in civil court when someone was found culpable in a case of accidental death? The girl's grisly demise was just a terrible mishap. He bore some responsibility, but maybe he could finally unburden himself of that. Hell, maybe he could even start sleeping peacefully again.

Gene still remembered Ben Malton's address from checking his ID back at the El Cortez. 418 Collins Avenue, Miami. Easy to recall since it was so close to where he used to live. With a little luck, he would find the guy and learn by bribery or force who'd hired him. Then he'd send an anonymous envelope with a fat roll of cash to put the whole matter to rest.

"You know something, Floyd? You just gave me a pretty good idea."

"What, using part of your cut to make the problem go away?"

"Precisely."

Manning shrugged, appearing less than convinced of his own suggestion's merit.

"What if it's not money they're after?"

Unsettled by the possibilities that question opened, Hoffman let it go unanswered.

Setting his empty glass on the table, Floyd's glance fell to the floor. He reached down and casually grabbed one of Stella's red pumps from where she'd kicked it aside, a smile on his face.

"Huh. I figured you for at least a size 10."

"Funny guy."

"OK, OK. Should've told me you had company. I would have made myself scarce in a hurry."

He gave a wink and rose from the couch, making a slow exit.

Gene started to relax, figuring he was in the clear, when he heard the bedroom door swing open. Both men turned at the sound. Stella stepped into the living room, a towel wrapped around her waist and a mischievous glint in her eye.

A moment of silence passed, equally comical and awkward.

"Well, well," Manning finally said. "I thought those pumps were familiar."

"You can wash that look off your face, Floyd. The movie's still a go."

Turning her gaze to Hoffman, her smile grew wider at the expression he wore, which was even more incredulous than Manning's.

"Oh, don't worry about Lenny. He'll come around if we explain it to him the right way. How's about the four of us have lunch and talk it over?"

14.

"So just who 'zactly is payin' to see this dirty picture?"

Corporal Hart exuded a calm geniality in asking that question. There was no hint of hillbilly rage in his voice. Not the faintest threat of bodily force honed to a deadly edge by virtue of military training and front-line combat experience. He couldn't appear more placid, really.

Sitting within arm's reach of the man who'd tried to choke him out less than forty-eight hours ago on one side, and the woman he'd screwed less than twelve hours ago on the other, Hoffman cultivated a state of hyper-alertness. Like he'd just downed two pots of coffee in ten minutes, wired to react on a hair trigger at the first hint of threat.

"It's a private buyer," Manning answered, taking an uneasy glance around the table. He wasn't thrilled to be seated in such tight proximity to Lenny and Gene, figuring if a fight broke out he'd be sure to catch a few stray blows. But it was a risk he had to take in order to keep this plan on track.

Floyd was just silently praying Stella didn't do anything to indicate the special relationship she'd recently established with her producer. Something stupid and careless, like stroking Hoffman's ankle with her bare foot under the table, which he'd seen her do twice already.

"Let me assure you, there's no possibility of public exhibition. I'm assuming your concerns lie in that area."

"Please don't assume anything," Stella said. "That's what got us off to a rocky start in the first place."

"Fair enough," Manning said, lifting both hands in a posture of mock surrender.

Bathed in a late afternoon glow, the anxious foursome occupied a table at the La Monica Ballroom, once a jewel of a nightspot catering to L.A.'s upper crust. Located at the far end of the Santa Monica Pier, the ballroom had in recent years fallen into disrepair. Largely deserted now except for seagulls and transients, it still offered a breathtaking view of the coastline, all the way from Long Beach to Malibu.

"Just tell us about the guy," she continued. "I mean, what kind of nut are we dealing with here?"

"For the sake of clarity, neither you or Lenny will have to deal with him at all. It's of paramount importance he never finds out you exist, Stell."

"That's right," Gene added. "As soon as we finish shooting, your involvement's over."

"We understand, cousin. Y'all made that part plain as day."

"So what's the problem, Corporal?"

"No one said there's a problem," Stella jumped in quickly. "We just want to know who's buying the film. It's only fair."

Hoffman nodded, turning his attention to Floyd.

"Been waiting for a few more details on that myself."

Taking a moment to acknowledge the three pairs of eyes pointed in his direction, Manning tried not to look like someone facing a hot lamp interrogation. Even if he felt that way.

"The man's name is Prewett. Henry Prewett. He's a personal acquaintance, though I'd stop far short of calling him a friend."

"That's nice," Stella said. "I'd hate to think you'd burn a friend with a phony deal like this."

Hoffman smiled. Then he felt her toes brush against his ankle under the table yet again, and the smile faded. He sensed she was getting off on openly cuckolding Lenny as the decorated war hero sat cluelessly present.

Shifty little minx, isn't she?

Yeah, but he liked her. Just didn't think the world needed to know about it. Gene couldn't risk rebuffing her game of footsie with even a telling frown, so he just tried to ignore it.

The Corporal had already offered what passed for a marginally sincere apology for attacking Hoffman at Stella's apartment. Sometimes a man can love his woman too much, that was the essential theme at the core of his words. Lenny faulted himself for being overly protective, saying it in such a way as to imply his lunatic jealousy was as much a personal asset as a failing.

Gene shook hands agreeably. What else could he do? He hardly had any moral ground to stand on.

Hart had attacked him before he'd given the man due cause, but that seemed like a fairly meaningless distinction.

All of Gene's keen instincts for self-preservation told him not to turn his back on him. Apology or no apology, this was a man trained to kill by the government who clearly felt his manhood had been affronted. Some kind of ambush was likely, regardless of the fact that everyone seemed to be cooperating on making this project happen.

"Henry Prewett? Why's that name familiar?" Stella asked nervously. "He's not in pictures, is he? I told you, I don't want anyone who might hire me someday seeing this."

"Set your mind at ease," Floyd said. "Henry's got nothing to do with showbiz. He's a big wheel in the strawberry and soybean markets. Owns roughly a hundred orchards stretching from La Jolla to Modesto. If you've eaten a California strawberry in the past ten years, odds are he grew it. Hence the name recognition."

"Produce magnate, eh?" Lenny said, scratching his dome in a vaguely simian pose of contemplation. "Wonder how he's holdin' up in this drought?"

"I wouldn't lose any sleep over Henry's welfare. His fingers are in a lot of pies. I hear he was the top single donor to both Ronnie Reagan and Pat Brown's gubernatorial campaigns, just to hedge his bets."

Stella was looking less convinced than ever.

"Why's an important fella like that want to waste his money on a lousy b.j. flick?"

"Oh, you'd be surprised by the predilections to which many a captain of industry finds himself held hostage. The heavier the crown, the more dire the need for esoteric pursuits by which to distract a clouded rationality."

134

"English, please," Stella said, rolling her eyes.

"The man's got a dirty mind," Floyd countered. "And money is definitely no object."

"OK, but ten grand just to see me doing that?"

"Not you, sugar," Lenny drawled with a leer.

"Right," she said impatiently. "Marilyn, I know. Still sounds like a ridiculous amount of bread."

Floyd's eyes met Gene's across the table. Hoffman was tempted to say something but held his tongue. He'd been a little irked at the lowball asking price Manning had mentioned to their reluctant starlet, who was promised ten percent off the top.

A thousand bucks, they told her. Indicating the total sale price was a mere ten large. Privately, Manning had assured Hoffman they looked to clear at least twenty times that amount. Didn't feel right to lie to her, but Gene wasn't about to offer a more accurate number if it meant diminishing his own cut. Business is business, and a cool grand was pretty good pay for this kind of gig. Truckloads of girls all over town would consent for a fraction of what she was earning. None of them, however, were blessed with the unique genetics that qualified Miss Chomsky for the role.

"Here's the thing to remember about our mark," Floyd was saying in response to her question. "Henry is stricken with the true collector's mentality. Nothing nags him more than the suspicion he doesn't own some item of value. The man's a slave to his enthusiasms."

"I can relate to that," Lenny said. "Feel the same way about firearms myself. Been collectin' 'em ever since my Daddy gave me my first .22."

He shot a look of jocular challenge at Hoffman.

"Ever fired a weapon, cousin?"

"Oh, I'm quite comfortable around guns."

"Good to know. You 'n me might hafta go out shootin' sometime. Bag ourselves a few coyotes up Temescal Canyon."

"Sounds like a hoot. Name the date, Corporal."

Each time Gene voiced Lenny's rank it came out with more pronounced disdain. No one at the table missed it.

"Let's try to focus on our shared purpose," Floyd said with some agitation. "You fellas can make personal plans some other time, OK?"

"Yeah," Stella added. "And be sure to count me out. The last thing I'm interested in is a dick measuring contest between you two."

Hoffman had to smile. The girl had real spunk, a trait he prized above all others in the fairer sex.

"Pardon us. You were saying, Floyd?"

"I first met Henry Prewett in the club house at Del Mar, a little over two years ago. He'd just pulled in a bundle on a 12-to-1 long shot. I found out later it was his own horse, he keeps a stable outside San Diego."

"That's where he lives?"

"He's got a dozen houses scattered around the U.S. Spends most of his time at an architectural folly he built from scratch in the foothills east of Tijuana. His very own Shangri-La, a humongous ante-bellum mansion just like the one he was reared in back in Louisiana. He calls it the Plantation."

"Wait a minute," Gene said, feeling a weird pulse of concern. "We gotta go to Mexico to make the sale?"

"Please, can you let me tell this my way?"

Floyd ignored the irritated look on Hoffman's face, then continued after a lighting a smoke.

"Henry was really living it up at the track that day, celebrating a big win. Funneling Mai Tai's into his gullet and prowling the bar for some two-legged

136

fillies to make his victory complete."

"Sounds like a creep," Stella said. "I'm sure you two hit it right off."

Taking a cigarette from his pack, she smiled sweetly to let him know it was at least partly a joke.

"We struck up a conversation with ease, that's true. The man styles himself an expert in the field of Hollywood arcana. His sphere of knowledge is limited, but the urge to acquire is quite keen. With that mentality and unlimited funds, I pegged him for a dream client. Turns out I was wrong."

"How come?" Hoffman asked, leaning forward. He'd forgotten about the simmering tension with Lenny. Despite some reservations, an intense fascination was developing with the man who just might provide deliverance from all his troubles.

"This is no ordinary collector," Floyd said, aware he had the group's attention. "In the two years I've known Henry, I have never been able to tempt him with any of my goods. Too commonplace, and too cheap. A man of his means figures if he doesn't have to blow six figures on something it's simply not worth owning. I offered to triple my price on a pair of Bogart's cufflinks just to put him at ease, no sale."

"So what's he know about our little home movie?" Lenny asked.

"He was the first person I called after I got a hold of the Bureau documents. I played it close to the vest, didn't claim to be in possession of the film but allowed him to believe that was possible. Henry wanted to fly me down that night on his private Cessna, I could practically hear him drooling over the phone."

"Glad I don't have to meet this guy," Stella said, making a face and brushing her foot against Gene's shin for the fourth time. "You make him sound like a nasty old perv."

"True enough," Floyd conceded, stubbing out his smoke. "The man's tastes run solidly toward the perverse. Claims the crown jewel of his collection is a solid brass dildo once the property of Mae West. I haven't seen the item myself so I can't speak for its authenticity."

"And it hardly matters," Gene said, casually pulling his leg out of Stella's range. He thought he caught Lenny glancing down below the table, but couldn't be sure.

"Given Henry's unique bent, the Marilyn film is irresistible. It has everything that turns him on. Not just a misappropriated piece of government property, one of only six in existence, but a dirty movie starring the most famous sex symbol of all time. Home run."

"Assumin' it looks real," Lenny said with a scowl of fairly naked doubt directed at Hoffman. "I guess that's where the big cheese here comes in."

"I'll handle my end as long as you handle yours, Corporal."

"Don't worry about that, cousin. Told you I'm real comfortable shootin' my gun off. Ain't that right, baby?"

Lenny grabbed Stella by the wrist, with more force than he probably intended. Allowing herself to be pulled in for a rough kiss, her pale blue eyes never left Gene's. They sent him a message of stark revulsion at the way she was being manhandled. And maybe they held a challenge as well.

Gene had to look away from her, before he did something stupid that wrecked the whole plan.

15.

Approximately twenty-four hours later:

"I just don't figure this for a two-man job," Hoffman was muttering uneasily. "How hard is it for a semi-capable adult to swipe a crummy bath towel?"

"I'd say that all depends on where the towel comes from," Floyd answered as they stood waiting for the light to change at the northeast corner of Hollywood and Orange. "This isn't like pulling a five-finger discount at the local Howard Johnson's. We might need to employ a bit of finesse."

Why argue? Gene thought to himself. Not as if he had any more pressing business today. He and Floyd had already passed several valuable hours marking off a list of pre-production concerns. With the cast, wardrobe, and location locked in, no major hurdles remained to prevent them from rolling film at the earliest opportunity.

Tomorrow was showtime.

Only one aspect of the plan still caused Hoffman some discomfort: the sale itself. Whenever he tried to press for more details, especially about the necessity of crossing the Mexican border to close the deal, Floyd found some way of dexterously rerouting the conversation to another topic.

It didn't really worry Gene all that much. Given his druthers they'd collect their fee right here in town and be done with it, but a short road trip to T.J. wasn't the worst of all potentialities. So he decided to pry for more specifics at a later time, once the loop was in the can.

The light changed. Gene and Floyd crossed over to the south side of Hollywood Boulevard.

Slanting rays of amber sunlight came in hard over the hills, sculpting long shadows across the glittery pavement. Reaching the opposite curb, they stepped out of the glare and into a massive shadow cast by the architectural behemoth looming above. Twelve floors of primo Tinsel Town legendry, constructed from tempered steel, a lake's worth of sandblasted concrete, miles of polished brass railing, and acres of beveled Italian glass.

The Hollywood Roosevelt Hotel.

Try as he might to maintain his standard cool bluff, Hoffman was semi-intimidated by this building. It stood as a mocking symbol of success in this cutthroat industry, where he'd barely managed to operate on the furthest margins despite fifteen years of frenetic full-time effort. The hotel's shadow grew in his vision the closer their steps drew them to the gilded entrance, which opened at an unseen door-man's pull as if to swallow them whole.

"Nothing but old time class, this joint," Gene said with an appreciative whistle as they walked inside.

"Naturally. You wouldn't expect Marilyn to make a stag flick in some fleabag, would you?"

"Good point."

Hoffman knew this was the site of the very first Academy Awards way back in '29. Few stars from the Golden Era of movies hadn't bunked here at one time or another. Who could say how many luminaries still remained in residence, either dead or alive? The ghost of Monty Clift had long been rumored to haunt his favorite room, 928, prompting numerous guests over the years to complain of a mysterious bugle playing in the wee hours from some unknown source.

Also widely accepted by those intimately versed with macabre Hollywood lore was that the restless spirit of Norma Jean herself paid an occasional visit to suite 246, overlooking the pool. For a host of reasons he didn't feel like examining too closely, Gene refused to ponder this particular superstition in much detail.

He followed Floyd's staccato footsteps into the cavernous lobby. Designed in a vaguely menacing Spanish Colonial motif, it echoed with countless memories from long lost nights of triumph and depravity. Gene took a moment to drink in the decor, then considered afresh their purpose for being here.

They needed a prop, something utterly simple and ordinary. A white bath towel monogrammed with the Roosevelt's iconic logo. Manning insisted the only way to proceed was with a bona fide towel taken from the hotel.

Hoffman didn't like the idea at first, proposing they take a plain towel to his favorite Chinese tailor and pay him a fin to stitch up a mock logo. But Floyd wore him down, and he took an eventual shine to the idea. It added a nice touch of verisimilitude to their bogus sex loop, and Gene had a feeling the more of those they could throw in the better.

"OK, kid. Laundry room?"

"Negative. We won't find any cocktails or bikinis down there, my friend."

"Gotcha. Poolside it is."

"Correct. No reason petty theft can't be an enjoyable pursuit."

"Snooty place like this, we'll drop more bread on a round of drinks than Mr. Wong would've charged. But fuck it, I'm game."

"You really don't give me much credit, do you?"

Floyd pulled a carefully pressed cocktail napkin from his pocket. One side bore the smudged shape of a lipstick kiss, imprinted in deep ruby red.

"The day shift bartender's got a major league hard-on for Angie Dickinson. Follow me? We'll knock back more than a few without dropping a dime, rest assured."

Twenty more steps brought them to the far end of the lobby. A ginger-haired doorman whose linebacker frame seemed oddly at ease with the European gentility of his voice stopped their progress cold. He stated in clear terms that only paying guests were allowed access to the pool area. A private party was underway, and unless they were on the register it was a no-go.

This was a wrinkle Floyd hadn't anticipated. He'd spent countless hours soaking up Vitamin D in one of the Roosevelt's reclining wicker chairs, acting as if he'd paid top dollar for a north-facing penthouse suite with a view of the hills. He'd never been asked to leave, on a few occasions latching onto a bored or desperately horny perfumed guest in need of some companionship. Those encounters usually left him feeling like a cheap gigolo, even more than usual.

"I'm sorry," he said in a solicitous tone to the doorman. "What's your name, friend?"

"Sven."

"A pleasure. Floyd Manning, I'm surprised we haven't met. Doesn't Philippe work here anymore?"

"He's not working here today. I am."

"And you're seriously saying my associate and I can't enjoy a simple drink?"

"Not unless I see a room key."

"Do you have any idea how much money I've spent at this hotel? Last year alone I must've put up a dozen of out-of-towners, all in premium rooms."

"Then you should appreciate our strict access policy to the poolside cabanas, *friend.*"

That last word came out with fairly plain hostility. A forward shift in Sven's posture added emphasis.

"What's the hubbub?" Gene asked, craning his neck to catch a glimpse of the activity beyond the doorman's beefy shoulder. Whatever party had booked the pool, it sounded like a wild one.

"Birchers," Sven muttered with a faint look of contempt. "In all honesty, I'm surprised the management allowed them to convene here."

Hoffman nodded sagely.

"That surprises me too, Sven. Class joint like this oughta have higher standards, don't you think?"

"Standards aren't what they used to be," Floyd said with a shrug, ready to turn away and try liberating a towel from the laundry room.

"Blame it on the economy," the doorman replied, now speaking solely to Hoffman. "We're barely at half capacity, and their money's as green as anyone's."

Gene offered a smoke. Sven declined, but made a show of providing him with a light.

"So what are those chuckleheads up in arms about now?" Gene asked.

"The war, what else?"

"I thought Birchers were opposed to the war."

"From what I've overheard they think Nixon sold us out when he signed that treaty in Paris. Who knows? Most of them belong in a rubber room, as far as I can tell."

Floyd was casually signaling to Gene that they should give up on the pool and make tracks for the basement.

"Look, Sven," Hoffman murmured, "I've always been curious to lay eyes on a Bircher rally. It'd make one hell of a yarn to lay on the wife back home. What do you say?"

"I don't think so."

"Just a peek. We won't linger."

Sven seemed to consider the request, his eyes darting to the concierge desk and back. He nodded.

"A minute, that's all."

"Good man," Gene said, stepping past.

After a beat, Floyd followed. The doorman laid a heavy hand on his shoulder.

"Don't make me come looking for you."

Manning briskly followed in Hoffman's direction, biting his tongue. The urge to stop and verbally dismantle this Scandinavian stooge was almost overpowering, but it could serve no valid purpose.

With Hoffman at the lead, they navigated a narrow pebbly pathway lined by lush palms, then turned a corner and reached a pair of iron gates leading into the pool area.

Luck was on their side: only a few feet away stood a handcart loaded with used towels. Floyd grabbed one quickly. He tried to pass it to Gene.

"No thanks."

"Come on. You can conceal it a lot easier than I can."

"Screw that. Looks wet."

"Yeah, and I'm gonna look like a goddamn pregnant broad with this under my coat!"

"Quit your crying, kid. It ain't dignified."

Going three shades of crimson, Floyd did what he could to conceal the towel under his sharkskin jacket. The cool damp cotton pressed against his silk shirt in a way that made him cringe. He felt the need to get back to his room at the Mark Twain and change into some fresh duds like the need for oxygen.

But Hoffman didn't appear in a hurry to go anywhere. He was peering with fascination over the gate.

About fifty men were gathered around the pool. Standing behind a podium placed at the foot of the diving board was a pudgy guy in horn-rimmed glasses and a tweed jacket. He was addressing the group over a crackly P.A. and getting interrupted by cheers every other sentence.

Floyd nudged Gene. "Ready when you are."

"Another minute. I'm wanna hear what this clown has to say."

"What for? Men of our intellectual acumen have nothing to learn from these knuckle-draggers."

"For entertainment."

Gene couldn't explain exactly why he felt like eavesdropping on the rally. Curiosity, mainly, fused with repulsion. He had always despised the John Birch Society on a gut level. The group's strenuously right-wing politics didn't bother him so much, it was their style that rankled.

From what he'd seen on the news, a typical Bircher gathering carried ominous similarities to a Klan rally. Hordes of lilly-white reactionaries, visually indistinguishable from one another in their matching crew cuts and ultra-square clothing straight from Ward Cleaver's closet.

Gene thought he picked up an anti-Semitic undertone to the Birchers' fevered protest against the propagation of Communist sympathies in American culture. Maybe he was wrong about that, or maybe it was a trait found exclusively in the southern chapters like the ones he'd heard of in Florida.

This rally's pasty-faced speaker might offer some clues. Clutching the podium, the dude was working himself into a pretty good lather.

"Well, what about it?!" he bawled at the audience. "Are you going to stand silent while our nation suffers a humiliating defeat in the eyes of the world?"

A slurred expression of audible disdain rose from around the pool. It made Hoffman think of a barnyard full of steers, lowing in mindless unison.

"No?" the speaker continued. "Guess what, people? It's too late! Tricky Dick gave away the last vestiges of American exceptionalism! He dropped our pants for the Fifth Column and no one's forgetting it! Waving the white flag to a bunch of barefoot mongoloids... is that the American way?"

The chorus of disapproval was growing more robust, and agitated.

The speaker didn't appear to want the crowd's support. He shook his head in a pantomime of scorn, leaning into the mic to drown out their cheers.

"You're all gutless! If you gave a tinker's damn about repelling the Red Menace and salvaging American hegemony, you wouldn't be here! What kind of patriot sips fruity cocktails in a pampered playhouse 8,000 miles from where the action is? Is that how John Birch, rest his soul, would answer the call of national duty? Answer me that, damnit!"

Unsure if they were being mocked or just goaded into more rabid support, the audience kept cheering, though with a shade less enthusiasm.

"Don't stand squawking like a bunch of hens! Take accountability for what you claim to believe, or take a hot seat with the Rosenbergs for all I care!"

The cheering had all but died by now, and a few tentative boos arose from the safely anonymous middle of the throng.

"Come on, Gene." Floyd was looking over his shoulder anxiously. "Let's show a heel before that doorman gets curious."

Glancing at Hoffman for agreement, Floyd was surprised to see pools of intense hatred fomenting in his eyes.

"Goddamn Birchers," Gene sputtered, clenching the iron rail hard enough to make his knuckles blanch. "Rabble-rousing bigots like this should be banned from assembling in public."

"It's a private party. Anyway, what do you care?"

"Ever live in the South, Floyd?"

"Um, no. I've traveled a bit. New Orleans, Atlanta... what difference does it make?"

"Unless you've lived down there you can't imagine how ashamed dumb crackers like this can make you feel to be a white man."

"Look, I'd love to discuss racial issues some other time. We got what we came for, so let's split."

Hoffman ignored him. The several dozen men by the pool seemed a bit dragooned by the speaker's aggressive challenge. Few showed any willingness to take the bait, either murmuring amongst themselves or wandering over to the buffet table.

"I just may vomit!" the speaker fairly shrieked. "Not a man among you takes umbrage when he's called a coward to his face!"

"Look in the mirror, you ignorant son of a bitch!"

It took Floyd a fraction of a second to realize that loud rebuke was delivered by the fleshy figure standing next to him. He wondered if Hoffman had gone temporarily insane, and actually laughed at the absurdity of it.

The speaker's head rotated, trying to identify the heckler. Gene helped him out by booming, "I don't see a rifle in your hands, asshole! Why not ship over there if you're so hot to drop napalm on civilians?"

At least half the heads in attendance had turned at the sound of his voice. If Hoffman was expecting some solidarity for confronting the man who'd been obnoxiously upbraiding the group, he'd miscalculated. Angry fingers pointed his way, accompanied by cries of outrage that a stranger had infiltrated the gathering.

"It's a spy!" the speaker squalled into the mic. "Probably sent by the Commie-loving *Free Press*!"

A distended moment of noisy confusion held sway. Floyd wondered if it was possible he was dreaming.

Then he heard a voice nearby wail, "There's two of 'em!"

A handful of Birchers were making a vigorous march around the pool in their direction. Apparently suffering some kind of pathological delusion, Hoffman showed not the slightest indication of retreat.

"Let's get out of here," Manning urged, tugging wildly on his arm. The difference in body mass made any coercive movement impossible.

Ready to run on his own, Floyd pivoted and stopped dead in his tracks. Emerging from the hotel, Sven cut a path toward the pool in long strides, pushing up his sleeves.

"I just knew you two guys were going to cause trouble."

148

Snapping to his senses, Gene grabbed Floyd's collar and lunged to the right.

"Come on, this way."

They bolted down the courtyard path in the opposite direction from which they'd entered. To their left was the poolside railing overgrown with expensively manicured shrubs, to the right a row of premium cabana rooms.

Five paces later Floyd was ready to ask where the hell they were going. Then he spotted the Fire Escape sign illuminated at the end of the pathway.

A beer bottle exploded against the wall behind him, inches from his head. Manning felt tiny shards nestle in his hair, maintaining enough presence of mind to be grateful none had found his eyes.

Hoffman slammed his full body weight against the door. He rebounded back a step, wincing with surprised pain.

"What kind of place locks a fire escape from the outside?"

"There!" Floyd said, pointing to the left.

Gene turned and saw an ax affixed to the wall by a brass bolt next to a fire hose. Grabbing the long wooden handle with both hands, he yanked it free and hefted the blade back over his shoulder in preparation to strike. Floyd barely managed to duck in time, avoiding accidental decapitation by a hair.

Hoffman swung the ax at the door in a forceful overhead motion. His aim was true, shattering the lock on impact. Dropping the ax, he kicked the door wide and barreled ahead.

Taking a hot step on his heels, Floyd was half-way through the exit when two powerful hands landed on his shoulders. Sven was trying to maneuver him into a headlock, with a cluster of clamorous Birchers closing in fast behind.

Floyd wriggled free from Sven's grip and dove out the exit, slamming the door closed behind him.

Pulling himself up from where he'd landed on the sidewalk, Manning turned to see Hoffman in a half crouch several feet to the right. He was struggling to push a bulky trash dumpster up against the exit.

"Grab the other end!" Gene grunted.

Floyd ran over and placed both hands on the dumpster's grimy rim.

His mind flashed to that night in Vegas, less than a week ago, when he'd gripped a similar trash receptacle's rim in an almost equally frantic effort to avoid bodily harm.

Weird, it was all very weird.

He didn't dwell on the coincidence, just pulled hard enough to induce a hernia.

The dumpster's metal feet scrapped noisily across the sidewalk. Hoffman's face ballooned, perspiring in wide sheets.

Just as the fire exit door swung open again, incensed oaths issuing from the other side, they managed to wedge the dumpster snug against it.

Both men collapsed onto the asphalt, utterly spent. A street lamp above flickered on and off in Floyd's vision, causing him to wonder if he'd blown out a capillary in his brain.

Gene didn't even ruminate on his own health, just took it for granted that some sort of major rupture had already occurred within his chest. Or would momentarily.

The exit door shook and rattled with the pounding of myriad fists, but it did not open. No chance that dumpster was budging an inch. But they couldn't afford to wait out here until the mob inside decided to circle around the Roosevelt's front entrance and bear down on them.

"You alive?" Floyd asked, his voice raw.

Hoffman wheezed something vague in reply. It sounded like a yes.

"Then let's get moving."

Staggering to his feet, he leaned over to lend Gene a hand. It was a clumsy maneuver, almost capsizing them both, but the big man finally got upright.

They started shuffling south down Orange as fast as their feet could carry them.

"Still got the towel?" Gene asked as they reached the first corner, tentatively judging no cardiac emergency was imminent.

Manning nodded with a wry smile and tapped the bulge beneath his buttoned jacket.

Taking a last look up Orange and not seeing any pursuers, they turned left on Hawthorn.

Just to play it safe they followed a wide eastern perimeter around the hotel before heading back north toward home.

"Sure glad we didn't waste five bucks on your tailor," Floyd said after a while, deadpan.

Gene had no reply to that. He started chuckling after a few steps, trying to stop himself which only succeeded in adding fuel to the fire. It grew in spurts to the level of semi-hysterical laughter. Floyd joined in soon enough. By the time they'd reached the next corner, both men were howling like jackals into the smoggy night air.

16.

"I think he suspects. Maybe."

Did she really have to say something like that right now? Not even allow for a minute or two of cozy postcoital silence?

Hoffman was still trying to catch his breath, just a few trickles of sweat making their way from his brow down onto the pillow. They'd been balling hard enough to splinter the headboard for almost an hour. He wasn't sure how many more sessions with Stella he was apt to survive, but figured it was as good a way to go as any.

"Are you listening, Gene?"

"Sorry, I was monitoring my pulse. What'd you say?"

"I said Lenny might be onto us."

"Come on. Don't tell me that."

"I could be wrong. Just thought you should know it's possible."

Nice work, Hoffman thought with a measure of reproach aimed equally at his brain and dick. *Couldn't resist making things more even complicated than they had to be, could you?*

He'd returned home tonight to find her on his stoop. Again. Lenny had lit out for Glendale to spend a few hours visiting an ailing friend, or so he'd told her. Stella was only too happy to see the Corporal go, and made a beeline for the Yucca Flats the minute he was gone.

Still jazzed with fresh adrenaline from the Roosevelt Towel Caper (as he and Floyd dubbed the ridiculous affair when parting ways a cautious distance from the hotel) Hoffman couldn't pretend he wasn't thrilled to see she'd come back for more.

He wouldn't have minded some time to cool down with a drink first, but Stella wasn't having any of that. Legs scissoring his midsection, she told Gene to carry her straight to the bedroom. He followed that and all her subsequent orders down to a tee.

What better way to close out the last day before production? It was actually starting to feel like, against any reasonable odds, every last detail had come together in proper fashion for tomorrow's shoot. And now, just as he should be focusing solely on how to capture the required 8mm images in the most convincing manner, Gene had to worry about blowback from Corporal Hart.

"So what happened? Did he say anything?"

"Not really. I catch him looking at me a certain way, especially when your name comes up."

"How often does my name come up?"

She shrugged, reaching for her Pall Malls.

"Practically all we talk about is the movie. We're both a little jittery, I guess."

"There's nothing to fret about, Stell. Thought we covered all that."

"Easy for you to say. I'm the one in the spotlight. There's no way to be sure this won't come back to haunt me."

"Still worried how it might impact your career options in this town?"

"Yes, and don't smile like that."

"I'm only smiling because I like looking at you." Hoffman sucked in a drag from the cigarette held between her fingers. "So what's the Corporal worried about?"

Stella returned his smile through a smoke ring.

"Thinks the woman he wants to marry might be a shameless whore."

"Marriage? Has he proposed?"

"Not in so many words. I know he's planning on it sooner or later."

"Would you accept?"

"God, no."

"Good. You can do better, a lot better."

"You, I suppose?"

"Sorry, doll. Not the marrying kind."

It came out too fast, too glib. The silence that followed felt uncomfortable. That's not what Gene wanted, especially in an intimate moment following such superb sex. Truth be told, if there was ever a woman to make him reconsider a life of dedicated bachelorhood, she was in his bed right now.

"So nothing specific from Len," he said, changing the subject. "He's just been giving you the fisheye?"

Stella nodded. "I guess he said something about wanting to use your face for whittling practice. I can't remember exactly."

154

"I see," Gene muttered, sitting up as the potential gravity of the situation became clear. "This is the last thing we need, Stell. Problematic talent is a producer's worst nightmare."

Well, not quite, he thought as a bloodstained buzzsaw appeared in his mind. He banished the image and rose to make them a drink.

"It's no picnic for me either," Stella said. "I can't stand being around the son of a bitch anymore. He's making me nuts."

"Just hang tight for another few days. Soon as we wrap and make sure the film's good to go, you can break it off."

"Oh, it's that easy? Don't you think I'd have dumped him by now if I wasn't too scared to do it? Screw the movie, I'd show him the door tonight if I didn't think he'd go totally bonkers."

She'd started to shiver slightly. Gene returned to the bed with a glass of scotch and put a fleshy arm around her bare shoulders.

"Don't worry. I'll back whatever play you want to make. Help you get a restraining order against him if need be."

"I can't take it any more, Gene. Even before you showed up he's been on me, gets all pissed every time some guy looks my way."

"Probably not too crazy about your job, and I can hardly blame him for that. Bunch of creeps pawing you in front of Grauman's every night."

"It's how we met, for Pete's sake. He tried to rip me off, two photos for the price of one. That should've told me he's a lousy freeloader. Never kicked me a single dime for rent all these months."

Together they drained the glass in a few healthy gulps. Gene set it on the bedside table and lay back down.

"The important thing is to not make any waves until we get the loop in the can. After that, we can figure out the best way to move ahead."

She crushed out her smoke with a wan glance.

"Sure. You'll head down to Mexico and I'll probably never hear from you again."

"You know that's a lot of crap. I gotta give you your cut, don't I?"

For the umpteenth time, Hoffman considered leveling with her about the potential payday he was in for. Then decided against it. No point in making that kind of decision until the cash was in hand.

"Will that be the end of it?" Stella asked. "A quick payoff?"

"Not unless you want it that way. I just said I'd help you deal with Lenny. Hell, you can shack up here till it blows over."

"I'm not gonna be forced out of my own home. Just need to figure out a way to make him leave so he'll think it's his idea."

Hoffman brooded in silence for a few moments.

"How about another woman? I could steer a couple young things his way. Know a few plucky gals from my softcore flicks, he's bound to not blow it with at least one of 'em."

"Young, huh? What's the implication there?"

"No implication, except that dumb cracker's more suited to a 19-year-old chippie than a class broad like you."

Stella regarded him when a long skeptical look.

"Anyway, I didn't come back just for another lay."

"I should hope not," Gene said, cupping a hand under her right breast. "My snappy repartee is pretty good too."

"I'm serious."

She pushed him away and rose from the bed, grabbing her bag from where she'd slung it over the back of his desk chair. She reached inside, rummaging through the random debris of her everyday life: combs, compact makeup kits, a small circular case holding her birth control pills.

Hoffman was content to lie there and admire the sumptuous view of her bare backside, until she turned holding a manila folder in one hand.

"I went to the library downtown," she said, returning to the bed. "Did a little research on our man Henry Prewett."

"I'm impressed," Gene said with a whistle.

Stella pulled out a loose-leaf stack of 8 x 10 pages. They were all photocopies of newspaper articles.

"Ever used the microfiche system before? It's incredible, you can find anything."

"Little snoop," Hoffman said, kissing her shoulder.

"I knew the name was familiar, and not just because I like fresh strawberries." She leafed through the papers and handed one to Hoffman. "This is from four years ago."

Gene scanned the copy. It was the front page of the San Francisco *Chronicle*, dated March 31st, 1969.

POLICE, PRIVATE CITIZENS QUASH
FIELD WORKER RALLY IN MODESTO

A gang of men and women claiming to represent workers in produce fields all across the Central Valley staged a protest rally in downtown Modesto yesterday. Intended as a peaceful demonstration, it turned violent when protesters clashed with both police and private citizens voicing opposition to the event. At least ten people were hospitalized as a result of the fracas.

The choice of yesterday's date for the rally was not accidental, explained Hector Colosio, spokesman for the protesters.

"March 31st is the birthday of César Chávez, the inspiration for equal rights among all migrant workers. We chose this day to shine a light on the unfair practices of growers across central California, and especially the wholesale cruelty shown by Prewett Produce toward its employees."

The rally began quietly, according to bystanders. A group of several dozen showed up in front of City Hall around noon. They waved banners defaming low wages and what the protesters described as a "total lack" of safety measures to prevent injury to workers in the fields.

The demonstration was not intended to come as a surprise, Mr. Colosio said. "We sent a letter of intent to Prewett Produce's headquarters in San Diego. They knew we would be in the streets today, and they had their strike-breakers waiting for us."

It was sometime after 12:30 P.M. when the event turned violent. Several squad cars from the Modesto Police Department arrived to disperse the gathering. Witnesses claim the uniformed officers were accompanied by more than a dozen men dressed in street clothes. One witness, speaking under the condition of anonymity, claimed the individuals not in uniform were armed with picks and clubs.

Among those hospitalized from injuries sustained at the rally were Ramona Mendoza, a 14-year-old girl employed as a strawberry picker by Prewett Produce, and Raul Torres, a 78-year-old veteran of various Prewett-owned orchards north of Modesto. Mr. Torres is not expected to emerge from the coma he entered upon arrival at the emergency room.

Gene scanned through the rest of the article and set the paper down.

"Doesn't surprise me all that much," he said with a resigned sigh. "Men like Prewett don't get where they are wearing kid gloves. I'm sure those workers had a gripe, but they should've known they were kicking a hornet's nest."

Stella shot him a dark look. "Your compassion is inspiring. Aren't artists supposed to side with the little guy?"

"I'm not taking anyone's side. Just saying they were asking for trouble, that's all."

"It gets worse," she said, shoving another clipping at him with some impatience.

Not seeing where this was headed but deciding she'd earned his indulgence, Gene took a gander.

This one was from the Sacramento *Register*, dated July 12th, 1969:

GRAND JURY WITNESS IN PREWETT STRIKE CASE FOUND DEAD; POLICE RULE OUT FOUL PLAY

The body of a man was found in a room at the Ambassador Hotel early Monday morning. Identified as Robert Hall of Modesto, age 36, he was discovered by a member of the hotel's maid staff during a routine room cleaning. Initial reports that the deceased hanged himself were verified in a statement by the Sacramento Police Department.

Hall had been named as a witness in a grand jury investigation of a public protest event that turned deadly last March. Field workers for Prewett Produce staged a rally in downtown Modesto to protest what they described as "cruel and inhumane" business practices to which they were routinely subjected. Beginning peacefully, the rally turned violent when police arrived to disperse the crowd.

Numerous witnesses described at least a dozen plainclothes men armed with handheld weapons acting in harmony with uniformed officers to break up the demonstration. The weapons were used with "indiscriminate and malevolent might," according to one eyewitness.

Widespread public sympathy with the field workers combined with outrage over the police department's heavy-handed tactics prompted a probe of the matter from the District Attorney's Office. Of primary concern was the contention that privately hired "strike-breakers" had been used in conjunction with uniformed officers as part of a premeditated strategy to quell the demonstration.

Modesto Police Chief Royal Blodgett has denied those allegations. In a separate prepared statement, Prewett Produce dismissed any claims of such collusion as a "deliberate smear campaign with no foundation in fact."

Last month, Robert Hall approached the D.A.'s office with testimony said to bolster the investigation. According to leaked court documents, Hall claimed to have been among the armed "strike-breakers." He testified to having been approached by a representative of Prewett Produce and offered $100 to assist local police in stifling the rally. Hall went on to state his instructions were to "crack open a few Spic skulls" in doing the job.

Hall arrived in Sacramento yesterday morning, and was scheduled to make his claims in open court on Tuesday, July 19th.

Hoffman stopped reading and turned to Stella. She was looking at him expectantly.

"What am I supposed to say? Prewett had the guy killed?"

"Pretty obvious, don't you think?"

"Not necessarily. People decide to off themselves for all sorts of reasons."

Gene wished those words carried more conviction. He didn't believe what he'd just said, and they both knew it.

"I just think you're reaching with this, doll. Or maybe not, but what difference does it make?"

"I figured you might want to know who you're messing with."

"Thanks. I'll think twice before taking the stand against him."

"This isn't a joke," she said, grabbing the clippings from the bed. "And it's not the only example, either. I couldn't spend all day making copies but believe me, Prewett's fingerprints are on a whole lot of ugliness."

"So what do you want? We're scamming the guy, aren't we? You might take some satisfaction from that."

"Big deal. He'll never miss ten grand."

Gene felt yet another twinge of guilt for lying to Stella about how much money was at stake in this scheme. Maybe he'd come clean with her after it was done, if he could be sure Lenny was out of the picture for good.

"OK, you're right. It's not a lot of bread to Prewett. Think of it as a symbolic victory. That's the best a couple of small fry like us can do to hurt the guy."

"It's not that," Stella said, her voice almost cracking. Gene placed a soft hand on her chin, lifting it so their eyes connected.

"Hey, what's the matter?"

"You're going to some place in Mexico to rip off a powerful man, on his own property. It's crazy, you should just drop the whole thing."

"C'mon, Floyd knows the guy. We'll be alright."

"So you completely trust Floyd? Interesting."

"He's putting his neck on the line as much as me. Why would he do that unless he thinks there's a real payoff in it?"

Now it was Stella's turn to grab Hoffman's face. She did it less than gently, fingers locking tight to make sure she had his full attention.

"I don't give a shit about Floyd. He's barely a friend, and I know he's headed for a bad end sooner or later. It's you I'm worried about. Can't you see that, you big dope?"

Hoffman's gut twitched with some unnamed disturbance. He pulled her close, partly to offer a calming hug and partly because he couldn't think of anything else to say.

Her warning made a lot of sense, but there was no chance of heeding it now. If only Gene could tell her about Ben Malton, and the debt he still carried from Florida.

Well, maybe someday he'd be able to tell her. But before then, they had a movie to make. And, damn it, they would do just that.

In a rapid shift Gene hadn't expected, it suddenly felt like there was far too much at stake to consider backing away.

His intention of optioning that script about the troubled Vietnam vet had metastasized into a much grander vision ever since the name Henry Prewett entered his mind. The financial possibilities offered by The Platinum Loop, remote as they may be, addled him toward an almost manic urge to break free of the morass he'd been living in since moving to Hollywood. The stink of failure to which he'd almost become accustomed over the past three years was now intolerable.

With some of that rich bastard's cash in hand, Gene could set himself up as legit producer. The kind who doesn't have to let his whole career ride on one project. Hell, he'd be able to option a whole slate of scripts, maybe hire his talented young screenwriting acquaintance to crank out a few more on spec.

Despite a gnawing sense of better judgment that tried to assert itself at odd moments when he let his guard down, Hoffman refused to consider these newly hatched designs as ludicrous. Anything was possible in this town as long as you had a little seed money and the right attitude.

All he had to do was shoot this phony sex flick, make it look totally genuine, and go down to Mexico demanding the kind of exorbitant sales price the real article would fetch.

Piece of cake. What am I worried about?

Well, a lot actually. Gene knew he'd opened a potentially hazardous door with Stella.

It was more than just the threat of Lenny catching on and causing some kind of chaotic disruption. Hoffman's own feelings were becoming an obstacle. The prospect of essentially pimping out this girl before the glass eye of a rolling camera and selling the film to some wealthy pervert was growing ever more odious.

It was bad enough when they'd planned to shoot right here in his own pad, but now that they'd moved the location to some hot-sheet dive on Wilcox, the whole endeavor started to feel unbearably sleazy.

Hoffman was, at best, a softcore exploiter. He'd never filmed any unsimulated sexual acts, nor had he ever planned to sink that low in his career. The mitigating fact that the general public would never actually see The Platinum Loop did little to set his mind at ease.

And Gene did not want to even consider the real emotional barrier he was approaching: jealousy. Now that Stella had come to him a second time, he didn't want Lenny to touch her again. Ever. Didn't matter how long they'd been together, or what they'd done before.

She was his now, period.

17.

Randolph parked the rented Datsun just beyond the mansion's driveway and killed the little pissant 4-cylinder engine with a sigh of disgust. It just about sickened him to be at the wheel of a foreign made automobile. He'd emphatically requested a domestic make but there had been some screw-up at the LAX rental desk and this was the best available vehicle. Those lazy shitheels at Hertz really could use a rough lesson in the value of attentive customer service, but Randolph didn't have time to waste on such petty concerns.

The car didn't matter all that much in the grand scheme of what he and Billy Bob planned to achieve here in Los Angles. It was to be a brief, focused visit. No sightseeing, all business. They wouldn't put more than a handful of miles on the Datsun before flying back to Houston on the red eye tonight.

This was Billy Bob's first visit to California and he'd made some noises about lingering for a while longer, but Randolph vetoed that notion. He had been to L.A. plenty of times and it never did a whole lot for him; far too geographically disjointed and spread out to make itself attractive. Other than an enviable assortment of primo snatch in every color of the rainbow, the whole damn city could tumble into the Pacific for all he cared.

Besides, there was little sense in sticking around once they'd settled Floyd Manning's hash in appropriately unforgiving Lone Star style. The prudent play was to get good and gone just as soon as they'd obtained some satisfaction.

It wasn't hard locating the Beachwood mansion with the help of a Thomas Guide purchased at the airport. Now they were here, and a long week of infuriated waiting since their last encounter with Manning in Vegas was at an end.

"Remember," Randolph said, making one final check of the loaded Colt Python in his lap. "This is for T-Ray."

Billy Bob nodded silently, jaw set tight.

"Goddamn crime what happened to that boy. And we ain't lettin' it go unpunished, hear?"

"I know, Randy."

Billy Bob silently wondered why his companion couldn't stop talking about their purpose for flying halfway across the damn country. Obviously, there was a score to settle. That devious little prairie dog Manning had the gall to burn them with some bogus merchandize in L.V. Then he'd inexplicably managed to call in some heavy artillery at the last minute and send the whole night into a tailspin.

The injuries suffered at the hands of that big man in the parking lot behind Binion's were no joke, but the humiliation stung worse. Such was Billy Bob's assessment. The pain of his broken wrist, still wrapped in a cast, didn't bother him all that much. He kept it effectively numbed with near-constant infusions of bonded bourbon and painkillers.

T-Ray was a different story altogether. He'd been thoroughly and properly fucked up by that hefty sumbitch. An initial round of reconstructive surgery had done little to reshape his face back into anything close to its original condition before it got implanted into the side of that van. Little Tommy Junior had run screaming from the hospital room the first time he saw his daddy with the bandages removed. Prognosis for a follow-up procedure was tempered by a cautionary note on T-Ray's chances for recovery. In all likelihood, he'd be left with a severe speech impediment for the rest of his life.

The whole sorry incident was just an outrage of the first magnitude.

So the two Texans were out here to make a few things right on behalf of their disfigured friend. That much was more than clear, which is why Billy Bob saw little need to keep jawboning about it. Yet for some reason Randy felt compelled to do just that ever since their plane left the ground in Houston.

Well, now that they'd arrived at the address printed on the back of Floyd's business card, the talking could cease and the sweet retributive action could commence.

Walking up the inclined driveway to the mansion, their shared reaction was similar to Gene's when he first saw the place. They couldn't quite believe their prey held claim to such an opulent hacienda, but were grateful for it nonetheless.

Couldn't ask for a more suitable location. Tucked away behind a wall of stately pines, it was hidden from the street and offered the kind of seclusion Randolph and Billy Bob needed. If they'd found that Manning lived in a more open area, the plan was to stuff him in the Datsun's trunk and drive out to the remotest regions of Angeles Crest National Park. Most likely they'd still make a trip up there for dumping purposes before day's end, but the freedom to perform the kill itself in a secluded residence simplified things greatly.

"Only one thing don't square up," Billy Bob said. "How could anyone be so shitass dumb to give his home address to the same folks he tries to rip off?"

"I don't think Manning's dumb. I believe the boy's crazy, got some kind of death wish."

"Well, then," Billy Bob nodded, rapping his cast on the wide front door. "Let's grant it."

Bristling with anticipation, they were both sorely disappointed when a husky gray-haired man in dirty overalls answered. Everything would have been so much easier if they'd found Manning alone, but it couldn't be helped.

Arthur refused to admit them entrance, at first. They pushed their way inside and the encounter got ugly fast. But not as ugly as it might. No more than a twenty percent stomping was required to extract a credible statement that Floyd Manning was no longer residing at this address. And merely another brief volley of blows was needed to eke out the name of a nearby hotel where Arthur believed he could probably be found.

In all, the handyman seemed a bit *too* willing to spill on Floyd's whereabouts, which had the unfortunate effect of causing the Texans to doubt his veracity. They assumed he was lying to cover for his boss, totally misreading the situation. Eventually they reached the conclusion that Arthur was too dumb to make up a fabricated story. He swore through a battered mouth he didn't know the hotel's address but insisted they could find it easily enough. How many Hollywood flophouses would have such an improbable name as the Mark Fucking Twain?

Before completing a total demolition of the guy, Randolph figured it was worth a shot at verification.

He tromped over to the nearest phone and dialed 411. Billy Bob stood over the fallen handyman, wiping off his rouged brass knuckles and waiting for a signal to finish the job. He was more than a little disappointed when Randolph hung up with a bemused grin.

"How 'bout that, boy? You wasn't lying to us after all."

His whole body shuddering with thankfulness, Arthur tried to stand. A blow to the head from Billy Bob discouraged any upward progress.

"That's a little excessive," Randolph said without much conviction. "1622 Wilcox is our next stop, I don't think it's far from here."

"Let's get going then."

And they did, but not after checking every room in the house for a trace of Floyd Manning. It was a fruitless search, only sharpening their anger for the wasted time.

The two Texans left Arthur lying unconscious on the parquet floor, lucky to be alive. As he slammed the Datsun's passenger door shut, Billy Bob silently vowed to himself that a certain lying little shit wouldn't be so lucky today.

* * * * * * *

The time for action was now, and Ben Malton finally felt ready. No more delay tactics, no more hiding from his own uncertainties. Malton knew the moment he awoke this morning he had to either pull the trigger on Gene Hoffman before the sun went down or hop on the first plane back to Miami and forget everything he'd discussed with Ms. Cheston.

Running with that shaky resolve, somewhat bolstered by frequent nips from a half pint of Old Harper, he'd driven over to the Yucca Flats around 9:30 A.M. The plan, such as it was, required no elaborate preparation. He was going to enter the building with a nylon stocking over his head, check the adjoining rooms to ensure the coast was clear, knock on the door to Hoffman's apartment, and shoot the big whale three times in the gut, figuring that was the hardest target to miss.

All that would remain once the gunsmoke cleared was providing Ms. Scarlett Cheston with proof.

Malton had come to regret his suggestion of offering a newspaper obituary to confirm the killing had been accomplished. It would require spending an extra day or two in Los Angeles, a prospect he didn't relish. He knew he'd want to get as far away from the scene as possible the moment it was over.

That was not an option. Ben would have to hang around long enough to make three anonymous phone calls. One to the police, to report the shooting. Two more to the respective City Desks of the Los Angeles *Times* and *Herald*, offering both an anonymous tip that a minor player on the entertainment scene had just been gunned down in a seamy Hollywood residence. A story like that was bound to generate some ink, he felt quite confident.

Even if neither paper chose to run a full obit for lack of biographical info on the victim, they'd never turn down the opportunity to cover a violent death with even tenuous ties to the movie world. A measly two-inch piece in the Metro section should be enough to satisfy his vengeful client, assuming it mentioned Gene Hoffman by name.

So Malton felt pretty good about how this was all going to play out. Well, not exactly good, but at least accepting of its imminent reality.

His well-crafted plan of attack took a surprise turn this morning as soon as he pulled onto Yucca and spotted Hoffman loading some sort of boxy equipment into that familiar champagne Eldorado. Cursing himself for not acting sooner, Malton followed the Eldo about five blocks south, eventually turning onto Wilcox. Hoffman parked in front of a crumbling pink stucco hotel called the Mark Twain and hauled the equipment inside.

Flummoxed, Ben drove to nearby DeLongpre Park and sat on a shady bench finishing the half pint. His sense of determination was fading fast and no amount of alcohol could kick it back to life. He needed to get this over with, regardless of any unforeseen contingencies. So after about thirty minutes of anxious dithering, he drove back to the Twain and saw with profound relief the Eldo was still parked out front.

Malton had no idea what Gene Hoffman was doing at this fleabag when his own lodgings were less than a quarter mile away, but he viewed the sudden shift of events as a good omen.

This dilapidated pile of a hotel was a far better location for the job than the Yucca Flats. As he loitered across the street, freshly loaded .38 pressed against his ribcage like a hot brick, Malton noticed a steady stream of riffraff shuffling in and out of the Twain's front door. Hippie trash, the lot of them. Invariably, each time some greasy longhair entered the hotel he (or she, it was hard to be sure in some cases) re-emerged a few minutes later, checking the street in both directions before hustling away.

Employing all of his honed detective's acumen, Malton concluded the Mark Twain was a bustling locus of drug activity. What a wonderful stroke of luck in his favor! He would easily blend in with the ongoing traffic of unwashed dopers. Even the sound of gunfire wasn't apt to incite as much blind panic in such a squalid den as it might at Hoffman's quiet if run-down apartment building. Nor was it too likely any pushers who used the hotel as a place of commerce would rush to call the police. With a little luck, he could stroll in, do the deed, and be halfway across town before any prowl cars appeared on the scene.

If Malton had returned from his regrouping session at DeLongpre Park a little sooner, he might have aborted the whole plan. A slight advancement of his schedule would have afforded him the opportunity to witness an unusual trio entering the Twain: two well-dressed men flanking a statuesque blonde who was all dolled up as if attending a movie premiere. Malton might have noticed something a bit familiar in her smashing figure and slinky walk, possibly recognizing her as the girl who'd accompanied Hoffman into Adele's costume shop four days ago.

But he didn't have a chance to make that association. Returning to the hotel exactly eleven minutes after Stella, Floyd, and Lenny walked into the lobby, he still operated on the assumption Hoffman was alone in there.

Telling himself this was a piece of cake, Malton slid the stocking over his head and marched across Wilcox. Twenty-three paces carried him through the entrance way of the hotel and into the lobby.

173

He was the only person around, other than a half-awake old man hunched over the manager's desk to the immediate left.

Malton tried not to inhale too deeply, not trusting the nylon to filter out any heavy particles of whatever might be in the air. The place smelled pretty much exactly as he expected, heavy on the Lysol with a few grace notes of urine, cigarette ash, and puke riding shotgun.

One hand on the .38, Ben approached the desk prepared to do anything necessary to find out what room the man he'd come to kill was occupying.

18.

Only minutes to showtime, assuming they were still on schedule. But why assume anything at this point? Alone in room 219, Hoffman made a final run-down of his checklist. Everything was more or less in place. He already knew that without having to verify, but any kind of busywork was beneficial to keeping his pre-shoot nerves at bay.

This small boxy room on the second floor was not the most pleasant place to spend a muggy afternoon. Gene had to laugh when he considered it was Manning's current place of residence, after presenting the grand mansion in Beachwood as his home only a few days before.

Well, they had somewhere to shoot. That's all that mattered.

The room itself, if a far cry from luxurious, was at least sufficient for their purposes.

He'd already shoved a bulky wooden dresser half a foot away from the corner where it stood, creating a cozy niche where Stella and Lenny could position themselves. A small portion of the dresser would be visible in the frame during the first shot, posing as the armoire described in the FBI documents. A cut crystal decanter, riding a smudged bronze tray, was set on the dresser's slightly nicked surface.

Gene had laid out the Roosevelt's white towel on the grubby carpet, careful to keep the monogrammed insignia in plain sight a few inches to the left of where Stella would plant her knees.

Out of frame on the opposite side, a single 1K lamp was rigged to a tall hat rack, aimed at a 45 degree downward angle.

Tilted on a tripod in the center of the room was Hoffman's vintage 16mm Mitchell. The same warhorse of a camera he'd used on at least a dozen productions, including the ill-fated *Crimson Orgy*. All things being equal, he'd rather have a different model at his disposal, but renting a camera for this shoot would have fractured their budget.

It was stupid to think the Mitchell carried any kind of malevolent secretions from that nightmare-inducing week in Florida back in 1965. Wasn't it? The camera had served admirably numerous times since then. Still, just seeing it perched on sticks, looming silent and motionless like some loathsome black raven, gave Hoffman the creeps. He'd be grateful to pack the damn thing back in its box and get rid of it for good. From now on, if everything worked out according to design, all future GH Productions would be shot exclusively in the respectable realms of 35mm.

For today's shoot, they'd be working with the cheapest film stock on the market: a 25-foot roll of black & white Cine-X 8mm. He'd already re-spooled the film so the sprocket holes would fit properly inside the Mitchell. Moviemaking didn't get much more primitive than this, yet as he fed the spool into the camera Gene felt that same familiar charge of excitement he always experienced in the moments before a new production commenced.

The Mitchell was equipped with the option to shoot at eighteen or twenty-four frames per second. Hoffman chose to set it at eighteen, which would create a slightly grainier image when projected. He figured a dirty home movie made over ten years ago would most likely have been shot at the lower frame rate, and besides the more they could obscure the fakery of this loop behind a layer of grain the better off they'd be.

Gene was determined to nail both angles quickly. Not simply for the budgetary purpose of burning as little film as possible, but out of a more basic impulse to just get the whole thing over with.

Checking his watch impatiently, he wished he had a cigarette to help kill the time. Floyd should've returned with Stella and Lenny by now. Gene had dispatched him to pick up their performers almost a half hour ago. With each tick of the clock, the chance of a last-minute change of heart from either only grew more probable.

Hoffman felt semi-conflicted by that prospect; though he still entertained visions of a fattened wallet at the end of this caper, another more prudent impulse told him everyone involved would be better off if it never came to pass.

A knock on the door invalidated those mixed feelings. Gene rose from the bed and any qualms he'd been harboring dissipated as he slipped into his focused producer mode.

Personal issues aside, this was an incredibly easy shoot. Should take no more than fifteen minutes. Twenty, tops. After that, Stella would never have to be with Lenny in an intimate manner for the rest of her life. And Gene would be one step closer to the kind of bankroll that would not only set him up professionally, but allow him to indulge the delectable Miss Chomsky with the kind of extravagance she so richly deserved.

Buoyed by that optimistic possibility, Hoffman opened the door and boomed a hearty greeting to the trio outside:

"Now that's one fine looking crew! Who's ready to make some magic?"

His enthusiasm wasn't overly contagious. Floyd and Stella offered rather tepid responses as they stepped into the room. Only Lenny appeared keyed up to make his on-camera debut, clapping Gene roughly on the shoulder as he closed the door behind him. It was a gesture that could be interpreted as equally amiable and hostile.

Hoffman barely noticed. He stood there semi-transfixed by the sight of Stella done up in her full Marilyn regalia. This was the only time since their first encounter in front of Grauman's that he'd seen her transformed into cinema's ultimate doomed sex goddess.

The illusion she created really was perfect. Hair coaxed into a curled platinum mound, fake mole expertly placed, lips gleaming with scarlet gloss, the lamé gown hung from each curve like tinsel from an expertly decorated Christmas tree.

Bombshell. That was the only word for her.

To be fair, Corporal Hart had shown up looking

more than presentable himself. He wore a tailored button-down shirt, pressed flannel trousers and, God willing, a pair of dark socks held up with clip garters underneath.

"Clean up real good, don't I?" he proudly beamed at Hoffman.

"Not bad, Lenny. I just hope that tattoo's all covered up."

"Done, cousin. Ol' Stell damn near used up two full bottles of vanishin' cream on me."

"Mind if I have a look?"

With an easygoing shrug, Lenny unbuttoned the shirt. Hoffman surveyed his contoured chest and was suitably impressed that no trace of the inked eagle was visible.

"Very good. You're what we call 'camera ready.' No distinguishing marks below the belt, I hope."

"Not unless you count my third nut."

Hart's halfway demented grin stretched wider. Rather than set Gene at ease, it was starting to unnerve him. The Corporal had never been remotely this friendly before. Hoffman had to wonder if it was a setup. Maybe Lenny did in fact suspect his dalliances with Stella, and had somehow wrung the truth from her before coming over here.

The best way to avert any potential confrontation was to proceed with haste. Under Gene's crisp direction, everything happened very efficiently. There wasn't a whole lot needed in terms of prep. Lenny took his mark next to the dresser, back to the wall. Hoffman adjusted the Mitchell's tilt position on the tripod so the top of the frame cut off just below his midsection.

Stella was standing in the opposite corner, as far away from the camera as she could without leaving the room. Her body language was hard to read, but her underlying tension seemed evident enough.

The Corporal began badgering Floyd about when exactly they could expect payment, for probably the twentieth time today based on Manning's irritated countenance.

Gene took advantage of the moment. He walked over to Stella and spoke to her quietly.

"How you feeling?"

"Ready. I guess."

"You look like a million bucks."

"I better. Spent all morning in front of the mirror. Besides, it's gotta look real, right?"

He nodded, resisting a strong urge to kiss her.

Stepping away from Lenny's barrage with a dismissive waving of his arms, Floyd asked in a loud voice if they were ready to get this show on the road.

"Sure thing," Hoffman answered without looking away from Stella. "Let's do it."

Lowering his voice again, he astonished himself by saying: "We can call it off right now. I'm serious."

She took a long final drag on her cigarette, peering into his eyes with a kind of detached appraisal he hadn't seen from her before. He didn't particularly care for it.

"Don't worry, big fella. You don't have to watch if it's too much for you."

Gene wasn't sure if her words came as a relief or not, but he gave her a nonchalant wink.

They turned and crossed the room. Stella broke left so she could she kneel down on the towel in front of her costar. Gene went right to step behind the camera.

"Um, OK," he muttered, bending at the waist to squint through the viewfinder. "I guess we all know what were doing here."

A shadow of discomfort fell over Lenny's face. "You can't see my kisser, right?"

"That's right, Corporal. Just try to relax, you've got the easy part. Ready, Stell?"

"Yeah, let's go."

"Alright. And we are rolling... now."

His finger depressed the drive button and the Mitchell started purring. Without hesitation, Stella unhooked the straps of her gown and pulled it down, exposing her breasts in the bright glare of the 1K. Floyd's eyes widened slightly from his vantage point next to the bed.

She reached for the fly on Lenny's trousers and yanked down with the businesslike application of force she might employ in ripping off a Band-Aid. It looked all wrong. Even Corporal Hart had to laugh, which invited a venomous upward glance from his semi-nude costar.

"Let's try that again," Hoffman said softly, the camera still rolling. "A little slower this time, Stell. It's all about the tease."

With an impatient sigh, she re-zipped the pants. Then, taking a deep breath, she began to coax the fly down again at an erotically languid pace. Her free hand stroked Lenny's chest and she planted a wet kiss on the small trail of hair below his navel.

Hoffman felt himself physically constrict with an almost nauseating mix of jealousy and anger. Tried to tell himself this was a stupid reaction, but knew it had nothing to do with reason. He thought he might involuntarily look away as Stella's head leaned forward to the task.

A knock on the door froze everyone in place.

19.

"Shit," Gene muttered, killing the camera. "Perfect timing."

"What's going on?" Stella snapped, annoyed to be
interrupted twice in a row.

"I thought you secured our privacy," Hoffman
said to Floyd, back popping as he straightened from
his crouch.

"I did," Manning replied, stepping over the bed toward the door. "Probably that decrepit old manager,
trying to finagle a quick peek."

"Get rid of him, for Christ's sake!"

"Don't yell at me, Gene. I'll handle this."

Unlocking the door, Floyd pulled it open with a
look of congenial frustration. It didn't have time to
fully form before his whole face went the color of cig-

arette ash as he beheld the two men standing on the other side.

"Howdy, Floyd," Randolph said warmly as if greeting an old friend.

"Dear God…"

"Naw, I don't think He'll be of any help to you now."

Opening his mohair jacket to reveal the sidearm tucked next to an enormous belt buckle shaped like a sheriff's tin star, Randolph gave a small nod to indicate Floyd should step back quietly. Billy Bob looked a lot more impatient to inflict some kind of bodily harm but was restraining himself to follow Randolph's lead, for now.

Manning retreated into the room, struggling for words. The Texans entered quickly and locked the door behind them.

It took Hoffman a full three seconds to recognize the men. His eyes made the connection instantly but his brain was a little slow catching up. It just didn't seem possible.

Floyd's lips were flapping but the words issuing forth were disjointed and lacking any clarity. Radio static that communicated mounting panic, nothing more.

Summoning a facade of composure with little to buttress it, Gene heard himself say, "What do you assholes want?"

The intruders didn't acknowledge his question. They were too absorbed making a perusal of the motley collection of people in the room, including a topless knockout who looked like a bona fide pinup queen.

"My, my," Randolph intoned, deriving great pleasure from the startled faces around him, "just what in the Sam Hill's going on here? Looks like we're breaking up a party, don't it?"

Billy Bob's focus was evenly divided by the tasks of keeping the gun trained on Hoffman and ogling Stella's blue-ribbon tits. She rose hurriedly from the floor and pulled up her gown, retreating into the corner behind Lenny.

"They're makin' a porney film," the denim-clad cowboy said, pointing jerkily to Hart. "That feller there was about to get his jimmy waxed, betcha ten to one."

Randolph nodded in agreement of his partner's assessment, adding a robust hoot of approval. The wildly fortuitous situation he and Billy Bob just walked into tickled him no end. Not only had they easily treed Floyd in a confined space with no exits, but they found that other sumbitch right in the same trap. Hell, it was almost too easy.

Lenny took his sweet time zipping up, looking only mildly put out by the disruption.

"These friends of yours, cousin?"

"Stay cool," Gene whispered, trying without much success to regain some self-assurance.

"Ya know, me and Stell never agreed to no gang-bang."

"Just shut the fuck up, Lenny."

A look of cold hatred stole across the soldier's visage. Randolph picked up on it. He nudged Billy Bob with a deep chuckle.

"If I had to guess, I'd say these boys got some bad blood a-brewin' over sugar-twat here."

Hoffman knew if he didn't make a fast move to assert himself the situation would spiral irrevocably out of control. Forgetting about Lenny, he took a step forward to address the Texans directly.

"Now see here, gentlemen. I assume you harbor some raw feelings from our last meeting. Can't say I'd blame you for that. I'm more than happy talk about any number of ways Floyd and I can set things right, but at the moment we're just a little busy. I hope you understand we'll have to table our business until later today. Isn't that right, Floyd?"

Manning, the perpetual slinger of effortless small talk, still hadn't located his tongue. The look in his eyes indicated a burning desire to start tunneling through the floor with his bare hands.

"That's far enough, pard." Randolph waved his gun to stop Gene's slow advance across the carpet. "I seen what you can do with them big gloves at close range."

Gene held both hands up to indicate no intention of violence. Not that he could move without getting instantly plugged anyway.

"Far as what we want, I'd give you three guesses but I don't think you need that many. Last time we crossed paths, you put a mighty hurtin' on a good friend of ours. Ol' T-Ray's jaw ain't never gonna heal up just right, the doc already had to rebreak it once and it turned out looking worse than what you done to him."

"Didn't do me no favors neither," Billy Bob snarled, holding up the wrist that Gene had snapped with such relish.

"Now why you saw fit to insert yourself into our dealings with this lying sack of dirt," Randolph continued with a sharp look at Floyd, "is beyond my knowing. Not all that interested in your reasons, truth be told."

Despite a rising swell of something not too far from outright dread, Hoffman was getting tired of listening to this shitkicker run his mouth.

"So I'll ask again," he said evenly, "what do you want? Whatever it is, spill it. We're working here."

"Your wallets ain't a bad place to start. Drop 'em on that bed, all of you."

The Corporal took a step forward, clearly tired of waiting for permission to get involved.

"You peckerheads picked the wrong room to rob, I'll say that much right off."

"Take it easy, Lenny. We have business ties with these fellows. Don't we, Floyd?"

"Sure," Randolph said with an open smile. "We're old acquaintances. Only thing is, we didn't get a chance to say proper goodbyes in Vegas."

"I never promised Sinatra would be there," Floyd croaked, his vocal chords back to at least a partially functioning state.

"Hell, we're way past that now." Randolph cocked the Colt, and everyone in the room heard it. "Now y'all do as I told you."

Gene reached slowly into his back pocket, pulled out his wallet and dropped it on the bed. Floyd followed suit quickly while Lenny stood rooted a few feet in front of Stella.

Randolph gave her a lazy once-over with his eyes.

"Don't you worry about no money, sweetheart. Just go on and tug down that dress like it was when we came in. Hate to think we interrupted a special moment."

"Like hell she will," Hart said in an emotionless cadence. Randolph shrugged, content to drop the request momentarily.

As Billy Bob rifled through the wallets, extracting cash, Gene's ear detected a faint, erratic scratching. It came from the door, and struck him as familiar in a way he could not name.

In next instant, it hit him. Someone was in the hallway, picking the lock. Quite clumsily, by the sound of it. Flooded with a disorienting feeling of *deja vu*, Hoffman knew exactly who was on the other side of that door, and how this new presence might offer a way out of what was starting to look like a seriously dire situation.

"This is really quite unnecessary," he said, speaking loud enough to mask the sound of the cheap lock's pins being crudely manipulated. "I realize we had a beef in Vegas, and I'm probably guilty of acting rashly in the heat of the moment. But seeing as we're all adults here, I know we can work it out in a way that will satisfy everyone. Don't you agree, Floyd?"

"Absolutely," Manning nodded as Billy Bob threw his cashless wallet to the floor in disgust. "If you gentlemen are still interested in those dice, I'd be willing to negotiate a discounted price to compensate for any inconvenience you've suffered."

Randolph turned away from Stella to look at Floyd as if beholding a mongoloid. Lenny stood poised with the tautness of an arrow pulled back in its bow to the furthest point before snapping.

With both Texans momentarily occupied, Hoffman was able to gradually inch toward the door. His intention was to leave as much open space in the center of the room as possible. He tried despairingly to figure a way to tip off Stella, Floyd, and Lenny about what might be about to unfold. But there was no time for that.

The scratching stopped. Very slowly, the brass knob started to turn.

Hoffman lunged for the door. Grabbing the knob, he twisted hard clockwise and swung it wide, flattening himself against the wall.

"Get down!"

Randolph spun around at the sound of his voice, finger closing on the Colt's trigger.

Ben Malton never had a chance. He stood there in the doorway wearing a look of stupefaction underneath the nylon hose. Concentrating so hard on picking the lock, he was totally unprepared for the door to open violently of its own will. The .38 was out of the holster and in his hand when he heard the report, thinking he'd discharged it accidentally. Then a dark splash of gore spread across his chest, soaking the Brooks Brothers shirt he'd bought just last month, and he realized he'd been shot.

Randolph was just as stunned to see the person he'd fired at was not Hoffman (who was crawling across the rug on all fours) but some skinny dude in a madras jacket who was now staggering back into the hallway, already half dead on his feet.

As he fell, Ben managed to squeeze off one round. Way off target, it hummed through the doorway a yard from Randolph's head, ripping straight through the palm of Floyd's right hand before sinking into the stucco wall behind.

Manning screamed, more from surprise than pain, realizing instantly he'd been shot without knowing who'd done it. Gunsmoke filled the small room and everything seemed to freeze in a surreal tableau.

Half a second of confusion was all Lenny needed to take action. He kicked the gun out of Billy Bob's hand and propelled himself forward in a flying tackle almost identical to the one he'd used to level Hoffman at Stella's pad. It yielded the same effect, driving Billy Bob flat onto the bed before both men rolled to the floor.

The Corporal landed on top. A thousand hours of hand-to-hand combat training kicked in from pure muscle memory. His thumbs went straight for Billy Bob's eyes, gouging deep into the sockets. The blinded Texan wailed, his own arms flailing instinctively for the Bowie knife he kept concealed in his left cowboy boot. Sightless and in agony but compelled by an animal rage, his fingers found the handle and he drove the blade clean into Lenny's stomach with a harsh upward thrust.

Dark arterial blood seeping at the corners of his mouth, the Corporal tried to corkscrew himself up away from the knife. It was no use. The blade was in too deep and his movements only succeeded in wreaking more damage to his internals. Looking down into that mashed pair of eyes as the last traces of life left them, Lenny knew it was over for him. He could see his innards dangling from the wound in his belly down onto Billy Bob's denim shirt. Groaning wetly, Corporal Hart collapsed forward on top of the Texan, horribly gutted.

Staring down the barrel of Randolph's gun, Hoffman pegged himself for a dead man. He stood there waiting for the bang.

It never came.

In a span of seconds, Randolph's face turned bright red, then plum colored, darkening to a deep turnip hue. Dropping the Colt, he clutched his wide chest with one hand while the other clawed madly at empty air. Foamy spittle sprayed from his contorted mouth, followed by a faint hissing sound. With a lurch he was on his knees, and then flat on his face.

Hoffman knew without any doubt what he'd just witnessed. His salvation had come in the form of a massive coronary, almost certainly fatal. He'd pictured himself experiencing the same type of collapse countless times in recent months as the angina episodes became more frequent. Seeing it strike another man, at precisely the most unlikely of moments, was almost too strange to process.

Reaching down to grab the gun, Gene rolled Randolph over onto his back. One last bubbly exhalation came from somewhere inside as the eyes started to glaze. In the time another heartbeat would have consumed, he was a corpse.

Hoffman stood with a brief last glance.

"Better you than me, pard."

Hysteria had overtaken the room to such a voluminous extent it took Gene a few hazy moments to determine who was alive and who was dead. Acting on thoughtless impulse, he ran out into the hallway and dragged the deceased private eye into the room, then closed and locked the door.

Then he just stood there for as long as a minute, ears ringing from the gunshots loud enough to stifle the throbbing in his temples.

Floyd was pacing one tiny corner of the room and emitting a reedy whine of intense discomfort. He'd wrapped the Roosevelt's towel around his wounded hand. A dark red stain had already halfway seeped through.

Stella draped herself over Lenny and lay with her face against his, quietly sobbing his name. It was a queer sight to Gene's eyes, seeing Marilyn Monroe clutching a prone dead man from behind, who himself lay in a pool of grue dripping down onto another bloodied corpse underneath.

It's just like Florida, all over again.

Either defying his state of intense stress or as a direct result of it, Gene felt his pulse slow to half its normal pace. He experienced a sense of almost startling clarity wash over his faculties. Everything was made obvious, denuded of any maddening veils of confusion.

This life he'd been pathetically trying to realize out on the West Coast was over, kaput. His dreams of making it as a legitimate producer in Hollywood? Ludicrous. How could he have conned himself with such a wafer-thin fantasy for so long? It was a sick joke, nothing more.

But there's a good minute or two of footage in that camera. Yes, there is.

"Let's go!" he barked, taking control. "Is there a fire escape, Floyd?"

Hearing his name spoken seemed to have a bracing impact on Manning. He stumbled to the window and turned with a vigorous series of nods.

"That's our way out," Hoffman said, signaling for him to open the window. "Can't chance being seen in the lobby."

Placing a hand on each of Stella's shoulders, he tried to pull her upright with as much tenderness as he could muster under the circumstances.

"Come on, sweetheart. We can't help him now."

She clutched Lenny's torso even more tightly.

"We're not leaving him like this!"

"It's no good staying here. We won't do him any good by getting locked up."

"We have to get him to a hospital!"

"He's a lost cause, Stell. I'm sorry but he is, look at him."

The explosion of obscenities she unleashed at that moment dizzied Hoffman almost as much as the violence of the last five minutes. But it didn't last long. She expended all her aggrieved rage quickly. Going into a kind of numb trance, she mutely allowed him to guide her onto the fire escape. Floyd was already standing out there, making furtive glances up and down Wilcox, expecting a phalanx of cop cars to arrive any moment. Taking Stella by the hand, he helped her down the metal stairway one slow step at a time.

Gene paused at the window to perform a quick scan of the room for anything incriminating. He was happy to leave the camera, it was too cumbersome to deal with right now and it had no markings that could be traced to him. Anyway, there could be little doubt after today the goddamned thing was cursed. Good riddance to it. As for the few other props, they could stay here too.

One foot out the window, Gene stopped cold. That old familiar gut twitch started acting up as an idea came to him. Highly dubious, without question. Almost mad, in fact, surely attributable to his jangled state of mind at the moment. But it was also an idea imbued with an irresistible pull of potential.

Pulling himself back into the room, Hoffman looked down at the whopping prostrate body of Randolph, purple face gaping blindly upward in a frozen death rictus.

Hell, he's just about my size.

There was no time to fully map out all the potential consequences of what he was considering. Driven only by a compulsion to shed every vestige of the past decade right here in this dingy room, Hoffman reached down into the dead man's hip pocket and grabbed a fat eelskin wallet. Made a quick check of the stats on his Texas driver's license:

Randolph Lee Faulks
DOB 5-16-1930
HT: 06-01 WT: 310

Not an exact match. A little on the small side in both height and weight. But close enough. Maybe.

This was a move from which there could be no turning back. If Hoffman just left right now without making the switch, it was more than reasonable to think no one would ever be able to connect him to these bodies. That was the prudent course, the sane one, but it would only leave him where he was before any of this happened. Still looking over his shoulder, knowing that whoever hired the dead private eye could easily send a more formidable presence to finish what Ben Malton failed to achieve.

"Gene!" he heard Floyd yell from the next floor down on the fire escape. "What are you doing?!"

Swallowing dryly, Hoffman went with the gamble. He grabbed his own wallet and made a fast scan of its meager contents: nothing much more than his California license and a few phone numbers jotted on cocktail napkins. Billy Bob had already dug out the $26 in rumpled bills he'd been carrying.

Extracting the napkins, he tucked his wallet into Randolph's pocket and stood, feeling a bit lightheaded. Then he retrieved his money from the other dead cowboy, along with two additional c-notes.

Realizing there was no way to wipe all potential fingerprints from around the room, it occurred to him that wasn't even necessary. Not if this course of action worked as he hoped. Let the cops find as many prints as they pleased, they'd never think to match them with the dead man. A couple of lowlifes shoot each other in a dive hotel in the bowels of Hollywood; no chance the homicide unit is going to expend any undue effort closing that one.

Hoffman had to let fly with a hoarse chuckle, feeling somewhat delirious. He was either a genius or a maniac. Either way, it was time to split.

Almost forgetting the most important thing, he rotated the Mitchell's crank handle until it came to a stop. Flipping open the housing case, he removed the roll of Cine-X and tucked it in his pocket.

20.

"I'll keep it running," Hoffman said as he parked the Eldo in front of Stella's place on Sierra Bonita.

Floyd nodded mutely from the passenger seat. There was almost no trace of white left on the towel twisted around his hand, but the bleeding appeared to have slowed if not stopped outright. At least none had spread onto the upholstery.

Gene got out and opened the back door for Stella. She wobbled a bit rising to her feet, still in the thrall of fairly significant psychological shock. Hoffman offered a steadying arm, though in truth he was feeling a long way from sturdy himself.

They silently crossed the grassy front walk to the building's entrance. She fumbled with the key for a moment and he had to help her open the door. He started to follow her in but she stopped him with a firm hand on his chest.

"You don't want me to come up for a minute?"

She shook her head. The smeared lipstick and eye shadow gave her face a slightly warped aspect, looking almost like some kind of ghoulish clown. The mole had come off in all the chaotic motion of the last thirty minutes. Hoffman found himself giddily wondering where it fell, and what someone who picked it up might think it was. He almost laughed out loud at the thought, feeling like if he started he wouldn't be able to stop. Gritting his teeth, he retained control.

"Listen, doll. Those were some real crumbs back there. I'm not happy to see anyone die, but believe me when I tell you they had it coming."

"What about Lenny?"

"Well... I really don't know what to say about Lenny."

"We'd be dead right now if not for him. That one man was ready to shoot us all, Lenny took his gun away and saved our lives. And now he's gone..."

The rest of that sentence dissolved into fresh shuddering tears.

Gene wished there was some combination of phrases at his disposal that felt appropriate, but they escaped him. She was right. If Hart hadn't acted so quick and viciously, most likely they'd all be on a trip to the city coroner's office.

"There's no doubt we owe the Corporal a lot," he finally said. "God knows I wasn't crazy about the guy, but he made all the difference in there."

Stella wiped her eyes, further smudging the makeup.

"Guess I don't have to worry about him smacking me around any more."

The emotions behind those words were totally

rudderless, containing relief, horror, and sadness mixed together into an indecipherable whirl.

"Here's the most important thing to remember. No one can tie us to what happened in that room. The manager never got our names, doesn't know the first thing about us. I saw to that."

"He knows Floyd."

"That's Floyd's problem. This will never come back to you, I swear. Lenny's name isn't on your lease, right?"

She shook her head, not seeming to really listen.

"Any friends or family of his come to visit here? Or even send a letter?"

"No."

"Then you're in the clear. I really need to know you understand that."

"Sure. It'll be just like none of it ever happened."

"I know that's hard to believe right now, but it's true. In a few days, this will all start to fade away in your mind."

Stella obviously wasn't buying anything he said, but she showed no interest in arguing about it. Hoffman leaned in to kiss her slick brow, then slowly retracted.

She grabbed his arm, squeezing hard.

"You're not still going to Mexico. Tell me you're not, Gene."

"Hey, the worst is behind us. Just a quick sale, that's all that's left."

"What the fuck are you going to sell? We barely shot anything!"

The furor she'd managed to bottle up was coming back to the surface. Hoffman tried to speak in as soothing a manner as he could muster.

"I think there's enough to make it look real, especially with the paperwork to back it up. We'll figure out some story to lay on Prewett about why the loop isn't complete. Probably have to settle for less than we'd hoped for. Maybe a lot less, but it should still be plenty to set us up in style. The kind of style you deserve, doll."

Stella was now looking at him in a way he found genuinely unnerving. As if seeing something in his eyes for the first time. Something distasteful. Even unhealthy.

"Just give me a few days," he muttered, unable to hold her gaze. "If I come back empty handed, I'll let you say I told you so till the cows come home."

"I don't want to say I told you so. I don't want any of this."

Her voice cracked again as a stream of recently implanted memories took hold in her mind. Blood spattered in abstract patterns on the carpet and walls. Visceral matter on the floor. Lenny face down on top of that eyeless cowboy.

Gene pulled her close even though she didn't make any show of welcoming the embrace.

"This will all be fine, Stell. I know it doesn't feel that way, but it will."

She pulled away from him roughly, her self-possession reclaimed in an instant.

"You'll never make it out of there. Prewett will see right through you and that'll be that."

"Nah, come on. The worst he can do is say no. If he's not satisfied with what we got, we walk. No harm no foul, but it's worth a shot."

"No it isn't. If he buys the loop it's even worse. He's bound to find out it's a fake sooner or later. He'll send someone, and they'll find you. I don't want to have anything to do with it. Don't come here again, I'm serious."

A loud persistent honk came blaring from the

curb. Manning was leaning on the horn with his elbow. Hoffman turned to glare at him, then faced Stella again.

"I promise everything will feel a lot better in a few days' time."

"Jesus," she said, greater clarity cutting into her weary tone. "You're just as crazy as Floyd."

Hoffman felt the situation slipping away. He heard the truth in her words, at least how they must sound to her own ears. Maybe he couldn't salvage this, maybe she was right and he deserved a cozy straight jacket for getting mixed up with this scheme in the first place. But he'd come too far to consider turning back now.

"Will you at least give me a couple days?"

"Goodbye, Gene."

Stella stepped inside and closed the door on him.

21.

They found a bit of luck at Yale Labs in Burbank. Thanks to a slow late morning shift, the film could be processed in less than an hour. Maybe that didn't qualify as a profound sea change in their fortunes, but Hoffman was willing to take any break they could get right now.

The long-haired kid behind the counter, bloodshot eyes betraying a recently smoked joint, halfheartedly tried to tack on a rush fee. Gene quickly browbeat him out of that notion. He explained no more than the first third of the roll required processing, barely five feet of stock in all. Demanding extra bread for such a simple job was uncalled for and seriously un-hip, as Gene made the clerk understand without too much resistance.

Manning wandered off while Hoffman haggled. He didn't return for twenty minutes, telling Gene he'd walked down to the Exxon on Pass Avenue for the purpose of getting some clean paper towels to dress his wound. A thick wad was now affixed to his right hand with some duct tape he'd mooched off the on-duty mechanic. The Roosevelt's towel was gone; Floyd said he dropped it into a trash can in the gas station's sulfurous men's room.

Speaking in a kind of weird monotone, Manning laid out a course of action they were to follow with total exactitude as soon as the processed loop was in their possession. They'd already reached an unspoken agreement that if this thing was still going to happen, it needed to happen right away.

The top priority, Floyd stated, was to reach the Hotel Caesar in Tijuana by no later than 4:00 P.M. He would call Prewett from the lobby immediately upon their arrival and a van would be dispatched from the Plantation to pick them up. Timing was critical because the trip from downtown T.J. to Prewett's property took a minimum of ninety minutes each way, and it was highly unwise to attempt after sundown.

Absorbing this new information, Hoffman started to voice strenuous objection. He had no intention of being picked up by any van at Henry Prewett's behest. For one thing, it seemed like an unnecessary risk to leave the Eldorado unattended in T.J. Far more importantly, having their own wheels might come in pretty goddamned handy if the deal went sideways and a quick departure became a necessity. Why leave themselves stranded out in the weeds with no means of escape?

Floyd irritably explained why there was no other alternative. The Plantation was situated high on a bluff overlooking a crevice in the foothills of some unnamed mountains forming a rocky perimeter to the east of Tijuana, eventually joining the aptly named Sierra de la Giganta range in Baja Sur.

Floyd couldn't find the place on his own even in broad daylight, much less darkness, and any attempt to follow Prewett's van in the Eldo would be useless. The terrain they'd be crossing was too treacherous, they'd end up stuck in a ditch if they didn't plunge off a hundred-foot gorge first. On top of which, they'd never find their way back to the city even if they had a vehicle at the ready. The route from the Plantation to Tijuana was not a straight shot by any means. Having traveled it twice before, Floyd recalled an incalculable series of hairpin turns, heavily forested dirt roads and several running streams of various widths.

As he listened to this ominous description of what lay ahead (all of which had been conveniently withheld until this late stage of the game) Gene couldn't quell a nagging urge to permanently part ways with Floyd Manning right now and never look back. Stella's warnings about the insanity of their plan, easy enough to dismiss at her apartment building less than an hour ago, now rang in his ears with total credibility.

Still, it might all work out... eyes on the prize, fortune favors the bold.. the means to start over with a clean slate are within reach...

With those self-enforcing thoughts maintaining a shaky hold, Gene determined to soldier on. Hell or high water be damned.

Forty-seven minutes after handing their 8mm roll to the clerk, they walked out of Yale Labs with the processed film. Hoffman carried the little circular canister in his hip pocket. Only three inches in diameter and about as heavy as a pack of cigarettes, it felt strangely laden with some kind of noxious moral gravity stolen from the lives lost in its creation. That was a ludicrous idea, of course, but one hard to shake with events so fresh in Gene's mind. He was a little creeped out just carrying the damn thing, like it was radioactive or sending out silent signals to every LAPD patrol car in a ten mile radius.

They could have rented a screening room at Yale to view the footage, but that seemed like a waste of time and money. Gene was confident in what the Mitchell had captured based on what he'd seen through the viewfinder. Even if the loop ended before the x-rated action got properly underway, there should be enough details in the frame to pass itself off as a portion of the genuine article.

"I'll drive," Hoffman said. Floyd didn't argue, and the Cadillac pulled out of the lab's parking lot onto the congested southbound lane of Barham, headed toward the 101.

* * * * * * *

Two hours and eighty-eight miles later, they stopped at a filling station in the minuscule coastal town of Las Flores. The needle had been hovering over E for some time and to push it much farther would have invited a breakdown.

"Gotta take a monster piss," Gene said, killing the engine. "Fill it up, then wash off that hand. I want to see how bad it is."

"I can tell you that without looking. It's bad."

Hoffman got out of the car without replying and stomped across the dusty blacktop to the restroom.

Floyd inserted the nozzle and stretched his legs. The freeway directly to the west was totally empty. Not too surprising on this highly isolated stretch, but eerie nonetheless. From across two lanes of paved road, the sound of breakers was crisp. Stereophonic. The ocean itself was invisible, hiding behind the veil of a foggy marine layer.

When Gene returned to the car, Floyd went to the restroom and gingerly unwrapped his improvised bandages.

The throbbing had not mellowed, in fact it was getting worse. But the bleeding had almost stopped. It was a clean wound, the bullet tearing straight through and leaving a perfect hole that had already started to close in on itself. Manning figured the heat of the gunpowder probably acted as a cauterizing agent, eliminating the likelihood of infection.

He had no idea where that concept came from, probably an episode of *Marcus Welby*. In any case, he wasn't of a mind to worry about it. Flinging the encrusted wad of used towels into a trash can, he enfolded the wound tightly with some fresh ones.

"How is it?" Hoffman asked when he returned to the car.

"Stings like a beast but nothing serious enough to throw us off track. Still, I think it's best if you keep driving. Only another hour or so."

"Let me see the hand."

"I just wrapped it up again," Floyd said, sliding back into the car. "Trust me, I'll live."

Hoffman stood there for a moment, weighing the situation. The hand worried him.

His concern was not based on Floyd's wellbeing, but his own. If the bloodflow had not abated, they would have to find a 24-hour clinic somewhere in San Diego before pushing further south. No way in hell he was going to cross into Mexico with a guy who might be bleeding to death in the passenger seat. That was one potential nightmare he'd take every possible step to avoid, regardless of what it did to their schedule.

"Come on, let's go!"

There was an edgy tone in Manning's voice that Gene had not heard before. Maybe a result of the physical pain, or maybe some kind of lingering derangement after the deadly confrontation in Hollywood.

Either way, Hoffman decided this was not an opportune moment for an argument. There didn't appear to be any blood visible on the new paper towels, in any case.

"OK," he said, easing behind the wheel. "Onward it is. But let's get something nice and crystal clear first. Gene Hoffman died in that hotel room."

Floyd blinked at him in the bright midday haze, a look of incomprehension on his face.

"You call me Randolph Faulks from now on. Got it?"

Almost grinning in a way that said he was too dazed to ask questions, Floyd nodded.

"Sure thing, Randy. I might have to come up with a fresh *nom de guerre* myself before it's all said and done."

"Shit, sit tight for a sec. We need smokes."

Gene got out and walked over to the attendant's office.

Floyd sat and waited. Using his good hand, he pulled his wallet from a trouser pocket. From its folds he extracted the photograph of Celia. The same one that had never left his person except when showering, sleeping, or screwing for the past fourteen months.

It looked even more cracked and crumpled than the last time he'd gazed at it. As if the deterioration process was accelerating, and within days or even just hours the 2 x 4 piece of thick paper and the image preserved on its glossy acetate surface would dissolve forever.

Faint as it was, Floyd could still see her face quite clearly. That same enigmatic smile he'd quite never managed to read, not when taking the photo or on the hundreds of occasions when he'd looked at it since. A smile that could just as easily convey affection as jest. Or, most likely, some combination of both. And behind her, barely readable now in the photo's decomposed state, those tall white letters planted in the hillside. Floyd had to wonder if he'd ever lay eyes on the Hollywood sign again.

The conversation Gene was having with the gas station attendant had inexplicably risen to the level of shouting. Manning turned to see what was going on, then took a last glimpse at her face.

"Hold on, *chica*. I'm coming."

Tucking the photo back into his wallet with care, he listened as Hoffman continued to argue loudly with the attendant over the price of a pack of Lucky Strikes.

Floyd shook his head in weary bemusement. Everything seemed to be a battle of varying magnitude since he and Gene crossed paths, not even the tiniest of transactions could be handled without some kind of conflict.

It didn't matter. The road south was waiting.

PART III

TIJUANA

22.

The lobby at the Hotel Caesar was a mob scene. Loud, cramped, colorful, aromatic, intoxicated. A microcosm of Tijuana at large, or at least the bustling Avenida Revolucion over whose most trafficked corner this faded relic of a more glamorous past stood guard.

Movie stars and diplomats once flocked to the Caesar back in its prime, stretching from the late twenties to well beyond World War II. A less elite clientele kept the coffers full this cool autumn evening of 1973. They were all on display tonight, mingling in semi-harmonious chaos beneath tall potted palms and magnificent wrought iron chandeliers:

Sunburned Yankees in Hawaiian shirts and polyester pantsuits sipping watered-down Margaritas from giant funnel-shaped glasses... working girls of the most exclusive caliber, elegantly clad in high heels and clinging gowns that advertised their charms to any customer with pockets deep enough to afford an hour of musky companionship... *mariachis* strolling in brotherly trios of collective song... a grubby smattering of barefoot street urchins who managed to sneak through the ornate brass doors and swarm confused *touristas* for some pocket change before being chased outside by musclebound doormen dressed in white tuxedos and shiny wing tips... and, filling out the melee, two busloads of conventioneers turned loose over the border from a gathering of orthodontic surgeons at the San Diego Ramada.

It was barely twilight, but the lobby's energy level might easily be mistaken for 11:59 P.M. on New Year's Eve. All in all, fairly typical for a Saturday cocktail hour at the Caesar.

Tired and bedraggled as he was by the events of the last twenty-four hours, Gene Hoffman perked up instantly upon entering the lobby. This was his kind of scene, no doubt about it. His mood elevated even more when he learned a room with two beds was available for the night thanks to a last-minute cancellation. He paid in cash, too wiped to even attempt any haggling. It was hardly necessary. Despite being the swankest hotel in all of T.J., the Ceasar's rates were dirt cheap compared to what they shook you down for at comparable stateside joints.

As Gene collected his change and the room key, Floyd Manning lingered several feet away. Staring into space with the same wordless, inscrutable expression he'd worn for hours. It was hard to say what was going on behind those zombielike blue eyes.

Hoffman had given up on trying to wring any small talk from him in the car. Something was really eating the guy. Gene suspected it was more than the bloody mess they left back in L.A. More even than their slim odds for success on this mission.

Part of the reason for Floyd's sour mood was easy enough to decipher: their tardy arrival in Tijuana. That was Gene's fault, and he took responsibility for it. About five miles south of Solana Beach this afternoon, he'd pulled the Cadillac over at a scenic rest area and killed the engine for what was intended as a brief catnap. Floyd would have certainly voiced objection to any delay, but he was sawing logs in the passenger seat at the time. Neither man had slept much the previous night, too jacked up with anticipation. Their shared adrenaline rush from this morning's craziness was followed by an inevitable crash.

Fuck it, Gene had thought as he closed his eyes. *We both need rest after what we've been through. Gotta be focused if we want to...*

Sleep hit him before he finished the thought.

He was awakened by a swift kick in the shin from Manning, followed by a string of vocal obscenities. Blinking in confusion, Gene saw the sun had already started its dive to the sea. His watch read 3:57, which meant they'd been parked for over two hours.

It was a costly gaffe, invalidating the possibility of keeping their carefully mapped out schedule. They wouldn't arrive at the Hotel Caesar before sundown, which ruled out any hope of getting to Prewett's place until tomorrow at the earliest. All of which Floyd pointed out in the sharpest language.

Gene didn't try to interrupt his rant, just hit the gas and decided to passively absorb the flack.

But after an initial outburst, Floyd switched gears and expressed his infuriation in silence. Lighting one Lucky after another, he sunk into a semi-catatonic fugue from which he still hadn't emerged.

Eager as Gene was to see this thing through, he didn't understand the manic emphasis on time. If they were too late to make the Plantation tonight, so what? Might do them a lot of good, actually. Why not try to get a decent night's sleep and move ahead tomorrow with recharged batteries?

Those were the questions Hoffman asked himself now amidst the chaotic bustle of the hotel lobby. But he knew his own buoyant spirits didn't have much foundation in reality. Manning was probably the saner of the two if he was reacting on a despondent gut level to the utterly fucked state of affairs in which they found themselves.

Four men dead in Hollywood, including a P.I. who'd been on Hoffman's tail for days.

A partial loop, at best.

A buyer with possibly dangerous tendencies, who was certain to be disappointed with what they were bringing him.

A potentially hostile environment in which to make the deal and get away with their skins intact.

Adding it all up, the mental picture Hoffman assembled from these fragments was not pretty.

Still, they'd gotten across the border in one piece and even managed to secure comfortable lodgings for the night. Gene decided to read these twin blessings as good omens. Snapping his fingers to get Floyd's attention, they crossed the lobby's gleaming terra cotta tiles to the elevator.

Their room was on the third floor, the top, with a wide southern window offering a startlingly clear panorama of Tijuana as night descended. Off to the east, Hoffman made out the low looming bulk of mountains, darker than the sky behind their peaks.

Their destination lay at an unknown point within that jagged range, ancient and impenetrable and wilder than the sea of lights spilling out from its feet. The thought that before very long he and Manning would be somewhere out there instead of ensconced in the madcap luxury of the Hotel Caesar made Hoffman shiver involuntarily.

He stepped away from the window, yelling for Floyd to get out of the shower before he used up all the hot water.

Twenty minutes later they were both cleaned up, freshly shaved and looking halfway decent despite the well-worn state of their clothes. Floyd's hand sported new bandages and if there was any gangrene in the works that was something he'd have to worry about later. Gene expected him to perk up a bit, but no dice. Even the restoration of some sartorial dash, which the guy seemed to prize on the same level as food, failed to snap him out of it.

His brooding silence, so uncharacteristic, was becoming bothersome. Their margin for error on this trip was flimsy to the point of nonexistence, and the last thing Hoffman needed to worry about was his partner spiraling into some kind of depressive funk. They needed to be communicating right now, poring over every last detail of their somewhat revised pitch to Prewett.

At the moment, Manning appeared content to lounge on his queen bed listening to one accordian-heavy love song after another on the AM radio. Hoffman wasn't having any of that. Talking a last look in the mirror, he tucked one of Billy Bob's hundreds in the bottom drawer of the cabinet.

"Let's get out of this fucking room," he said briskly. "Dinner's on me, and all the *cervesas* you can stomach."

Floyd nodded, flicked off the radio, and grabbed his cigarettes from the night stand.

In what Gene chose to view as another positive portent, a four-top table opened up just as they hit the cantina adjoining the fevered lobby. Hoffman grabbed a seat with proprietary assurance, turning his back on a quartet of outraged stares from two *gringo* couples (doubtless part of the convention-eering group) who'd been waiting in the wings for a chance to sit. Gene was pleased to note a slight grin from Floyd as the orthodontists dragged their irate wives away from the table rather than initiate a con-frontation.

"I don't know if it's my size or your crazy eyes that scared 'em off, but there's no way in hell I was giving up these seats."

A curvy waitress in a leather miniskirt sashayed over and Gene ordered two shots of the hotel's best mezcal with Bohemia chasers. The drinks arrived quickly and disappeared even faster.

"I called the Plantation," Floyd said, abruptly breaking his silence.

"What? When?"

"When you were in the shower. It was a quick call, shouldn't cost much."

"Hell with that, what did he say?"

"I didn't talk to Henry, he was unavailable. Prob-ably buried under a pile of poon."

Floyd winced slightly at his own words, looking like he wished he hadn't spoken them.

"So who'd you talk to?"

"Rodrigo, that's one of his main guys... driver, bodyguard, pimp, God knows. He answered the phone."

"And?"

"He told me what I already knew. Henry's going to be voluminously pissed about the delay. It could end up costing us plenty."

"One lousy day really matters that much?"

"When I spoke to Henry earlier in the week, I assured him he'd see the loop by tonight. At the time, that seemed like a realistic agenda."

"OK, so we're a little behind. I just don't see the seriousness of the problem."

"That's because you don't know him. He isn't a man accustomed to having his schedule adjusted by anyone but himself."

"Fine," Hoffman said, feeling his stomach growl with hunger as a waitress passed with a tray of steaming tamales. "But let's try to consider things from a detached perspective. We're offering him the chance to purchase an item of tremendous value. Why should he be the one to dictate terms?"

"He doesn't transact business any other way. Don't you understand that yet?"

"This isn't a normal transaction, kid. I say we act like it's a seller's market, show a little goddamn confidence."

"If we'd shot the entire fucking film," Floyd answered, voice rising, "we could show plenty of confidence. But that's not the case, is it?"

A few nearby heads turned, then looked away.

"Calm down," Gene said with a hard glance across the table. "No point in brooding on what we *don't* have. Celluloid is highly delicate material. It erodes with time even in the best conditions. Sunlight, dampness, too much heat, any number of factors can take a toll. It's entirely plausible, even likely, that an 8mm loop made in the early '60s would no longer be in cherry condition."

Their waitress brought another round. Gene's mind was so engaged with a fresh thought, he forgot to ask for some tortilla chips.

"What is it?" Floyd asked, reading his face.

"I'm just thinking, we might be a couple of lucky bastards here. You could even make the argument we're better off this way. The whole thing looks more legit now, doesn't it? Why would we intentionally disappoint him if we were pulling a scam? It would make no sense to offer an incomplete loop if it's a fake we made ourselves, see what I'm saying?"

Floyd nodded without looking any more relaxed.

"I won't argue with you, Gene. But none of that makes any difference. Henry Prewett expects to see Marilyn Monroe giving head, and we can't deliver. That's the problem, and if we're bringing him bad news it would have been far preferable to do so in a timely manner. Making him wait to be let down is not going to help our cause."

"Ah, fuck it," Hoffman muttered, wishing he could summon a more credible tone of nonchalance. "Let's order."

He grabbed a menu with keen interest.

"Look at that. Says this is where they invented the Caesar Salad, right here in this hotel. I'm order-ing one for starters, how about you?"

Floyd was starting to reply when a gaunt bellman appeared at the table.

"What?" Gene asked. "Didn't I tip you already?"

"*Teléfono para el caballero*," the bellman replied with a nod to Manning. He raised a spidery arm to motion toward the front desk.

"Stay here," Floyd said, but Hoffman was already following him out of the cantina, across a Mayan-themed carpet spread across wide hexagonal tiles.

Grabbing a phone at the front desk, Floyd vainly tried to block Gene from earshot.

"Yes. I'm aware, Henry. We were unavoidably de-tained, but I know you're a man who values anticipa-tion as much as the experience itself."

Hoffman couldn't make out all the words coming through the earpiece, but the voice itself arrested him. Low and coarse, it spoke in sharp bursts like a drill instructor ladling out abusive orders on his recruits. And yet the man was not shouting, rather speaking in a conversational tone which somehow imbued the most banal cadence with a sledgehammer impact.

The voice almost scared Gene, and he didn't know why.

"I understand, Henry." Floyd's head bobbed like a oil derrick set to turbo. He was having a hard time getting a word in edgewise. "No one is casting aspersions on your frustrated state of mind, let me assure you of that."

"Don't let him steamroll you," Gene whispered.

Floyd flipped him the bird and turned away.

"That sounds perfectly agreeable to us, Henry." A pause. "My associate, Ge... Randolph Faulks. I'm sure I mentioned him to you before."

Now a longer pause, and Hoffman didn't like the look spreading across Floyd's face.

"I'm positive I did. He helped me come by the merchandise. No, he's not with the Bureau, more like a go-between."

Another sustained rumble from the phone, then Floyd nodded with apparent relief.

"Fine, we'll be ready. See you then."

Hanging up, he gave Gene a shrug.

"The van will be here at 10:00 sharp tomorrow morning."

"Sounds good. You said it's an hour and a half each way?"

"Give or take."

"Perfect. No matter how he reacts, we'll be back in time for cocktail hour. This place is a real scene.

I wouldn't object to another night here, especially with enough bread to swing separate rooms and live it up in style."

"Well, I guess we'll know soon enough."

As they walked back to their table, Manning added, "Maybe I should have said something about the loop."

"Nah, better to do that in person. Let's get in the door first, whet his appetite with the documents. Hell, it worked on me."

Gene flagged down their waitress, feeling ready to order every item on the menu. The phone call seemed to have snapped Floyd out of his funk, which was a good thing. Hoffman didn't intend to spend this evening fretting about what tomorrow might bring. The best way to stave off any jitters was to eat and drink with abandon, then head out and see what kind of entertainment this town had to offer.

23.

The pounding would not stop. For what felt like a long time, Hoffman couldn't be sure if it came from within his head or from some external location. Eyes fluttering open to a stinging wash of sunlight, he determined it was probably both. And that this was almost certainly the worst hangover of his entire life.

Laying on his back staring up at the cream colored ceiling in whose center a rustic fan was gently turning, Gene felt a profound sense of relief despite his physical misery. He was in the safety of his room at the Hotel Caesar, and for that much at least he was grateful.

Exactly what happened last night to leave him in this condition was a question Gene felt ill-equipped to address at the moment. At least not until he had the benefit of some strong coffee. A fistful of aspirins and a B12 injection wouldn't hurt either.

That goddamned pounding. It assaulted him at a syncopated tempo. One slow throb matched the pulse in his temples while another sharp staccato kept up a faster pace.

Finally, Hoffman realized someone was knocking on the door. Staggering out of his queen bed and seeing the other one empty, he figured it must be Floyd. Hopefully the kid woke in an industrious mood and hit the lobby to bring back some java and fresh fruit.

As he lay a hand on the dead bolt to open the door, a startling realization set in: Floyd's bed was not just empty, it hadn't even been slept in. The sheets and pillows were in a state of perfect order that Gene couldn't believe Manning would have taken the time to achieve this morning.

A fresh volley of knocks jolted the door, and a thin sliver of memory surfaced from the bleary haze in Gene's cranium. They got separated last night, sometime well after dinner but before a black curtain of utter mezcal-fueled oblivion descended. Gene could just barely recall swiveling on a barstool at some point and seeing that Floyd was no longer sitting next to him. Where he'd gone, and where Hoffman himself had been at the time, qualified as incomprehensible mysteries right now.

"That you, kid?" he asked, his voice scratchy and slightly tremulous.

"From Prewett," a deep male cadence with a hard Spanish inflection answered through the door. "Van's ready, got tired of waiting downstairs."

Hoffman looked at his watch and was dismayed to see it was almost 11:00. Holy hell, he really must've tied one on for the books to sleep this late.

Leaving the chain on the door, he opened it a few inches. Through the crack one half of a dusky, unshaven face leered back at him.

"You Rodrigo?"

The man's stubbly chin descended a few centimeters as if refusing to offer a more committed sign of affirmation.

"Ten minutes," Gene said. "I'll meet you in the lobby."

Not liking the cold stare greeting those words, he shut the door fast without waiting for any further response.

Then he shambled to the bathroom to soak a towel in cold water. The bloated, bloodshot face staring back at him from the mirror did not look like a man ready to execute a complicated bluff of a merchandize sale. Or conduct any transaction more involved than purchasing a pack of chewing gum, for that matter.

Fortunately he'd had enough presence of mind to undress before collapsing on the bed last night. His shirt and pants were neatly draped over a chair by the dresser. Slipping into his scuffed black Florsheims, Gene tried to formulate a plan of action. The most urgent priority, obviously, was to locate Floyd. With their luck, Gene wondered if the kid had been snatched by some *federales* and was now fending off a cell full of chancrous pederasts in some godforsaken jailhouse. Or maybe he'd been stabbed in an alleyway by some hardened eleven-year-old pickpocket.

OK, don't panic, but Jesus! Letting him out of my sight was the fucking dumbest thing I could possibly do!

Swirling some tap water around his mouth, careful not to swallow any, another thought occurred to

220

him. What if Floyd had lost his nerve and pulled the plug, headed back to L.A. and kiboshed the whole plan? Or, to the contrary, what if he'd decided to cut Gene out and had driven on to the Plantation by himself?

A glance at the night stand put both those paranoid theories to rest. The rabbit's foot key ring lay where he left it. And the small valise carrying both the loop and the accompanying documents was still here. Checking the dresser, Gene found the spare c-note he stashed, kind of amazed in retrospect he'd taken that risk. But glad he did, as it would have almost certainly been pissed away during the course of last night's bender.

Alright, the kid didn't bail. So what the hell?

Pulling himself together as best he could, Gene picked up the valise and stepped out of the room. Whatever was going on, he needed to start making some moves to find out.

Riding the elevator downstairs, Hoffman knew his first challenge was stalling the mean-eyed *cholo* who'd been dispatched for them. Running more than an hour behind schedule already, this might be a little dicey. Gene felt that with twenty or thirty minutes to canvas the immediate area, covering a perimeter of about five blocks in each direction, he had a good chance of picking up Floyd's trail. How many *gringos* were apt to be strolling the Avenida Revolucion this morning wearing a sharkskin suit and with one hand wrapped in bandages?

Stepping into the lobby, a virtual morgue of inactivity now compared to last night's rumpus, Hoffman saw to his chagrin Rodrigo had not come alone. He sat on a brown leather sofa near the concierge desk, flanked by another man so similar in size, dress, and bearing they could have passed for twins.

Both stood brusquely as Gene approached. Clearing his throat, he tried to ignore the jackhammer inside his skull and summon everything he had in terms of commanding stability.

"Gentlemen," he boomed, extending his right hand to the guy he thought but could not be entirely sure was the door-pounder. "My most sincere thanks for providing such courteous passage to our destination."

The men deigned to offer a pair of bonecrushing shakes, and Gene was able to learn Rodrigo's partner was named Jaime.

"That the merchandise?" Rodrigo asked, pointing to the valise.

"In fact it is. I'll be happy to show it to Mr. Prewett at the appropriate moment. However, there seems to have been a slight..."

"*Vamos*," Jaime interrupted, jerking his head toward the lobby's front entrance.

"As I was saying" Gene calmly intoned, "I'm afraid there's been a misunderstanding regarding today's itinerary. My associate and I were led to believe you wouldn't be coming to meet us until noon."

"Wasn't no misunderstanding," Rodrigo bluntly uttered. "Mr. Prewett said 10:00 sharp. I was standing right next to him when he said it on the phone."

"Must've been a bad connection," Gene shrugged. "What can you expect from Mexican utilities anyway?"

Apparently Jaime's grasp of English was too limited to pick up on the oblique insult, but Rodrigo's pupils dilated with fiery indignation. It was more or less the reaction Gene had intended. A potent sense of confrontation, impossible to miss, acted as a dose of adrenaline just when he badly needed to clear the cobwebs.

"*Embustero*," Rodrigo hissed under his breath with barely enough force to be audible.

"In any case, I'll ask you for a bit more patience. I have some important business to take care of before we depart." A casual glimpse at his watch, which read 11:14. "How about we split the difference, meet back here at quarter of?"

The *cholos* traded a wordless look that said they were debating the wisdom of knocking this fat *gringo* over the head and stuffing him in the van right now.

"*Comprende?*" Gene said, putting perhaps just a bit too much inflection into it. The affronting slight implied by his utilities comment was now explicit. He realized he may have pushed it too far with these guys, and for no good purpose whatsoever.

Rather than wait to find out, Hoffman pushed past them toward the hotel's front doors. Half expecting to feel a hand on his neck after two or three paces, he was faintly relieved to reach the arched entrance way unmolested. But not alone. Jaime and Rodrigo were following close at his heels.

Fuck this. Let's see 'em stop me by force right in front of the doorman. Even for T.J. that's a little bold.

That false bravado evaporated the moment he emerged outside.

Hoffman physically shuddered at the outrageously intense sunshine, feeling woozily unsteady on his feet. He took a few cautious steps toward the curb, hoping to shake off or at least disguise his momentary disorientation.

Something bumped his legs from behind. He turned and looked down at a flea-ridden donkey wearing a sombrero and painted snout to tail with red and green zebra stripes. It was such a surreal sight to behold in the grip of a hangover, he could only stand and blink stupidly. Then the dirty beast brayed at him with the volume of a fire alarm, causing Gene to lurch back like an elephant recoiling from a mouse.

He heard some high-pitched giggles and looked around to see a grouping of young children openly ridiculing him. And there was little doubt his two escorts found his jittery state a source of amusement as well. Summoning as much poise as possible, he turned back to them.

"Well then, gentlemen. See you in a short while."

Rodrigo shook his head in a gesture of total refusal.

"There," he said, pointing to a blocky four-door passenger van of unidentifiable make. Gleaming spotlessly in the crisp daylight, it was by far the most well-kept vehicle in sight. The van's pristine condition suggested a heavy owner, and was sufficiently intimidating to keep even the most assertive beggars at a respectful distance.

"Very good," Hoffman said, pretending not to understand the intent of Rodrigo's pointing finger. "I know which conveyance to look for when I come back."

With speed that took him off guard, the two men advanced. Each grabbing an elbow, they started shuffling him toward the van. The last time Gene Hoffman allowed another human being to bodily move him anywhere he didn't want to go was back before his balls dropped. But these *cholos* were strong, and determined. And he was in no shape to resist them.

"Wait a minute, goddamnit! My associate isn't here yet. He's the one who knows Prewett, not me!"

This plea had no effect on Rodrigo or Jaime. Gene realized too late it was a bad mistake to confirm he had the item in question on him. The two men may have been ordered to bring the loop, with little concern for who was carrying it. In any case, as Jamie used his free hand to open the van's rear door, it became clear they were leaving now, whether Floyd was on board or not.

Feeling a stab of genuine panic as Jaime prodded him into the back seat, Hoffman's head performed a wide rotation in hopes of laying eyes on Manning.

And there he was, walking briskly around a corner opposite the hotel. Even from this distance, Gene espied an unusually furtive air in his gait, but was too relieved to make much of it.

"Floyd! Over here!"

Starting as if someone lit a firecracker nearby, Manning identified the location his voice and made a beeline across the bustling intersection. Hoffman shook himself free from the hands of his two rude escorts.

When Floyd got close enough to speak he said their names with a notable lack of affection. The *cholos* didn't seem all that thrilled to see him either.

"Our chariot awaits," Gene murmured, trying to sound carefree as his heart rate gradually ramped down.

Manning and Rodrigo launched into what sounded like a fairly terse exchange. Entirely in Spanish, which was greatly halting on Floyd's part, Gene couldn't make heads or tails of it. But just from the tone he gathered they'd met previously and formed unflattering opinions of each other.

Hoffman considered interrupting to offer a rebuke of the way he'd just been manhandled, but restrained himself. Better to keep his powder dry for now and see how the situation panned out. He may have an opportunity to pay back one or both of these thugs in kind, regardless of what happened with Prewett. Then again, if the deal went down agreeably, there would be little sense in dwelling on such a minor point of contention.

Turning away as Rodrigo was still speaking to him, Floyd climbed in the back seat of the van. Hoffman followed, pulling the door closed.

"I assume the goods are still in the valise?"

"Yeah, of course. Where the fuck were you?"

"Had to run an errand. Sorry, it took a little longer than I anticipated."

The *cholos* got in front, Rodrigo taking the wheel. He gunned the engine and peeled into the busy intersection, coming within inches of running over an elderly man pushing a taco cart.

Banging a hard u-turn that almost made Hoffman part ways with last night's dinner, the van tore eastward along Avenida Revolucion. It was clear Rodrigo didn't intend to pay much attention to traffic signals, nor any vehicles or pedestrians that might be sharing the road.

"You don't look all that green around the gills," Gene said, taking an appraisal of Floyd. The kid actually looked disconcertingly sharp. His suit, badly wrinkled the last time Gene saw it, had been pressed. A fresh, smaller bandage snaked around his hand, looking more like some kind of odd fashion statement than a makeshift tourniquet.

"I didn't indulge to the degree you did," Manning replied with a wry grin. "You were really on a tear, big man."

"So, uh, how exactly did the night end?" Gene asked, not sure he wanted to know.

"I can't speak for both of us. We split up around midnight. I went back to the hotel, you were raving about finding an all-nude cabaret in the Zona Rosa. Doubt you had much luck, you stumbled back into the room no more than an hour or so later."

Floyd's words threatened to arouse a pile of clouded memories Hoffman didn't feel like revisiting right now. He could vaguely recall a long taxi ride during which he became convinced the driver was taking him in circles.

"Christ, I should never drink mezcal."

"Famous last words if I've ever heard them."

"What really threw me was seeing your bed all made up this morning."

Manning nodded with a smile. "A habit drilled into me by my mother. There's no shaking it by this stage of life."

They hadn't traveled another ten blocks before Gene's chest started flaring with a type of pain that had become all too familiar in recent months. Jesus, not now. Manageable if unpleasant enough under normal conditions, an angina episode felt like more than he could handle on this particular morning.

The van came to a rough stop at a red light on the Paseo de los Heroes. A lengthy funeral procession was traversing the intersecting avenue and the idea of plowing into a carload of mourners simply to maintain a good pace of acceleration was apparently too hardcore even for Rodrigo's standards of road etiquette. As they idled, Gene found himself staring out the grimy window at an unlikely monument. Planted in the middle of a wide traffic circle was a towering bronze statue of Abraham Lincoln.

Hoffman was almost ready to ask if Floyd knew why the Great Emancipator's image should be preserved in the middle of downtown Tijuana when something else caught his eye. Acting on impulse, he leaned forward to speak to Rodrigo.

"Park at the corner. I need to do something."

The man in the driver's seat didn't bother to turn as he replied.

"No more stops. We're late already."

"It'll just take a minute, for Christ's sake. Pull over or the deal's off."

After a protracted pause, Rodrigo decided to do as Gene said.

Floyd tapped his arm. "What's up?"

"Got an errand of my own to run, kid."

Indeed. The instant he saw that building on the corner with a sign reading *Farmacia* over the front door, Gene knew exactly what to do. He needed every possible advantage to get back to even right now, and it would be foolish not to exploit any helpful opportunity. Being south of the border had certain advantages in the realm of self-medication, after all.

The van ground to a stop by the curb. Ignoring an irritably curious look from Floyd, Gene hopped out and stomped across the crowded sidewalk. He was glad there were still a few small bills in his wallet, as a c-note would be useless for this type of purchase.

The *Farmacia* was empty save for a withered druggist behind the counter, smoking a cigarette and reading a bull fighting program. Hoffman realized soon enough the language barrier wouldn't be a problem. It took less than two minutes to convey what he was looking for, hand the clerk five bucks, and walk out the door with a box of amyl nitrate capsules in his pocket.

Stepping behind a bushy pinyon tree that kept him out of sight from the van, he ripped open the box and hunched down to crack a capsule under his nose.

With one deep sniff a thunderbolt of revitalizing energy coursed through his entire body, instantly wiping away any trace of the dull ache in his chest. For maybe the first time since those cowboys made their uninvited appearance at the Mark Twain, Gene felt one hundred percent on top of his game. Hell, he never felt better in his whole goddamned life! Hangover obliterated, the back of his throat would gladly welcome an ice cold beer this very moment, but he wasn't going to push his luck by ducking into a ratty cantina situated at the end of the block. The next drink would have to wait until they arrived at the Plantation.

Almost skipping with enthusiasm, Hoffman headed back to the van and jumped in.

"Alright, let's hit it! What are we waiting for?"

Rodrigo cast a jaundiced look in the rearview mirror but Gene didn't notice. He slapped Floyd on the shoulder a bit harder than was probably necessary.

Manning almost asked what the hell was the matter with him, but a gander at Gene's pupils gave him a good enough idea.

"For God's sake. Are you losing all control of yourself?"

"Cheer up, kid. This thing's gonna go our way, I got no doubt whatsoever."

And with the help of some amyl nitrate he believed those words, he truly did.

If Hoffman's senses were a bit less fogged and he was paying more attention, he might have discerned a lump under Floyd's jacket. A familiar sight that might have brought to mind the first time he laid eyes on Ben Malton, lying on the floor of his hotel room in the El Cortez. But Gene was too distracted by visions of cramming his pockets with Henry Prewett's money to notice the gun.

24.

It was a hellacious drive by any reasonable measure. Once they'd cleared the eastern perimeter of Tijuana's city limits, the wide paved boulevard gave way to a two lane dirt road. After another fifteen miles, it was little more than a rocky cart path, but at least it was relatively flat until they reached the foot of the mountain range.

When the van started navigating this new terrain's sharply sloping grade, things got unpleasant in a hurry. Bouncing around the back seat, Hoffman was shocked at how steeply the hills jutted upward, almost instantly and without warning. His chemically induced euphoria faded faster than he would have believed possible without so much as a parting glance. He didn't dare crack another capsule until they reached the Plantation; way too difficult to hold one still under his nose the way Rodrigo was piloting the van over the wildly uneven path, making it jump, shimmy, and bounce like an improbably malicious amusement park ride.

Besides, there were only four capsules left. Gene cursed himself for not shelling out a few more bucks for another box. It would be wise to conserve his limited stock and only dip in judiciously until they got back to T.J. If the situation with Prewett should grow strained, he might need an artificial jolt to clear his head and prompt decisive action.

Jostling into each other in the back seat as the van careened ever higher into the deeply overgrown foothills, Hoffman and Manning didn't speak too much. Both men's minds were focused with nervous intensity on what lay ahead. Their imminent arrival, growing nearer by the minute, seemed to amplify the foolishness of the scheme they'd traveled all this way to enact.

After another half hour of unabated vehicular abuse, the van pulled to a stop in front of a large gate of bulky gray stones built into the mountainside. Only a narrow wedge of the gate was visible, with thick clusters of trees covering much of the rest, but Gene got the impression the stone foundation stretched around the entire property, however large it may be. It reminded him of a moat, or a medieval fortress's protective wall designed to cut off any unwanted entry.

Rodrigo reached out the window and opened a sturdy metal box implanted in the stones. Dialing a seven-digit number on the keypad inside, he slammed the box shut. The gate opened silently, swinging inward to reveal a paved driveway twisting up through the trees.

The van gunned forward, climbing higher until what could only be the Prewett Plantation came into view. It was just as Manning had described, but Hoffman still didn't quite believe his eyes. Though Floyd had spoken of the place in considerable detail, Gene never imagined it would measure up to those hyperbolic descriptions. He'd be hard pressed to conceive of a manmade structure that looked more out of place with its surroundings than the elegant monstrosity looming above them.

The main house, a two-story mansion constructed in the quintessential ante-bellum style, stretched almost half a football field in length. It gave the impression of having been plucked whole from a patch of land in the deep American South and carefully situated on this bluff. During his time in Florida, Hoffman had made a few pleasure trips to the Gulf Coast region stretching through Mississippi all the way to Louisiana. He'd toured a number of former plantations preserved in their original forms as tourist attractions. None of them could hold a candle to Henry Prewett's outsized version. In terms of nakedly hubristic scale, it dwarfed any of the historical properties Gene had laid eyes on.

Perched on a ridge overlooking a gorge that dropped an indeterminable number of vertical feet into a mass of chaparral-rich overgrowth, such an extravagance could only be affordable to an obscenely rich person. But there was more than just wealth on display. The flagrantly incongruous style of the place, its stubborn refusal to blend it with the bordering environment, advertised a man of iron will. Someone aggressively unconcerned with propriety, and perhaps a bit mad to boot. Who but a lunatic would go to the trouble and cost of erecting such a monument in these far-flung wilds?

Floyd's elbow prodded the gape-jawed look from Hoffman's face as the van parked.

"Quite a spread, huh?"

"Unbelievable."

"'In Xanadu did Kubla Khan a stately pleasure dome decree.' Close enough, anyway."

"Kubla Khan?" Gene said with a raised brow, opening the door. "Let's not build up this asshole too much in our minds."

"A wise suggestion," Manning nodded as they climbed out of the van.

The four men trudged up a column of wide marble steps toward the main house. Gene clutched the valise like a life raft. In the absence of his brief amyl high, something more intense than simple anxiety was starting to take hold.

Fear. The kind of paralyzing fear that had only visited his mind during the throes of nightmare these past few years. Hoffman wasn't accustomed to feeling this way when wide awake, nor could he pinpoint an exact source. The news clippings Stella had brought from the library swam before his mind's eye for a moment.

This is no good. No good at all.

Stopping for a moment, Gene bent down and pretended to tie his shoe. With a bit of crafty stealth he dug out another capsule and cracked it under his nose. It had the same effect as the last, and Hoffman briskly bounded three steps at a time to catch up with the others.

He and Floyd followed their escorts toward the main house, taking it all in. They were not alone. Scattered about the lush grounds facing the property were at least twenty stoop-backed Mexicans toiling at extensive tasks of upkeep. Some operated hoses, some hefted gardening tools, others carried away baskets of trimmed leaves and branches. Stationed at regular intervals were tall silver watering machines similar to the kind used on exclusive country club golf courses. These sophisticated contraptions pumped out a fine mist that seemed designed to both dampen the assortment of nearby greenery and create a kind of humid canopy above.

It took Gene a moment to recognize how incongruous much of the lawn's varied growth was to this terrain. Magnolia, sycamore, honeysuckle, and palmetto plants mingled in riotous harmony, emerging from dry sunbaked soil never intended to nurture them. The hot morning air was redolent with their conjoined fragrances, almost sweet enough to induce a swoon. Standing tall in a manicured front courtyard was a weeping willow so perfect in size and symmetry it might have been swiped from the set of *Gone With the Wind*.

Hoffman was no horticulturist, but he felt pretty damn sure little if any of the delicate vegetation around him grew naturally in this region of the globe. Prewett clearly spared no expense in recreating his ancestral Southern upbringing down to its finest points, even if that required a round-the-clock squad of groundskeepers to maintain the facade.

They were not an overly nourished lot, by the looks of them. Comprised of both sexes, all of them wearing the same short canvas pants with not a stitch of clothing on above the waist, Gene thought he caught a few of the workers cast reflexively frightful looks at Rodrigo and Jaime. He may have imagined that, but there was no fancy behind the whip marks plainly visible on a number of brown sweaty backs, some of the grooved patches of flesh still freshly blooded.

"I get it," Gene muttered lowly to Floyd, feeling dumb for taking so long to piece together this jarring tableau. "It really is a Plantation. With honest to goodness slaves, just like down in Dixie."

Floyd turned to him quickly.

"Ixnay on the aveslay. I should probably have mentioned before, never use that word around Henry. He prefers to call them sharecroppers."

"I'm sure they appreciate that distinction."

Hoffman's eyes had taken on a glassy quality Manning recognized from his inexplicable outburst at the Bircher rally. It was an unsettling thing to behold, now of all moments.

"Actually," Floyd said, "the distinction is pretty substantial. No one's kept here by force, I'm told they can quit at any time. And he pays them extremely well, many times more than they'd earn from menial labor in Tijuana."

"Of course he does," Gene replied through tightly set teeth. "I'll lay ten to one he's not just paying 'em to till the soil either. It's the power trip, that's what he gets for his pocket change. Freedom to wield the lash out of sight from anyone who might object. It's all pretty clear even before I meet the son of a bitch."

"You're about to do exactly that, so let's try to focus."

Jaime trudged through an arched doorway into the main house. Floyd started to follow but Rodrigo stopped him with a loud whistle. He led them around to the right side. A winding red brick path flanked by tall and immaculately pruned boxwood hedges opened up on a patio adjoining the mansion's southern facade.

A garden party of sorts was underway. Spread amongst three tables were roughly a dozen people, all dressed for a formal affair. Bare-breasted servant girls circulated among the tables, refilling drinks and clearing plates.

Executing a quick visual scan of the patio, Hoffman had no difficulty picking out Henry Prewett from his companions. Sprawled in a semi-reclining position on a long wicker settee, their host was holding the hand of a shapely young women in a floral dress while apparently regaling her with some humorous anecdote. In any case, she was laughing hysterically at whatever he was saying to her.

Still unnoticed by the assembled, Hoffman took a moment to size up the man. There was an aura of faded decadence about him, at least that was the immediate impression. Fleshy, long-limbed body stretching the seams of a seersucker suit, bald pate gleaming in the bright sunlight, he seemed a virtual parody of the courtly Southern gentleman gone somewhat to seed. All that was missing to complete the image was a riding crop.

Rodrigo noisily dragged two unused chairs to the nearest table, which was empty except for a pair of heavily made-up middle-aged ladies speaking in high-pitched French slightly slurred by whatever had been in the empty pitcher in front of them. He waved for Manning and Hoffman to sit but they remained on their feet.

Pausing midsentence, Prewett turned to face them from across the patio. His reaction upon seeing Floyd revealed itself as an almost exaggerated pantomime of delight, even from a distance of twenty paces. Eyes sparkling as a slightly lopsided smile reached across his moon face, he rose with some evident difficulty from the settee and executed a stately waddle in their direction.

Hoffman swallowed dryly and shot Floyd a quick wink.

"Showtime, kid."

236

25.

"As I live and breathe, the man of the hour has arrived," Henry Prewett crooned in a gravelly voice lightly tinted with a Bayou drawl. Extending a hand that pumped Manning's with vigorous affection, he continued, "Such a pleasure to welcome you to my humble home once again. Of course, we were all hoping you might join us last night but that's of little consequence at the moment. All that matters is you're here."

"And we couldn't be more excited to be here, Henry."

"I assure you the feeling is pointedly mutual, my boy."

"We're lucky to have made it at all," Gene broke in, "the way your man handles these canyon roads."

Prewett adjusted his gaze to take in Hoffman for the first time, frowning slightly as if even a jocular comment on the transportation he'd generously offered caused offense. A friendly expression swiftly returned as he held out a pink hand.

"Mr. Faulks, I presume."

"Call me Randolph," Gene said affably, responding with a firm shake. He couldn't help noticing that Prewett's hands were both disproportionately small for his wide frame and also slick with some kind of oily perfume.

"If it's all the same, sir, I'd prefer to maintain a more formal mode of address for the moment. At least until we've had an opportunity to break bread together."

"No sweat off my ass, Henry."

The smile froze on Prewett's face. Floyd made a soft choking sound, looking like he'd just swallowed a lit cigarette.

Then the ample gent in the seersucker began shimmying with laughter. It came with some reserve at first but soon enough broke free into a chain of lusty guffaws.

"Very good, Mr. Faulks. I can see you're a man who doesn't believe in standing on ceremony."

"No offense intended."

"And none taken. You'll forgive me for not introducing you to the assemblage on an individual basis," Prewett continued with a slightly dismissive wave toward the other seated guests.

Most heads were now turned their way as if awaiting some kind of instruction from the man of the house.

"Truth is," he continued with a conspiratorial leer, "I only know about half their names. Shameless freeloaders, most of them."

Another barrage of laughter announced this was a joke. Taking their cue, the guests showed appreciative mirth at his good-natured jest. Prewett motioned towards the empty chairs.

"Sit, sit."

Only when Floyd and Gene did as they were told did Prewett join them. The two French ladies rose in response to some silent message and moved to another table.

"In all seriousness, gentlemen, I'm afraid you've just missed out on the most sublime luncheon. But I'm sure some kind of repast can be conjured with a little imagination. If you didn't have a chance to sup earlier, the kitchen can throw something together from our table scraps."

Gene didn't particularly like the way he said that, nor the shit-eating grin that seemed to be welded onto the man's face on a semi-constant basis.

"Don't go to any trouble," Floyd said, his manner becoming more solicitous with each passing second. "We're just fine."

Even though he was starving, Hoffman nodded amiably. "Sure. Throat's a bit dry, if there's anything you can do about that."

"Certainly!" Prewett semi-shouted, then turned and clapped his slick little hands together. The image of a trained seal leapt into Gene's mind.

At the familiar beckoning sound of command, a servant girl came shimmying over to stand beside Prewett. Barefoot in a light blue peasant dress, the only one present whose breasts were covered from public view, she could have been anywhere between eighteen and twenty-five. No matter how old, she was a natural dazzler who carried herself in a way that indicated she had little concern for her own beauty. And her beauty was profound. No amount of distractions could have prevented Gene from noticing that.

He noticed something else too: Floyd and the girl were locking eyes with a strange intensity. She looked away first, and the loaded moment barely lasted more than a few seconds, but it was pretty hard to miss. If Prewett picked up on it, he made no sign, just slipped an arm around the girl's slender waist and pulled her closer.

"*Refrescos* for our new arrivals, Celia."

She stood rooted in place, eyes flicking from her master to Manning and then back again.

"*Pronto, chica!*"

Prewett retracted his arm and gave her a hard slap on the rump. Not even blinking, she stood for half a beat longer before moving away.

Hoffman was watching how Floyd's attention closely followed her footsteps when he felt a tap on the elbow.

"I hope you'll forgive an indelicate question, Mr. Faulks. As you're a man who puts great stock in direct language, I'll risk a breach of decorum by asking it aloud despite my natural hesitation."

"Whatever's on your mind, Henry. Spit it."

"What a marvelously crude way you have of expressing yourself. I can't help wondering, sir, if the item that inspired this delightful visit is not located within your satchel."

He pointed to the leather valise Gene still held in his grip.

"That's where it is alright."

At those words, a tiny trickle of drool bubbled at the corner of Prewett's puckered mouth. He licked it away and nodded.

"Splendid. Most splendid, indeed."

"On that topic, there's a word or two that needs to be said about the item," Manning uttered nervously.

240

"I tried to bring it up on the phone last night but couldn't seem to..."

"Please, Floyd," Prewett cut him off with a raised palm. "This isn't the proper moment to discuss business. We'll have plenty of time for that, I assure you. And here are your drinks."

The girl reappeared with a tall frosted glass in each hand. Topping the rims were lush green leaves, which had been muddled to mix with the concoction within. Gene was expecting a Margarita and wondered how his constitution would react to more tequila after last night's debauch, but he tasted minty bourbon with the first tentative nip.

"Gentlemen, if you ever should ever set foot in an establishment that serves a finer Julep," Prewett commanded in a mock sinister tone, "tell me where it is, and I'll buy the doggone place!"

At this he bawled some more hoarse laughter. Floyd and Gene smiled and sipped their drinks. The girl had already started to move away, presumably to escape another squeeze or slap.

"And just where are you going?" Prewett said, any indication of mirth immediately washed from his voice.

Wordlessly, she stepped back closer and waited to see what came next.

For a weird moment Hoffman felt certain Prewett would strike her, but he merely gave a mournful sway of the head.

"I'm tempted to utter a few choice phrases about the difficulty of finding good help in this godforsaken country, but that would not be appropriate in front of guests."

Out of nowhere the threat of some kind of violence permeated the air, almost like a ripe odor. Gene was sure they all sensed it. Glancing across the table, he saw Floyd's entire body tense into a posture ready to either run or attack.

"Celia," Prewett purred in a much softer tone, "please show the gentlemen to their rooms. I imagine they'd like to freshen up from the dusty drive."

Manning relaxed with an audible exhalation as it seemed the possibility of any display of wrath directed at the girl had passed. But Gene's tension level was now shooting further northward.

"I'm sorry," he said, crimping a confused brow. "Our rooms?"

"Yes, Mr. Faulks. I've arranged accommodations that should more than meet your satisfaction. Separate sleeping quarters, of course, each equipped with a private bath. All the amenities of a five-diamond hotel. If there's anything wanting, you need only ask."

An awkward pause elapsed, with the only sounds to be heard coming from the other tables. Oblivious to the odd little drama unfolding in this corner of the patio, Prewett's lunch guests were occupied with smoking cigars, quaffing drinks, and making small talk amongst themselves in a fluid mix of at least three languages.

"Wait just a minute," Gene said, since the barefoot knockout's presence seemed to reduce Manning to a worthless mute. "I think there's been a slight misunderstanding. We came for the sole purpose of showing you the item in question."

"And indeed you shall, Mr. Faulks. It will be no less than the main attraction at tonight's revel."

Floyd nodded briskly as if finally hearing the words he'd been waiting for.

"A superb plan, Henry. We'd be delighted to stay."

He strenuously avoided looking across the table

at his traveling partner, and was thus spared the ocular daggers pointing directly at him.

Hoffman felt this had gone far enough, and he stood to emphasize his next words.

"Let's all get clear on what's happening here, OK? Mr. Manning and I appreciate your hospitality, but we have no intention whatsoever of spending the night."

Sensing Floyd was about to chime in, he continued in a slightly louder voice.

"An overnight stay was never part of any plan I agreed to. Therefore I suggest we find some private space to look at the merchandize. I mean now, Mr. Prewett. If you're interested, make us an offer. If not, we'll accept a ride back to the city."

Gene stopped speaking and gave Floyd a look so fierce it halted any words he may have been itching to add.

Prewett's countenance had grown notably less genial while Hoffman spoke. For the first time since they arrived, the man appeared genuinely displeased.

"I'm afraid that's far from satisfactory, Mr. Faulks. My intention is to experience this piece of cinematic history with an audience of like-minded film enthusiasts." He motioned toward the other guests. "You see, I've been regaling the assemblage here with some titillating hints about tonight's grand entertainment. I've shot my mouth off quite a bit in that regard, if the full truth be known. You wouldn't want to make me look like a naive blowhard in front of my friends, would you?"

All traces of comity, of that polished Southern charm, gone. It suddenly occurred to Gene that Rodrigo had probably been standing a few feet away the whole time, but he'd forgotten all about him until just now.

"It's alright, Randolph," Floyd started murmuring. "We can leave first thing..."

"Be quiet."

Hoffman forced himself to stay calm as he continued:

"Of course we'd never dream of embarrassing you, Mr. Prewett. Frankly, I don't see how that's possible. You're free to screen the loop for your friends any time you like, after we've closed the deal. By which point Mr. Manning and I will be on our way."

Hearing a boot scuffle against brick, he rotated his head a few degrees. Rodrigo was now standing directly behind him, close enough to touch. Glancing to the left, Gene saw Jaime posed rigidly across the table. The second *cholo* had materialized without any noticeable command.

Prewett was now smiling again, like there'd never been a hint of confrontation to begin with.

"Come now, Mr. Faulks. We've all had enough sun for the moment, so I'll ask you to indulge me. I promise it won't be a cause for regret. The most sumptuous of feasts is in the early stages of preparation as we speak. Tonight we shall dine like kings, ventilate our heads with some of the finest *pulque* in all of Mexico, and then we'll gather to view the item you've gone to such trouble to deliver. It will truly be a night to remember, and I'll brook no further argument on the subject."

Waiting a short moment for more words of resistance he knew would not come, Henry Prewett smiled with hearty amusement.

"What's life without a sense of showmanship, after all?"

26.

Celia led Gene and Floyd up a winding staircase to the second floor. The ceiling above was so high the exact shade of paint covering it was hard to determine. Hung from the wall opposite a grand colonial bannister were oil portraits in wide gilded frames, arranged in a climbing pattern that mirrored the steps. They depicted ladies in elegant hoop gowns and men dressed in the easily identifiable slate gray military uniforms of the Confederacy.

"The Prewett family tree, I suppose?"

Hoffman posed it as a rhetorical question, mainly to diffuse the suffocating silence generated by Manning and the servant girl. He was a surprised when she answered in perfect English graced only on the edges with a Spanish lilt:

"He wants you to think that, but I can tell you they're fakes. That one there," she said, pointing upward, "was done only last month. Henry liked the face of one of his guests, a man from Germany I think. He asked if the man would be willing to sit for a picture."

A shy smile started to part her lips but she didn't allow it to fully develop.

"This man was so surprised to look at the picture. I don't think he expected to be made into an old... what's the word..."

"Soldier?"

"No, the one who orders the soldiers."

"A general."

"*Sí*. Henry wants people to believe every man in his family was a general."

They continued upward until they arrived at the second landing. Floyd had taken on a slightly cow-eyed aspect during the girl's brief exchange with Hoffman, as if the sound of her voice acted as a kind of narcotic.

Celia motioned for them to follow her down a broad carpeted hallway, which led them along the mansion's western flank. Stopping at the second to last doorway, she opened it, revealing a quaint room with a four-poster canopy bed and a mahogany-paneled sitting area. She gestured inside, and then toward another doorway at the end of the hall.

"Your rooms, *señores*."

"Thank you," Gene said. "Have the bags brought up whenever you can."

She gave a quizzical look, full lips slightly pouting. It only made her lovelier, if that was possible.

"Forget it. Dumb joke. I'll take this one, Floyd."

"Fine with me," Manning answered, peering directly at the girl in a vain effort to catch her eye.

With a small nod she started to move away. Floyd reached out to gingerly lay a finger on her shoulder.

"*Perdóneme.* I have a question about my room, *señorita.* Would you please come for a moment to see if you can help me?"

"I'll send a man up," she said brusquely. With that, she moved down the hallway with assertive strides and made her way back to the first floor.

When she was out of sight Gene wrapped one hand around Floyd's collar and yanked hard.

"What the fuck is going on?"

"Take your mitts off me right now."

He shimmied himself free and Gene refrained from grabbing him again.

"Talk to me, Floyd. What's this shit about spending the night?"

"I've tried to make one thing clear to you from the beginning. Henry Prewett is a man who transacts business on his own terms. If he wants us to stay the night, that's what we need to do to make the sale."

"Did you know he was going to insist on that?"

Floyd hemmed and hawed for a moment before answering, "I recognized it as a possibility. Didn't see any reason to mention it until we knew for sure."

"Terrific. So now we're running the loop in front of a crowd. All that does is raise the chances of someone calling bullshit."

"Please. The last thing any of those cretinous sycophants would do is question the loop's validity if it would leave egg on Henry's face. They're all quite terrified of him, I can assure you."

"Maybe we should be too. Especially since we only got about twenty percent of what we came to show."

Now it was Floyd's turn to look exasperated.

247

"That's what I've been *telling* you. Forget the audience, that's irrelevant. Of total fucking relevance is addressing this issue proactively, which I tried in vain to do outside. One way or another, we need to cushion his disappointment in advance."

Hoffman brooded for a minute, then nodded.

"I think we'll be OK. Sounds like he doesn't plan on screening until after dinner. That should give us ample opportunity to drag him aside and make clear he's not going to see as much as he's hoping for. Then he can communicate that to the others so there's no potential for embarrassment."

"Couldn't have said it better myself. Now if you'll excuse me, I think I'll grab forty winks."

That was exactly what Gene planned to do, but he needed one more question answered first.

"What's up with you and the mamasita?"

"Huh?"

The look of feigned incomprehension on Floyd's face was so transparent it might have caused Gene to laugh under more casual circumstances.

"Don't give me 'huh'. I saw the way you two were clocking each other. It's a goddamn miracle Prewett didn't notice, unless he just decided not to let on."

"Don't worry, it's nothing serious. And it's got nothing to do with you."

His dismissive tone was really not the right approach to take right now. Gene clutched Floyd by the neck, fingers closing roughly on soft tendon.

"Listen to me, kid. Against all odds, things seem to be going pretty well. If Prewett doesn't totally flip over the incomplete loop, we might just walk out of here with some fat pockets."

Manning refused to acknowledge the painful pressure Hoffman was applying. He didn't even try to free himself, just quietly said, "You're correct. But we need to be razor sharp, and some of us are clearly suffering the effects of a late night in T.J. I'd advise you to grab some sleep, big man."

"I'd love to, believe me. But when I see you getting into a fracas with the little hoochie there, it makes me very worried. So I'll ask again, for the last time. What's going on?"

Floyd tried to shake his head to show he was insulted by this line of questioning, but he couldn't keep it up for very long. Pulling away from Gene's grasp, he took a step back.

"She's an old acquaintance. It's nothing."

"Didn't look like nothing."

"I guess she's not all that happy to see me."

"No shit. I thought she was getting ready to rip your tonsils out, and I was halfway rooting for her to do it."

Manning sighed heavily. There was as much relief as weariness in it.

"Celia and I had a little romance."

Gene nodded, already taking a dislike to what he was hearing.

"How long ago?"

"Two years. No, more than that. I met her on one of my regular pleasure trips to Tijuana. She was selling candles in a booth at the Mercado Hidalgo. We just hit it off, immediately and in a very deep way. I brought her up to Hollywood with me. It was supposed to be a long-term thing. A lifetime thing, actually. It didn't work out, for a lot of reasons."

"You mean you blew it."

"That's about right."

"How? Not that I really give a crap."

"Some cocktail waitress at Boardner's. The most costly one-nighter of my life."

He grimaced at the memory, then continued.

"Anyway, Celia made me drive her down to T.J., she was going to move back in with her family. God knows why, but I convinced her to come along to the Plantation. I was making a short visit, this was the time I tried to sell Bogart's cufflinks to Henry. He was a lot more interested in her, and didn't take long to ask if she wanted a job with the house staff. She accepted, primarily to spite me. At least that's what I thought at the time. We haven't seen each other since, and obviously her feelings are still raw."

"Her feelings? What about yours? I thought you were going to faint or start blubbering a goddamn love song when she first walked up."

Floyd could only smile. It was the most forlorn smile Hoffman had ever seen.

"I won't pretend I'm ever getting over her. But that doesn't have anything to do with why we're here."

Did Gene believe those words? Was there any way he could, given the plainly battered emotion behind them? He was too tired to contemplate it right now. That potent Julep he'd downed outside completely wiped away all effects of the second amyl capsule, and his brain and body were both screaming for a temporary shutdown.

"I really don't give a shit if that's the whole story or not, Floyd. You and I are gonna dump the loop and part ways as soon as humanly possible. That's the only thing of any importance right now."

"No argument here. I'll see you in a few hours."

Manning shuffled off toward his room, turning before he got there.

"Just remember this, Randolph. No matter what happens, we will have ourselves one hell of a story to tell when it's all over."

Sure, Gene thought but did not reply out loud. *Assuming we live to tell it.*

27.

The torches were lit at sundown. Dozens of them in all, burning bright atop tall brass sconces placed in serpentine trails winding both within the porticoed rooms of the main house's first floor and throughout the immaculately manicured clusters of greenery outside.

Darkness did not arrive silently in these foothills. The plaintive yelps of coyotes echoed across distant ridges, only to fight for aural supremacy with an unbridled cacophony of birdcalls and the circadian thrumming of an unimaginable assortment of insect life.

Despite the natural world's evening tumult, Henry Prewett was not an individual who allowed for any confusion as to who claimed the title of master in this land. He'd invested untold thousands into a stereophonic system wired to pump sound from a central tower to speakers hidden in the walls of certain rooms of the main house. In response to the atonal symphony of wildlife that greeted nightfall, some unseen hand flipped a switch and the swirling adagios of Mozart wafted forth from all directions.

Taking a last look in the oval mirror of his private bathroom, Hoffman did not fail to admire the surge of classical music as a consummate touch. Clearly the man in whose house he found himself an unwitting guest was possessed of a genuine appreciation for the dramatic. As this was a quality Gene prided in himself, he had to acknowledge Prewett was someone whose style of presentation could not be easily dismissed. Indeed, it was something to be well considered in the negotiations that lay head.

A large bell was rung in formal announcement that cocktail hour had begun. Its ponderous reverberations reached the very foundation of the house, as if to state in the most unequivocal language that everyone present was expected to appear for the nightly ritual of opening the bar. Hoffman didn't need to wait for another toll. He felt rested after a deep dreamless nap that lasted over two hours, and was ready for a cool beverage.

Stepping out of his room, he encountered Floyd in the hallway. The last traces of sunlight from the opposite windows were dying, leaving only the flicker of candles to offer illumination. They wordlessly nodded to one another, both understanding there was little left to say until the business that brought them here had been concluded. Whatever grudges or misgivings either may have harbored over the past week could wait until they stood safely on the American side of the border, cash in hand.

The two men walked downstairs and followed a trail of other guests who'd been summoned by the bell into a cavernous dome-ceilinged den looking out onto the rear patio. Gene overheard a gray-headed man tell his beehived companion that just a week ago it would have still been warm enough to serve cocktails outside. The fresh chill that had arrived with the shortened days indicated an imminent end to this summer's season of regular soirees at the Prewett Plantation.

Once ensconced in the den with fresh drinks, Hoffman and Manning stuck fairly close together. They exchanged greetings with a handful of the other guests, but names and faces blurred together. Most apparent was the broad range of nationalities represented by this group, comprising American, South American, and European citizens of a certain class. Hoffman found himself idly scoping for an Asian to round out the mix but couldn't find any. The single obvious factor linking these people was money. It was a prosperous crowd, to be sure. Aside from the half-naked servants incessantly refilling everyone's glass, Gene and Floyd were without doubt the poorest people on the entire property.

Prewett circulated among the group, playing the role of jovial host to the hilt. Whether he was genuinely enjoying the company of these people or if his derisive description of them earlier today was a truer indication of his feelings, Hoffman could not say. Nor did he care.

Cocktail hour dragged on endlessly, the den growing steadily dimmer. Or maybe that was just an optical illusion rendered by alcohol and a pervading sense of weirdness. Gene was determined not to get drunk, but that hardly felt possible given his wired state of mind. He didn't even anticipate needing to revisit the box of capsules, though it was kept secure in his hip pocket just in case.

Everyone seemed more or less crocked by the time the bell rang once more, announcing that dinner was served. In they filed to a significantly smaller dining room, almost all of which was occupied by a long narrow table. One corner held an open brick fireplace, around which stood a quartet of shriveled old Mexican women rolling fresh tortillas.

Gene grabbed the nearest chair he could find, Floyd sitting opposite a few seats down. Prewett took the head of the table, too far away to engage in any private conversation.

Patience, Gene told himself. *The right moment will come, and it'll be easy to recognize it when it does.*

He ended up flanked by the two women he'd first seen on the patio today. They spoke across him in a nonstop barrage of French, pausing once every few minutes to favor him with a truncated translation before resuming full bore like he was not within earshot. As best he could tell, they were in the fashion industry, one a designer and the other owning a boutique on Rodeo Drive.

Across the table, Floyd was locked in discussion with a bronzed young couple who spoke proudly of their deep roots in the thoroughbred game. It tickled them no end that he and Henry had first crossed paths in the paddock bar at Del Mar, where they spent most of their time during racing season.

Despite a feeling of something that was not quite confidence but at least a healthy reach from worry, Gene could not fully banish a repetitive memory of Stella's warning as the first course was served.

That guy who was found at the end of a noose in Sacramento, just days before taking the stand against Prewett...

254

This line of thinking refused to dissipate, so he tried to wash it away with a deep draught from the gilded chalice set by his plate.

Which proved to be a mistake. He'd wrongly assumed it contained more of the same pleasant sangria the servants had been proffering in the other room. Instead, his tongue withered at the hellishly sweet kick of something with bracingly high alcohol content.

Hoffman set the goblet down roughly, sputtering a bit.

"What do you think of our *pulque*, Mr. Faulks?" Prewett asked with an amused chuckle. "Packs quite a wallop, doesn't she?"

Working hard to keep a composed face, Hoffman drained the chalice, then wiped the corners of his mouth with a napkin.

"Delightful," he managed to say in clear voice. "What is it, exactly?"

As if waiting all day for someone to ask, Prewett launched into a lengthy description of the traditional native beverage of Mexico, how it was distilled from the fermented sap of the maguey plant, and a host of other details Gene had no desire to learn.

The banquet staggered along over the course of several hours in full circus-like swing. Courses were introduced with assembly line regularity, one after the other. Gene couldn't recognize half of the items he crammed into his mouth, and he didn't really care. He hadn't eaten anything since last night and it all tasted good. Whatever his faults, Henry Prewett was clearly a man who appreciated the finer things, and knew how to treat guests in the most opulent manner.

At a certain point, Hoffman looked up from his plate to see Rodrigo and Jaime positioned at the end of the table. He didn't notice them come in, and was wondering what their appearance portended, when Prewett got the room's attention with his standard obnoxious clapping.

"Pardon the interruption, but I'd like to take a moment to honor one of our most valuable assets here on the Plantation."

He motioned toward the two brawny men standing watch over the feast.

"Rodrigo Fernandez has faithfully piloted me in any number of vehicles for... what, a good five years now. That sound about right, Rodrigo?"

The mustachioed driver gave a noncommittal nod as if he didn't remember or particularly care how long he'd been working for this man.

"I usually don't allow non-kitchen staff into the dining room, but I wanted to take this occasion to offer a toast to such loyal service. Let's raise a glass, everyone."

All the guests did as they were told. A servant girl walked up to the two *cholos*, offering a tray. Gene noticed it only held one goblet, which Rodrigo took in hand. Apparently Jaime would not be treated to any refreshment tonight.

"To Rodrigo!" Prewett bellowed, and the others followed suit.

Everyone drank. The *pulque* went down just a bit easier with each swallow. Rodrigo consumed it naturally, bespeaking a long association with the sturdy concoction.

"That's it, my boy," Prewett encouraged. "Savor every last drop."

It seemed to Hoffman an unusually sadistic smile was entrenching along their host's face. Its source became clear in a moment, when Rodrigo started gagging loudly. The goblet fell from his hand as his eyes bulged from the result of some kind of harsh physiological distress.

"In the future, you'll be a bit more careful about keeping the Bentley properly oiled, won't you? Those vintage British makes require a special amount of care, as I've explained to you before."

The driver couldn't answer, or probably even hear the words being spoken. Tears were streaming down his face, which had turned a shade of red Hoffman had never seen human flesh assume. It reminded him of what the real Randolph Faulks looked like at moment of his death, only worse.

Jaime took a step back, alarmed by what threatened to be an imminent explosion of his partner's visage. But the spectacle acted as a sight gag for Prewett, who started laughing. A few coarse guffaws grew into an eruption of sincere mirth.

The seated guests were looking at each other nervously, some casting openly alarmed glances at the end of the table.

"Oh, don't worry about him," Prewett said, picking up on the growing unease. "Nothing fatal was in his *pulque*, I assure you. Just a finely crushed habanero pepper grown to prodigious size by my own hand. You see, I've been experimenting with some cross pollination lately. It's quite a diverting hobby. I believe the strain placed in our friend's beverage is the hottest hybrid I've yet been able to cultivate."

Rodrigo was struggling to remain upright as the crushed pepper's juices ate into the linings of his mouth and throat, burning a fiery trail down his esophagus. He used both hands to clutch his stomach with as much dismay as if he'd been stabbed, a lacerated gurgling sound coming from within.

Prewett eventually tired of the joke and collected himself.

"Be a stalwart companion and take him away, Jaime. Cold milk is the best thing for him, water will only make it worse."

Jaime followed the instruction, silently guiding his stricken colleague from the room. And thus ended the high point of this evening's dinner.

Quite some time afterwards, the dessert plates and coffee cups were finally cleared, and the guests started stumbling out of the dining room. Their host announced that hand-rolled Cubans and a variety of digestifs would be available shortly in the southern sitting room.

Gene and Floyd tried to position themselves off to the side, to catch Prewett as he worked himself away from the table. He made it easy for them by taking a proactive approach.

"Let us three break off from the group for a short while, gentlemen. There is a rare item in my private vault I dare to hope you may find worth a gander."

"Wonderful idea," Floyd said with audible relief that they would have some time alone with him. "Lead the way."

28.

It took a bit of caution to walk down two narrow flights of subterranean stairs that led to the Plantation's vault. Along the way they passed a cavernous wine cellar and, if Gene was not mistaken, a private crypt. Prewett didn't comment on that area so Hoffman decided not to inquire.

The vault itself was designed to be more than just functional in storing valuables. A semi-circle of leather backed chairs surrounded a small table on which several polished bottles sat next to a gleaming silver bowl. This was an inner sanctum of sorts, almost archly sinister it its gothic design. Lit only by gas lamps placed at regular intervals along the sharply converging walls, the ambiance was one of monastic claustrophobia.

"Gentlemen," their host said with a finger pointing at the table, "I'd like to suggest you'll find no more impressive collection of nightshades within the bounds of any privately owned property. All grown right on these grounds."

"Your personal reserve?" Gene asked, stepping closer to look into the bowl, which was filled to the brim with an assortment of greasy chili peppers.

"A small representation of it, sir. Cream of the crop if you will. In this room I keep the most promising specimens of certain strains too intense for casual company."

He reached down to extract a small pepper. Barely the size of a matchbook, shriveled to a pointed tip and pale ochre in color. It looked evil, or malignant at the very least.

"This little devil is found only in the fertile lowlands of southern India. Natives call it the 'ghost pepper' for its alleged power to steal souls. I've had to import a rare type of soil to nurture it."

Hoffman could smell the pepper from three feet away. Sweet yet acrid, the fragrance stung his sinuses with enough force to yield a shiver.

"Arguably the hottest pure member of the nightshade family I've come across, putting that habanero at the center of my little prank on Rodrigo to shame. In fact, once a scientifically valid way to measure heat in these exotics has been proven, I'm confident the ghost here will find no rivals for supremacy. I don't suppose anyone would care for a taste?"

Not getting a reply from either man, Prewett took a small knife from the table and sliced off the pepper's pointed tip. Barely the size of a #2 pencil's eraser, he licked it from the knife edge and chewed with a foul wet sound.

A fairly stark show of bravado, one laden with

a message of challenge: did either of the other two have sufficient balls to match it? Floyd exhibited no sign of being tempted, but Gene had to force down a surge of ego that prodded him to swallow one of those peppers whole, consequences be damned. That would obviously be idiotic. Why allow this windbag to draw him into some pointless contest he couldn't possibly win?

"No takers? Pity, but I won't belabor the offer. In truth, I didn't bring you down here to sample my peppers. There's another item that should be of some interest to purveyors of odd curios such as yourselves."

"Mae West's favorite dildo?" Gene asked, getting somewhat tired of hearing this man talk.

Prewett frowned slightly, looking displeased that he may have stolen some thunder.

"I'd be happy to show you that as well, Mr. Faulks. But I had something else in mind."

Opening the latch of a compact cabinet, Prewett stood to block their view of what was inside. He turned, brandishing a small booklet in his hand.

"I take it you worldly men are familiar with Tijuana Bibles?"

"I've seen a few eight-pagers in my life," Hoffman answered. "Stopped reading them around the time I grew hair on my sack."

"I agree, they are rather childish in terms of content. My interest in these volumes lies in the rarity of their publication. This little number, in particular. It's believed to be the only such work featuring the woman at the center of tonight's main attraction."

Handing the booklet to Manning with an air of reverence, Prewett seemed to be holding his breath with anticipation as to what kind of reaction it would yield. Floyd gave it a cursory once-over and passed it to Hoffman. The pages were yellowed with age and thin as tissue. Gene tried to mime a look of appreciation as he beheld the cover.

The title, rendered in a looping scrawl, read: "Marilyn Monroe in *Lost at Sea*." A moderately accurate caricature of the starlet leered up from the cover with a lascivious wink. Skimming the pages, Hoffman saw the expected assortment of dirty jokes and smudged but highly explicit drawings that depicted Marilyn in a wide range of sexual situations with a boatload of horny sailors.

Returning the booklet to Prewett, Gene saw a weird gleam in the man's eyes.

"I'll never forget the first time I beheld dear departed Marilyn on the silver screen. *Niagara*, summer of 1953. It wasn't much of a movie, truth be told. I hardly even noticed who else was in it. My gaze never left that blonde goddess. The soft music of her voice, the way she filled out those tight sweaters. I guess you could say it was love at first sight, after a fashion."

For the first time Hoffman realized Prewett was quite inebriated. He held it extremely well, but there was no doubt he'd started to flush. From alcohol or some strange sentiment, it was hard to tell.

"I realize how foolish that sounds, forming an emotional fixation on the projected image of a woman I never had the great fortune to meet in person. But I'm not the only one she affected so powerfully, as her legions of fans would surely attest. I must have gone to see *Niagara* ten times, and never missed another of her pictures."

He looked down at the booklet in his hands as if he'd forgotten it was there.

"When I came upon this volume of silly little etchings in a specialty bookshop in Prague, I'm not ashamed to admit it cast a powerful spell upon my erotic imagination, which is prodigious even without any external stimulation. It's really quite special to me."

Prewett tucked the eight-pager back into the cabinet with the type of ardent care a museum curator might show for an original Rembrandt.

"Well," Gene said, "if those doodles float your boat, you're gonna cream when you see what we've got."

"Precisely what I was hoping you'd say, Mr. Faulks. I believe a sufficient anticipatory mood has been established, and my guests upstairs are surely chomping at the bit. Shall we?"

Floyd loudly cleared his throat.

"Henry, we need to explain something first."

"I don't think I like the sound of that, Floyd. It gives me a distinct feeling you're preparing me for some kind of disappointment."

"Disappointment is a strong word. This is really just a matter of calibrating your expectations."

Prewett's face took on an unusually lifeless mien, the twinkle in his eye quickly deadened.

"My expectations are quite clear, based on what was promised me. Any calibration had best be done on your end. Now let's get on with it."

Turning, he made for the door without allowing for further discussion.

"Jesus Christ," Manning said to Gene. "This could get ugly."

"At least make him look at the paperwork first. The more we can do to establish authenticity, the less chance he'll blow a gasket."

Neither man felt too convinced of that idea, but they had little choice but to follow their host out of the vault.

29.

The housebound sharecroppers had been hard at work turning the den into a screening room. All the chairs were placed in a theater arrangement, facing the south wall. A roll-down screen, the largest Hoffman had ever seen at about fifteen feet square, was positioned in front of the fireplace. Across the room, just behind a sectional leather couch that had been left conspicuously vacant, a black Bell & Howell projector stood on a thin wooden stand.

Most of the guests had already streamed back into the den to claim seats. A few stragglers roamed in search of a good viewing spot. The air was thick with cigar smoke. Two bare-breasted servant girls, neither more than a year or so past the crest of puberty to Floyd's circumspect eye, moved through the murmuring audience collecting empty glasses.

Prewett sank onto the leather couch and clapped his oily hands together. The nearest servant girl hurried over, lowering the tray for him to discard his glass. But he didn't have a glass. A jerk of his head told her to set the tray down. She did. A quick pat on his knee told her to sit. She followed that order as well.

Even from several feet away in the low light, Manning could see the girl shiver as Prewett's left hand closed over her scarcely developed breast. It was a disturbing sight. He had to look away, over to behind the couch where Gene was carefully loading the loop onto the projector.

Trying to keep his eyes averted from the under-aged domestic, Floyd held out the FBI documents for Prewett's inspection.

"As I was trying to explain, this is an archival piece of footage. In order to fully appreciate what you're about to see, I implore you to peruse the accompanying paperwork."

"Later," Prewett huffed, hand still idly caressing the girl. "My guests have waited long enough, and so have I."

Manning stubbornly thrust the papers at him.

"I'm afraid I have to insist."

"Insist, Floyd? Did I hear you correctly? I take it you've lost all sense of where you are right now, otherwise you wouldn't abash yourself with such an uncouth remark."

And that was very clearly that.

"No dice," Manning bemoaned as he walked over to the projector. "Son of a bitch won't budge."

"*Que sera, sera,*" Hoffman said after a long exhalation. "Guess we'll just have to see what happens."

At that moment, wired by a bolt of telepathy, the

same delirious thought rocketed into their minds, one they'd avoided considering for the last twenty-four hours:

They had no idea what was on that roll of film.

The action looked alright to Gene through the viewfinder in the hotel room, but that was no guarantee the image had been captured with any fidelity. It could all be one big hazy blur, or just an empty black square.

And they were fresh out of time to worry about it now.

Prewett reached around the girl to clap his paws together, generating a hushed silence in the room.

"Ladies and gentlemen... *damen und herren... madames et monsieurs... señoritas y señores...* I pride myself on offering all guests to the Plantation not simply fine food and accommodations, but entertainment of a most rarefied kind. Adult entertainment, if you please, that not even the kinkiest salons of Amsterdam nor the most exclusive brothels of Paris might hope to rival. I'd like to think my efforts have been successful to date, but you must consider yourselves hugely fortunate to be here this particular evening."

A dramatic pause, which Prewett used not only to heighten the room's palpable buzz of anticipation but to issue a terse wave at Manning.

"I give you the most towering and indelible icon of female sexuality since Cleopatra, as you've never seen her before. Roll it!"

Gene and Floyd exchanged the kind of look that two people on the top floor of a burning building share before leaping to what they can only pray will be a soft landing.

"Here goes nothing," Hoffman whispered, flicking the projector's switch.

For an agonizing moment, they thought they were fucked. Both of the projector's reels were turning properly, a beam of light shot across the smoky darkness and filled the screen. But nothing was visible within that white box.

Then the screen went black, and a bold numeric countdown appeared at intervals of two seconds.

5... 4...

Hoffman sighed with relief and comprehension. When he filled out the work order at Yale Labs yesterday morning, he'd neglected to request that any leader be spliced onto the loop. The lab technician did it anyway, either out of habit or simple courtesy. That explained the blackness followed by the numbers.

3...

2...

Another few frames of black.

And then there she was.

Their handmade movie star, looking in every conceivable way like the real deal. Gene's heart clutched unexpectedly at the sight of Stella made up as Marilyn. For a second he forgot all about his immediate surroundings and allowed himself to drink in every inch of her counterfeit glamour. The grainy black & white image projected across a befogged room only added to the unreal likeness.

Her tousled blonde hair was rendered a slightly blurred white glow in the light of the 1K. The lamé of her gown glittered on the screen like breathing silver and her glossy lips shone with the allure of black diamonds. But it was her eyes almost made Hoffman shudder. They spoke to him with a message of plucky élan, even amusement, radiating outward as they flashed briefly at the camera before turning to address the headless male torso in front of her.

No one in the den blinked as Stella hooked a finger under the right strap of the gown and pulled it down. Her breasts popped free into the light as if bothered by confinement beneath the fabric.

Floyd twisted himself around the couch, trying to get a look at Prewett's face. He couldn't discern any kind of reaction from the murky profile view, but it seemed undeniable the loop had fully claimed the man's attention. He was leaning forward on the couch in a posture of the most intense concentration, threatening to crush the pubescent girl on his knee.

Stella reached and unzipped Lenny's trousers. She paused and turned to face the Mitchell's lens, a bemused grin on her painted lips as she absorbed some silent off-camera instructions. With a visible shrug, she zipped him back up.

Gene froze with apprehension, having totally forgotten that he'd asked her to do it over. Was that liable to make the loop seem more or less authentic?

He got a quick answer when Prewett rumbled, "Wonderful! A pro to the end, always willing to take direction!"

On the screen, Stella rolled her eyes at where Hoffman had been standing outside the frame, then turned back to Lenny and began Take 2. Fingers languidly closing over his fly, she unzipped him again with measured sensuality. Then came that wet kiss she placed below his navel, the tip of her tongue leaving a moist dot on the pale skin. It was an intensely erotic image, claiming the entire room's rapt attention. Not a sound could be heard but the ticking hum of the projector.

With a brief glance upward, Stella slid her right hand into Lenny's pants and started to pull his manhood out for some proper attention.

Then the screen went black once more. And this time, Gene and Floyd knew it was going to stay that way.

A buzz of agitated confusion almost immediately arose from the audience. Prewett remained a statue on the couch, eyes fixated on the screen as if attempting to produce a resumption of the imagery through sheer will.

Floyd startled Hoffman by cupping his hands around his mouth and shouting, "That's it, folks! I hope you all appreciate what a rare piece of celluloid you just viewed. If I were to disclose exactly how it came to be in our possession, you might not sleep so well tonight. At least not if you have any reason to suspect the Federal Bureau of Investigation is keeping a file on you. But, I digress..."

"A fragment of true cinematic history," Gene broke in as Manning seemed to lose his way. "Something to tell your grandchildren about. Once they reach an appropriate age, of course."

Their mincing patter fell flat. The general grumbling had started to shift in tone from confused to maddened. Floyd thought he heard someone in the dark breathe a word that sounded distressingly close to "*phony.*"

Prewett pushed the girl off his lap and rose from the couch. He stood there with the beam of light shining directly into his engorged face.

The loop had traveled all the way through the Bell & Howell. Its tail end was spinning on the feed reel, flapping softly against the projector's outer casing. Gene killed the power and the reel came to a stop.

Seeming to anticipate their master's next command, the servant girls began turning on lamps to offer some illumination.

"What's this all about, Floyd?"

The sound of Prewett's voice did not suggest anger, just the abysmal disappointment of someone who doesn't want to believe a truth that's impossible to deny.

"If I led you to expect more, Henry, I can only apologize."

"But this is most confounding," the host said with a bit more volume as a sense of communal discomfort began to take hold. "Surely I'm incorrect in thinking we just saw the entirety of what you gentlemen have brought tonight."

"That's it," Gene said. "Of course, the original negative probably ran a bit longer, but it's really a miracle even this much still exists."

Noting that their host was showing signs of being equally out of sorts, the guests started grumbling amongst themselves with greater vehemence.

"What kind of hokum is this?" one man with an aristocratic British accent inquired of the person next to him, while a floridly drunk American woman seated across the room more bluntly stated, "We didn't even see cock!" A few pejoratives in French and Italian also cut into the air as a general mood of offense held sway.

Hoffman nudged Floyd with an elbow.

"They'd never dream of embarrassing him, huh?"

Manning could only answer with a perplexed shrug.

"Hush, everyone," Prewett said to the audience, almost pleading. "I appreciate your consternation, but you must try to contain yourselves."

His admonition was largely effective, though not as much as it might have been ten minutes earlier. The host was losing face with his guests to a certain degree, that much was evident.

Every eye in the room was by now trained on the two men behind the projector, none more glaringly than Prewett's. Even in the thick air, it was easy enough to see a volcanic reaction building within. To accentuate or perhaps muffle that point, he stepped around the couch to speak privately to them.

"Gentlemen, I can only hope this is some sort of joke? One made in poor taste and with flagrantly bad timing, but a jest nonetheless. I'm correct in that estimation?"

Neither Floyd nor Gene could think of anything especially smart to say. They just shook their heads in unison, and the reality of this situation finally set in.

"I see. Well, it appears I've been made quite the jackanapes. A remarkable turn of events, to say the least."

"Still interested in buying the loop?" Gene asked agreeably, figuring there was no harm in going for broke at this point. "We could talk numbers over a nightcap."

Floyd almost dove behind the nearest chair at those words, thinking Hoffman had definitely pushed too far this time. But Prewett seemed to take it mildly enough.

"Out of the question, Mr. Faulks. My sense of inner turmoil is far too grave to even consider the matter right now."

While some indignation was evident, there was no doubt the man's overriding emotion was a kind of sadness. Like someone might react upon learning a long held promise that always sounded too good to be true has turned out to be just that.

He clapped his hands, as meekly as Gene had seen him do, and the same young girl who'd been in his lap scurried over. Lacing an arm around her shoulder, Prewett gave a parting nod.

"We can revisit the matter tomorrow morning. I won't deceive you gentlemen into thinking I hold the slightest interest in the... item. But out of respect for the effort made in coming here, I'll give it the benefit of a night's repose."

Holding the girl tight, Prewett turned to face his guests, most of whom had been engaged in a strenuous if largely ineffective bit of eavesdropping for the past few minutes.

"Friends, I can only express regret for failing to live up to my rather boisterous grandstanding in regard to tonight's program. Please take every liberty to entertain yourselves as you see fit. I bid you good night."

And with that, clinging to his tiny companion, he shambled out of the screening room.

Floyd watched him leave, not quite believing it. Gene carefully unspooled the film and returned it to the canister.

"I gotta say," he mused. "All things considered, it could've gone a lot worse."

"Your capacity for self-delusion is admirable, big man."

Hoffman nodded as if to concede there may be some truth in that assessment.

"Well," he said, tucking the loop into his pocket. "I don't know about you, but I think I'll see what the bar has in the way of brandy. Anything to get the taste of that goddamn *pulque* out of my mouth."

30.

The pathway from the main house to the servants' quarters was poorly lit. On a cloudy night it would have been tricky to navigate, but the moon was full and the sky clear so Floyd didn't have too much trouble following the grassy trail. All about him the grounds were quiet except for buzzing insects and the occasional far off yip of a coyote.

Manning took his time walking the path, making sure he knew the right things to say when he found Celia. He'd waited until well past midnight to seek her out. The main house had been dark and largely silent for almost an hour. Floyd planned not to leave his private room until he was sure all Prewett's guests were asleep. That probably wasn't the case, given the conjoined amatory groans of what sounded like at least three people coming from a room somewhere on the first floor, but it didn't matter. All he wanted to do was get out of the main house undetected.

He'd done that. The next step was to make his way inside the servants' quarters, locate Celia, and coax her out to an area where they could speak in private. Ideally without waking the untold other male and female sharecroppers with whom she shared sleeping space.

The pathway sloped downhill at a manageable grade. Before long he could easily discern the angle of a low slanted roof set against the treeline. It was a single floor structure, long and narrow, resembling a barracks more than anything else. Floyd arrived at the entrance, which was screened but unlocked. Taking a deep breath, he pulled the door open and stepped through.

The room was much darker than outside. From all around him came a sonorous fanfare of slumbering noises. Snores, wheezes, and a few faint murmurs in Spanish.

The meager beds, if they could properly be called that, were arranged in two rows. He had no more practical plan than to go from one cot to the next until he found the right one. Even in this near blackness, with only a few slivers of moonglow coming through the narrow windows, Floyd knew he'd have no trouble recognizing her.

As it turned out, Celia recognized him first. She was in the second cot on the left, and bolted upright as he was leaning down to confirm it was her.

Holding a finger to her lips, he really thought she might scream or bite it off. The fury in her eyes almost carried its own illumination, but she stopped herself from making a sound. Floyd pointed to the front door, and she seemed to realize the futility of resisting him. Celia rose from her bed and they quietly walked outside and around to the southern flank of the barracks.

As soon as they were beyond earshot of the sleepers, she wheeled around and slapped him hard across the face. Manning didn't mind; at least it was a direct acknowledgment of his existence.

"I told you not to come here," she whispered. "*Nunca parar*, Floyd?"

"Let's not argue about whether or not this was a good idea. I'm here."

"But why? I'm not going back to L.A. with you. I've told you that a hundred times."

"Listen, I have no illusions about us reuniting. I know that ship sailed a long time ago."

She shook her head, indicating a deep lack of faith in those words.

"*No te creo*. But, OK, fine. So what do you want?"

"A couple of things, really. Making sure you're alright, for one."

"Please don't worry about me. I can take care of myself. I told you that on the phone."

"I heard you, but I came anyway. Maybe you can tell me why."

"Because you think I might still give a damn about you."

"Already told you I gave that up a long time ago. Try again."

"You feel some kind of stupid guilt. Let me ease your mind, Floyd, so you can forget all about me. I chose to accept Henry's offer. *Fue mi decisión*, understand?"

"The choice would never have been yours to make if I hadn't introduced you to him."

"Maybe so. Why should we play that kind of game after so much time?"

"This is a poisonous place, Celia. I know you hate it here."

She shrugged, but it didn't look as cavalier as she probably intended.

"Staying has some advantages."

That fairly cryptic remark hung in the air without further illustration. Floyd wasn't entirely sure he wanted to know what those advantages might be.

"If it's money..."

"That's part of it. I have other reasons."

"Don't tell me it's love. If you're going to lie, at least come up with something more believable than that."

The girl shook her head, black hair shining in the lunar blaze, and a portion of a laugh escaped her lips.

"You can relax, Floyd. Henry hasn't touched me in a long time. Not that it's any of your business, but we only slept together once or twice."

Manning hoped it was too dark for her to see the expression on his face, which he imagined must be similar to that of a man who just ingested a saddle burr. While he'd always assumed in a vague way Prewett had enjoyed carnal relations with Celia, to hear that fact directly confirmed struck hard.

"I suppose it must've been a challenge refusing his advances."

"Only at first. I didn't have to refuse for long. He lost interest fast, and hasn't bothered me for sex in at least a year."

"I find that hard to believe."

"Then you must not know him very well. I'm too old for Henry. Any girl over sixteen doesn't get him excited. He can't... perform?"

Manning acknowledged it was the correct word with a terse nod.

"And he likes virgins," she continued. "So that was a problem from the start."

Even this oblique reference to the fact she'd once given Floyd her maidenhead, freely and with passion that was only made more inflamed by her innocence, momentarily robbed him of speech. Celia misread the brief silence.

"What? You didn't know your rich friend was a pervert?"

"Not... like that. Jesus."

He didn't have any difficulty believing what she'd just told him, especially after seeing the grotesque display of Prewett fondling that young girl on the couch earlier tonight.

"But look, if Henry doesn't hold any amorous claim on you, there's no reason he should object to your leaving."

Celia laid both hands over her face with the exasperation of trying to communicate with a concrete wall.

"How do I get this through your head, *cabron*? He's not keeping me against my will. I can leave any time."

"So what are you waiting for? You'd never stay this long just to spite me."

"*Es correcto*. I'm staying for someone else's sake, not yours."

Manning almost asked who, then it came to him. He felt ashamed not to have considered it before now.

"Rita."

"He finally understands."

"No, not really. How does your little sister figure into this?"

With a faint sigh, all the irritation fled from Celia's manner. She sat on a rough wooden bench, and after a cautious moment Manning joined her.

"You're not the only one who wishes they could change things. I did something so stupid, now I have to deal with it."

Such regret came through her words Floyd instinctually reached out to stroke her hair, the way she used to love him to. And she didn't push his hand away.

"What is it? Tell me, please."

"One day, eight or nine months ago, I let Henry drive me into Tijuana. *Nunca había hecho eso antes*, usually Rodrigo takes me when I want to make a visit. I tell him to drop me off at the Mercado and from there I walk. I don't want anyone to know where they live. But that day, Henry talked me into it. He wanted to meet Mama, give her a crate of fresh avocados. I didn't know about his problem with young girls then. The minute we go in the house I knew I made a mistake, a bad one. The way he looked at Rita... *que me dieron ganas de gritar.*"

Floyd didn't know exactly what those words meant but the feeling behind them required no translation.

"As long as I'm here," Celia continued quietly, "I know he doesn't have her."

"So you're going to stay for the rest of your life to protect her?"

"No. Just until she's too old for him to want in his bed. Another three or four years, then I can be sure."

"What if..." Floyd uttered tentatively. "What if he decides he wants her anyway, even with you around?"

"Then I kill him, that's all. I cut his throat while he sleeps."

She spoke those words with no change in her emotional register. It made Manning think she'd visualized the act many times, down to the most min-ute detail. And he knew she'd do it.

"Let me assure you, such extremes won't be nec-essary. This time tomorrow, you'll understand that."

Placing a kiss on her brow too quickly for her to withdraw from, he stood.

"Good night, *chica.*"

Floyd started walking up the pathway to the main house. When he turned his head after about twenty paces, she was still sitting there like a statue in the moonlight.

31.

The floorboard creaked just as he was passing Hoffman's room. But that didn't make any difference, because Gene was already waiting for him in the open doorway. He laid a hand over Floyd's mouth, signaling for him not to make a sound. Then pulled him roughly into the room and closed the door.

"What are you still doing up?" Manning asked with an inauthentic casualness.

"I heard you leave your room, asshole. Followed you out of the house a little ways down that path. Wasn't hard to figure out where you were headed."

"Very nimble for a man of your carriage. I'm impressed. Now I'm going to sleep, and so should you."

Floyd tried to move for the door. Placing a hand on his chest, Hoffman shoved hard enough to make him stagger back on the bed.

"This was never about money, was it?"

"What the hell, Gene?"

"Just tell me if I've got it lined up correctly. You had some beef with the girl, now she's Prewett's. You needed a way in the door, and some backup in case shit got heavy. An all-around chump to carry your water, and I fit the bill."

Floyd didn't answer. Shaking open his pack of cigarettes, he crumpled it into a fist finding it was empty.

"OK, it's true I had an ulterior agenda. Only reason I didn't fill you in is that it doesn't overlap on our purpose for being here."

"My ass it doesn't. I came to sell a piece of film, not settle some personal score. Hell, if that was the case you really think I'd take your side against his?"

"You're right. I couldn't do this alone. I knew the documents weren't enough to garner Henry's invitation. I needed the loop."

"You already had Stella. Why didn't you try it a year ago?"

"Never believed it would work. Not until you showed up out of the blue."

Hoffman shook his head weightily.

"Worst mistake of my fucking life."

"It didn't feel like a mistake to me. Felt like, I don't know, divine intervention."

That characterization of the events at Binion's Horseshoe yielded a snort of contempt.

"How else could I explain it?" Manning pressed on. "A total stranger saves my life in Vegas. A guy of your imposing nature, who happens to have real filmmaking experience? A guy who might be in need of some quick cash himself? Who might even be a little desperate? I would've been a blithering idiot not to take advantage of such an opportunity."

"You took advantage of *me*, you lying little cock-sucker!"

"Gene, you know what it means to have remorse. Don't you? To know you've done wrong by someone in a way you'll never be able to shake off?"

Hoffman wanted to act like he didn't have any idea what Floyd was talking about, but Florida wouldn't let him. And they both knew it.

"I did Celia a terrible wrong, whether she accepts that or not. Did it intentionally. I knew Prewett was a rotten bastard, and I was furious she didn't want to be with me anymore. I brought her here, knowing damn well he'd offer her a job with too big a salary for her to refuse. And why should she? She had no way of telling what a sick fuck he is. I opened the door to this snake pit and let her walk right in."

"That's a heartbreaking story, Floyd. But I don't give a shit about your personal problems. We're selling the loop tomorrow, and that's all we're doing."

"Are you totally delusional? The loop's a lost cause. Regardless of any subterfuge on my part, we clearly failed to deliver something Henry wants."

Hoffman shook his head, smiling just a bit.

"I don't think so. I smelled bluff tonight. Sure, he was pissed the loop's incomplete, but he didn't say he thinks it's fake."

As Gene was speaking, he thought about the way Prewett had waxed romantic over the Tijuana Bible with Marilyn in its pages. That memory convinced him even more he was right.

"Prewett will pay us," he continued. "I'm absolutely sure of it. Probably a fraction of what we want, but he'll pay."

Seeming to weigh the risks versus benefits of making one last revelation, Floyd nodded.

"You're right, big daddy. But he won't do it by choice."

He reached into his jacket and pulled out a nickel-plated revolver. The one he'd just barely had time to purchase at the flea market in Tijuana this morning with his last ten bucks, along with a full load of rounds. A throwaway Saturday Night Special, scuffed and scratched from usage, the gun at least worked. He'd fired a test into the ground before buying it.

"Just what the fuck do you intend to do with that?"

"Call me cynical, but somehow I don't think Henry reports all his income to the IRS. I'm not greedy, not looking to take him for all he's got. Just enough to make everything you and I have been through worthwhile. And to set up Celia and her family with a nest egg big enough to build a new life on. Someplace far away from here."

Listening to this, absorbing the entirety of Manning's scheme finally laid bare, Hoffman could only think back to what Stella said right before closing the door on him.

You're as crazy as Floyd, she'd said.

The hell I am.

Something tore inside him, some last veil of restraint. It was a numbing sensation more than anything else. He didn't even feel particularly angry as he reached out and took the gun away. He gently set it down on the bed, then he grabbed Floyd's wounded hand and squeezed with every ounce of his strength.

A glass-shattering shriek from Manning got muffled by a handkerchief Gene stuffed into his mouth. All the color drained from his face and Hoffman only squeezed harder, deliberately crushing the damaged tissue. The bandage started seeping redly at the edges. Floyd's eyes glazed over with gathering shock and it was clear in another few seconds he would pass out.

Gene let go. Floyd's knees buckled. He collapsed onto the floor, whimpering like an abused animal. Hoffman bent down in a crouch so they could be eye to eye.

"Listen close," he said softly. "I'm going to pretend I didn't hear anything you just said to me. First thing in the morning, we sit down with Prewett and find out how much he's willing to pay for the loop. You will remain as silent as possible without drawing attention to it, and let me handle the negotiation. In the end, we'll accept whatever he offers. Then we're leaving this place, just the two of us. And all you have to worry about is whether I decide to give you your cut or keep it myself. Now get out of here."

He pulled Manning upright and yanked the handkerchief from his mouth. Some pinkness had begun to return to Floyd's face. He stood for a moment, weaving slightly. Gradually refocusing onto Hoffman's eyes with a wordless expression of naked hurt that was much deeper than just physical.

"Do you read me?"

Manning nodded, barely. Hoffman led him across the room and pushed him into the hallway.

Closing the door, Gene walked over to the open window and tried not to think for a few minutes. He was utterly beat, but the prospect of trying to sleep repulsed him. Far too many nasty images spiraling around his brain, both in plain view and hidden just below the surface of consciousness.

Noticing a pad of stationary on a rolltop desk in the corner, he stepped toward it and sat down.

The idea of writing a letter to Stella soothed him somehow, even knowing he'd probably never mail it.

Taking a pen in hand, he tried to compose a few thoughts that might shed some illumination, to himself as much as her, on the events of the past few days and his own decisions that helped to shape them.

It was a futile, maddening exercise. What could he say now that would make a damn bit of difference? Angrily tearing up the letter, he walked over and lay down on the bed, hoping in vain for a few hours of dreamless sleep before seeing what the next day would bring.

32.

The buzzsaw. The blood. Barbara in pieces.

Hoffman bolted out of bed with a scream. A sense of utter disorientation gripped him for a few seconds. Shakily pushing the sheets aside and rising, he realized his face was wet. He'd been crying in his sleep.

Crisp sunlight filtered in through the eastern window. The antique bedside clock read 8:15. Gene was surprised and somewhat taken aback he'd slept this late. His intention before nodding off had been to get up around dawn and take some time to gather his thoughts before the next encounter with Prewett.

Only feeling halfway returned to the waking world, he was still trembling slightly as he pulled on his clothes. The nightmare had never hit him so hard before.

He thought he knew why, but didn't want to brood on it.

Even if things went as well as they possibly could today, nothing that had defined his recent state of being would change.

With Ben Malton dead, any chance of buying off some measure of guilt from Florida was gone for good. He'd never find out who'd hired the private dick, never mail that anonymous payment in the dim hope it might bring some succor to whoever mourned Barbara Cheston. Hoffman would spend the rest of his life carrying his burden of culpability and there wasn't a damn thing he could do to alleviate it.

Freshening up as best he could in clothes he'd been wearing for three days straight, Gene took a last look in the mirror. He refrained from dipping into the box of amyl nitrate. Maintaining a calm rather than hyper focus seemed the wisest approach.

He didn't hesitate to slip Floyd's revolver into the back of his belt, however. No point in leaving himself without a viable option that, Lord willing, wouldn't be necessary.

He stepped out of his room and knocked on Floyd's door. There was no answer, and for a moment Hoffman flashed on a paranoid certainty that he'd done something nuts.

But then the door opened. Manning stood there, looking like he hadn't slept a wink. The blood around his bandages had dried to a dark paste, almost brown in color.

"How's the hand?" Gene asked, feeling bad about what he did last night despite the ample justification Floyd have given him.

"Never better. Thanks for asking."

They were both very close to murmuring an apology to the other, but the words didn't come.

287

"Ready to wrap this thing up?" Hoffman said, trying to inspire maybe a small shred of the unlikely camaraderie that had just barely sustained them in each other's company thus far.

"Sure. Let's go see what we can shake loose from the bastard."

They found Prewett seated alone at a table on the southern patio. The other guests seemed to have taken an order, either overt or implied, to make themselves scarce. The Plantation was as quiet as it had been since they arrived yesterday. Even the sharecroppers were not out on the grounds in any visible formation.

A bowl of fruit and a tray of baked goods sat on the table in front of Prewett, who was finishing a cup of coffee as he perused a leather-bound volume of Neruda.

"Have a seat, gentlemen. I trust you found your sleeping accommodations comfortable."

"No question," Floyd replied, pulling up a chair as Gene did the same. "Best night's rest I've had in some time."

"Delighted to hear it," Prewett grinned, setting down the book. "I feared perhaps your slumber might be disturbed by worries about that unpleasant outburst following the screening."

"Didn't cross my mind once," Hoffman said, wondering what the man thought he had to apologize for.

"Very good, sir. I must beg your pardon for venting my disappointment with such infantile theatrics. In front of guests, no less. Truly an abominable breach of etiquette I hope you're willing to forgive."

"More than understandable, Henry. You reacted with great equanimity."

"Kind of you to say, Floyd. Would you gentlemen

care for coffee? I've made due with no more than a continental breakfast, as you can see."

They both nodded and Prewett picked up a small bell from the table. He shook it vigorously, its chimes ringing in the silent morning air.

"Where's everyone else?" Gene asked

"If you mean the other guests, they're dining in the east hall. I thought it preferable for the three of us to have some time alone. I'm sure you're both eager to be about your business."

Celia appeared from the house with a carafe of coffee on a tray. Jaime walked out behind her, positioning himself by the next closest table.

"Thank you, my sweet. Perhaps you could linger nearby in case the gentlemen should decide they've an appetite for anything else."

She retreated to a shady corner of the patio, sitting at an unused table.

Dumping three spoonfuls of sugar into his coffee, Floyd wondered why, of all the servants, she'd been chosen to attend to them. A coincidence only, or had his late night foray to the barracks been noticed by someone other than Hoffman?

"Funny," Prewett said, somehow reading his mind. "I'd almost forgotten it was you who brought this fair damsel to my attention. Don't suppose I've ever properly thanked you for that."

"No need. I'm sure it's been a mutually agreeable situation."

"Oh, indeed. Most agreeable."

"Getting back to our business," Gene broke in, figuring nothing helpful could possibly come from discussing the girl, "it really makes no difference what we didn't bring. The question is, are you interested in the loop as it exists?"

"I admire your directness, Mr. Faulks, even if it

chafes somewhat at my sense of propriety. I'll try to be equally blunt in the interest of time."

Rather than continue, he reached for an orange from the bowl and began pulling off the skin in tiny little pieces. Gene figured he planned on letting them stew in anticipation until the entire peel had been removed, and that's exactly what happened.

Licking grossly on a liberated wedge, Prewett gave a nod.

"I'd be willing to offer you gentlemen a total of ten American dollars for the loop and the accompanying documents. Foolishly wasteful, I have no doubt, but it pains me to consider letting this visit conclude as an utter failure for all involved."

Manning's response was to sit with a purely blank face.

Gene waited half a beat to allow for some sign that this was a joke, but saw none was coming.

"Mr. Prewett, I hope you'll recognize that I speak with all due respect when I say you're wasting our goddamn time. I'll ask that you either put a serious figure on the table or instruct your driver to get the van ready."

It was hard to tell what impact those words had, if any. Their host seemed more interested in the peeled orange.

"Very well, Mr. Faulks. Since my initial offer fails to meet your satisfaction, allow me to sweeten it. In compensation for the woefully incomplete and quite possibly *bogus* piece of celluloid you've brought into my home for the purpose of humiliating me in front of my peers, I'll grant you and Floyd the freedom to leave this place. On foot. Your departure will not be impeded in any way by members of my staff, nor will you be stripped of whatever lint and small change may be lining your pockets. A fair deal, is it not?"

Draining his coffee cup, Prewett clapped his hands for Celia to pour him a refill.

"Maybe we should all take a deep breath," Manning said. "Randolph meant no disre..."

"Still your lips, Floyd. Rest assured most of my pique is pointed squarely at you, whom I'd almost come to think of as a friend. It's only thanks to a lifetime of practice in the finer points of decorum that my hands haven't found their way to your neck. Now I suggest you be on your way, gentlemen. The sun reaches its zenith in approximately four hours. It's your great fortune most of the trip is downhill."

A look of not quite total panic stole across Manning's face. He barely even noticed Celia had rejoined them and stood waiting to see if Prewett had any more orders for her.

"Henry, for God's sake. We'll never make T.J. on foot. We'd be lost within a hundred yards of the property line."

"Don't fret over that unduly, Floyd. I'm providing you with an escort who surely knows the route well enough by now."

The twittering of birds was the only sound that held the air for a long moment. Catching a look of budding comprehension in Celia's eye, Prewett nodded sagely.

"That's correct, my dear. I'm giving you your walking papers, if you'll pardon a rather weak pun. The service I've come to expect from you is far from satisfactory of late, marked by what I can only brand a laggardly or perhaps even defiant attitude. In any event, I have no further use for you here."

He took a sip of coffee. Then added, as if it just occurred to him, "Perhaps there's another member of your lineage who'll be more appreciative of the unique opportunities I have to offer."

Floyd jerked his head to check for a reaction for Celia. Probably too subtle to be noticed by anyone not watching for it, but to his eye an icy aspect fell over her countenance. He saw her looking at the butter knife on the table and felt momentarily positive she was going to lunge for it.

"What if we don't feel like leaving just yet?" Gene demanded, interrupting whatever action she may have been about to take.

"Of course I'd never dream of forcibly ejecting invited guests from my property, Mr. Faulks. No matter how crude their behavior."

Prewett shot his cuff to look at a gold watch.

"Twenty-eight minutes ago I placed a phone call to the central office of the *Policía Federal* in Tijuana. Captain Ramos and I are on rather friendly terms, you see. I informed him there were three thieves found in my house, including one individual whom I'd naively taken into my employ. He promptly dispatched a jeep full of highly capable offers, I'd say they should be here in less than an hour."

He let those words sink in, raising another wedge to his mouth.

"Now, you three can wait here to be arrested, though I should caution I've heard some disturbing rumors about the treatment of prisoners in the Mexican penal system. Or you can take your chances on the road. They'll be looking for you, of course, but if timing breaks in your favor you may be able to hide in some underbrush and allow the jeep to pass you by unnoticed. The choice is entirely yours, but if you do elect to take it on the hoof, I'd advise against wasting any more precious time."

Accentuating the point, Jaime stepped closer to the table. Floyd seemed to have reached a point of total speechlessness. Again.

Hoffman simply stood, hands behind his back in what might easily be mistaken for a casual pose.

"Very well. You've laid out the situation clearly enough."

And then the gun was out and pressed squarely against Prewett's temple. The *cholo* instinctively lunged forward but halted at Hoffman's voice.

"One more step and it's brains for breakfast. Back off."

Gene was pretty impressed with how calmly Prewett reacted. Setting down his coffee cup without spilling a drop, he nodded to Jaime.

"Do as he says. Let this pantomime of ludicrous desperation play itself out."

"You," Gene barked at the *cholo*. "Sit."

Jaime took another glance at Prewett for confirmation. Getting it, he lowered himself into the seat Hoffman had been occupying.

"Where's your pal, Rodrigo?" The lack of an answer encouraged a hard nudge. "Hey, I'm talking to you."

"*Trabajando,*" Jaime grunted. "*En el garaje.*"

That bit of news seemed to please Prewett.

"Applying some overdue care to the Bentley, I should hope."

"Good," Gene said, thinking this guy really had ice water in his veins. "Makes it easier not having another pair of hands to worry about."

Hoffman stepped around and positioned himself behind the table. Drawing the gun back like a pitcher on the mound, he swung down against the base of Jaime's neck, muzzle finding exactly the right spot behind his ear. The blow folded him down hard onto the table, unconscious.

Then Gene returned the gun to its previous position with Prewett in the crosshairs.

Manning jumped out of his seat and asked, "I'm assuming you have some sort of plan in mind?"

"As much as you did, probably."

He turned to face the girl.

"Celia, right? Go get some rope, the thicker the better. A sharp knife, too. You know where to find that?"

She nodded.

"Good. Go with her, Floyd. Bring as much as you can. Make it snappy, I'll keep an eye on our host."

"You really have a plan?"

"I'm working on it. Come on, no lollygagging."

Celia had already started walking toward the house. Floyd gave a shake of the head and jogged over to catch up with her.

Sitting, Gene helped himself to more coffee.

"This is a remarkably stupid thing you're doing, Mr. Faulks."

"You may be right. It's getting to be a habit with me."

"You seem like an intelligent man. I wonder if you're intelligent enough to recognize when it's not too late to change a disastrous course of action."

"Hell, I'd say we passed that point a long time ago."

It took only about five minutes for Celia and Floyd to return to the patio. He was hefting a braided coil of rope, she carried an eight-inch sterling butcher knife, which Manning was unable to keep his eyes away from.

"Perfect, tie them to the chairs," Gene said, waving the gun at Prewett and Jaime. "Both of 'em. Wrists and ankles, and make sure it'll hold."

Floyd got to work on Jaime while Celia knelt behind Prewett's seat. He craned his neck to speak lowly to her.

"You can't even begin to imagine the dire consequences of this betrayal, *putilla*. Nor will you be the only one to suffer them."

Hoffman pointed the gun a little closer to his chest.

"Pipe down and let her work."

Trading the butcher knife, Floyd and the girl were able to slice the rope into eight long segments and tie up the two men as Gene instructed. After about ten minutes they were both bound to the heavy metal chairs in which they sat. Hoffman tested the ropes for security and nodded in approval.

"Alright. We don't want to wear out our welcome, but there's still one order of business left. See, Floyd has an idea you've got some folding money stashed around this joint, maybe a lot. I tend to think he's probably right. So the question is, do I have to hurt you to find out where it is?"

"I don't believe you're possessed of sufficient gumption to act on that threat, Mr. Faulks."

Hoffman stepped behind him and out of view.

"You really want to test that assumption?"

"Even if there was a handy pile of cash I'd never be apt to miss, my lips are sealed. I'll take my chances waiting for the *federales*."

Floyd noticed the butcher knife was still clenched in Celia's hands. He shook his head wildly, trying to catch her eye.

With a fuzzy groan, Jaime started to lift his chin from the table. Gene drilled him with the gun again.

"I really didn't want to do that," he said to no one in particular.

"This is all so pointless," Prewett clucked.

"I know where he keeps money," Celia said, dropping the knife.

A triple take from the three men. Their collective look was so weighted she hastily added, "I don't know how much."

"We're listening," Gene said, making an effort not to sound too impatient.

"In the bedroom. There is a... I don't know the word. Like a wooden box with doors."

"A cabinet?"

"*Sí*, next to the bed. Henry keeps a lot of Yankee dollars in there. He likes to roll around on them in the bed, when he... you know. It helps him perform, and he needs a lot of help."

The silence following that revelation would have made a bizarre tableau to any detached observer. Prewett finally started to lose his cool.

"Why, you devious little slut!"

"Don't get excited," Gene warned him.

"How do you know I still do that?" Prewett demanded of Celia. "I haven't bothered to touch your indigent brown hide in God knows how long."

"I've been stealing it," she said matter of factly. "A little bit at a time so you don't notice, *puerco*."

To Floyd she added, "I told you I had more than one reason to stay."

"Well, that's very interesting," Manning sputtered, voice quivering with relief that there may be a nonviolent route to what they wanted. "Gene, what say we mosey on up and see how much is there?"

"By all means," Hoffman agreed. "And let's take something to carry it with, assuming she's right."

"Come. I'll show you."

With a last baneful look at the fuming Prewett, Celia turned back toward the house. Floyd was close behind. Hoffman started to follow, then paused and turned around.

Brows raising with the inspiration of a good idea,

he grabbed a napkin from the table. He folded it down the middle and started draping it around Prewett's eyes.

"Hold still, damn it."

Prewett was rotating his head with acute agitation as Gene tightened the makeshift blindfold until there was no way it could be shaken loose.

"Really, sir. You may have gained a momentary advantage. Why bother with such needless foolery?"

Gene's face broke into a deeply satisfied grin, his first in some time.

"Indulge me, Henry."

33.

Exactly eighteen minutes later they followed Celia down the driveway, branching off to the right where a garage sat partially hidden behind a grouping of mesquite trees. Hoffman felt a little lightheaded, carrying a large paper sack with a tight grip.

Stealing the money had been accomplished with almost hallucinatory simplicity. She'd led them up to the second floor master bedroom, with a private verandah overlooking the canyon. Just as she said, an unlocked chest of drawers sat squatly next to the four-poster bed. Pulling open the top drawer, she stepped back to let them look inside. It was stuffed end to end with American legal tender. The money was not stacked neatly or bound in packets but carelessly strewn about. Most of the bills were badly wrinkled and creased, presumably from Henry Prewett's currency-riddled sex romps. At least they didn't appear to be stained.

Still, Gene wished he had some rubber gloves to use in moving the money from the cabinet into the sack they'd brought up from the kitchen. There was no point in worrying about it. He could wash his hands with industrial strength lye later.

Floyd and Celia watched as he bent on one knee and filled the bag. By the time he reached the brim, the remaining bills in the cabinet couldn't have comprised much more than five percent of the original amount. Might as well leave something for the gods, Gene reckoned. He knew there was little chance this cache represented more than a small fraction of all the available money scattered around the house, but it would have to be enough. Reproving himself not to get greedy, he stood up and told Celia to guide them to the garage.

As they now trudged down the hillside, it occurred to Gene he'd so feverishly stuffed the sack he didn't keep too close a watch on the bills' denominations. Many looked to be hundreds. If he was in a more relaxed state of mind he might try to guess how many c-notes it would take to comprise a pound, and then multiply that estimation by five to get a handle on roughly how much he was carrying. But such a pleasant diversion would have to wait, at least until they'd cleared the property line.

Prewett's garage was of a prodigious scale in keeping with the rest of the Plantation. A half dozen different autos of various makes were lined spotlessly next to each other. One end of the structure housed a large trailer used to transport these luxury vehicles to flatter ground. The van they'd come in on was parked off to one side.

A vintage silver Bentley Mark VI tilted up on a jack, a pair of legs protruding from beneath.

Hoffman handed the money to Floyd. Then he pulled out the gun and cocked it, primarily for the sonic effect.

"That you, Rodrigo? Get up nice and easy."

The burly *cholo* pulled himself from under the car and rose slowly. His face looked rather waxy and drawn, a lingering aftermath of the intense gastric punishment he'd endured for the table's entertainment last night.

Rodrigo stood eying the threesome warily, a heavy wrench held in one hand.

"Drop that," Gene said, keeping the gun trained on him. "Don't be stupid, I got no beef with you."

After a beat he obeyed, the wrench clanging to the floor.

"Good. Now give us the keys to the van and we'll be moving along."

Another loaded pause as the man grimly pondered his options. Not finding any, he walked over to a patch of wall where numerous key chains hung from nails. He tossed one over.

"Get it started and pull out," Gene said, handing the keys to Celia. "Floyd, you get in the back seat."

They did as they were told. Rodrigo cast a particularly hateful look at Manning as he stepped past.

She backed the van out of the garage and Hoffman walked over to open the passenger's door, gun still aimed at the *cholo*.

"You boss is tied to a chair on the patio, can't move a goddamn finger. Blindfolded, too. If someone were to walk up there and crack his head open with a blunt object, he'd never know who did it. In fact, he'd probably think it was me."

Getting in the van, he leaned out the window and

added, "Thought you might want to know that."

Rodrigo just stared coldly for a moment. Then Hoffman thought he saw the slightest suggestion of a smile curl underneath the thick mustache.

"Hit it," Gene instructed Celia, and she did not wait for further directions. Pumping the gas, she steered the van down the steep driveway.

Before they reached the first bend, Hoffman looked in the rearview mirror and caught a glimpse of Rodrigo trudging up toward the main house. The wrench was back in his hand, and he was swinging at the empty air like a batter on deck taking a few practice cuts in anticipation of knocking one clear out of the park.

They descended rapidly through the twisting lane until the gate came into view. Gene was about to ask if she knew the combination when Celia jammed with greater force on the accelerator. Her two passengers barely had time to brace themselves before she plowed straight into the gate.

The steel frame gave way with a metallic screech followed by a jarring snap. It fell forward onto the ground like a huge mousetrap. The van's heavy tires bounced over the twisted frame and kept chugging onward. Hoffman shook his head silently, knowing they were incredibly lucky to have gotten through.

"What?" Celia asked him with a challenge in her voice.

"Nothing. Eyes on the road."

They next twenty minutes or so passed in silence. It was a breakneck trip, effected at a much more expeditious pace than the one that brought them here despite the sharp downhill grade. Celia piloted the van with a lead-footed zeal that would have bordered on sheer recklessness were it not matched by her expert handling of the rough terrain.

As she plowed over hairpin turns and sudden drops without tapping the break, Floyd could look through the window over the path's edge, far down steep chasms plunging into masses of leafy overgrowth. More than once, he was at least marginally sure they were a goner.

Neither he nor Hoffman uttered a word of admonition for her to slow down. Even during a few tense moments when it really did feel like the van would career over a cliff's edge or slam into the mountainside with sufficient force to kill them all. Somehow at the last second Celia always managed to ease up a tiny bit before pressing on at greater speed.

After they'd put about eight miles between themselves and Prewett's land, the road narrowed to its most treacherous stretch of the journey. Coming around a high twisting peak bordered by shrubbery on one side, Celia slammed on the brakes for the first time. Floyd's face smacked into the back of her seat and Hoffman almost swallowed the smoke he'd been struggling to light.

Gene was about to ask what the problem was, then he saw it through the bug-dotted windshield. His mouth went dry.

Fifty feet ahead, a shiny green and white jeep clearly marked with the words *Policía Federal* was advancing up the hill in their direction. Prewett hadn't been bullshitting. That Captain Ramos had responded to his call so promptly said much about the man's clout with municipal authorities in Tijuana.

"I can't get past," Celia said. "There's no room."

"Yeah," Hoffman murmured, "but sitting still might be the worst thing we can do."

"They're expecting us to be on foot," Manning said. "And they probably don't know what we look like."

302

"That's true, but if we're going to bluff our way past we need a little more road to work with."

He looked at Celia for confirmation. She nodded, hands tightening on the wheel.

"Get down, Floyd," she instructed. "They're looking for three people."

"Good thinking."

Manning lay flat on the floor of the van, brushing aside various garbage and assorted debris. He stuffed the sack of money under the back seat as far as it would go.

"We could always try to buy our way out," he said.

"Hell with that," Gene grumbled. "We didn't go through all this just to pay off some thug with a badge."

Celia tapped the gas, easing forward at a crawl.

They hadn't moved more than another few yards when the jeep pulled into the center of the path, completely blocking their ability to advance. The bulky outlines of two officers were just barely visible through the windshield, and Hoffman was quite sure they were not alone in there.

Celia had nowhere to turn. It was just rotten luck to encounter the jeep at this point the road, barely wide enough to accommodate a single vehicle. To their immediate right loomed a muddy hillside, to the left nothing but empty air and a long fall to whatever lay below.

Gene pulled the gun from his pocket and checked to see how many rounds were in the chamber. It occurred to him he'd neglected to do this earlier today, and could have been holding a blank to Prewett's head for all he knew.

"Please don't be stupid," Celia said, looking at the revolver. "The *federales* carry machine guns."

"Just want to know what all the options are."

There were four rounds in the chamber.

The jeep flashed its highbeams, which would have been impossible to see if it hadn't been partially parked under a fir tree's thick covering of branches.

Celia responded by planting an elbow on the horn and leaving it there.

Floyd reached up from the floor to lay an alarmed hand on her shoulder. "What are you, *loco*?"

"*Talvez*," she nodded in partial agreement. "But I'm not going to wait here all day."

Hoffman silently admired the girl's moxie, even if he agreed with Manning it was almost suicidally rash.

After what seemed a very long time, the jeep backed up with a shudder and positioned itself into a narrow culvert on the right side of the road against the hill. The driver flashed his highbeams again, inviting them to pass.

"OK, easy does it," Gene said even as his fingers closed around the revolver.

Celia drove at a slow pace, veering left to advance around the parked jeep. Both the van's wheels on the driver's side came within an inch of leaving the road. That they didn't tumble side over side downhill was as much attributable to sheer dumb luck as to her skilled wheel work; if Hoffman was not sitting with all his weight in the passenger seat they'd never have stayed anchored on the path.

Another few yards brought them within a single vehicle's distance from the jeep's front bumper.

"Any last words?" Floyd asked from the floor.

Celia ignored the comment.

Gene considered it, then nodded.

"Yeah. Were those really Sinatra's dice?"

From their respective positions, neither man

could see the yielding smile appear on the other's face.

"Absolutely," Manning answered. "At least I thought so when they first came into my possession. Then the keno dealer who sold them to me was locked up for mail fraud, which caused me to suspect I may have been ripped off."

"Sounds like poetic justice to me."

"*Cállate!*" Celia hissed as they pulled a few more feet ahead to advance around the *federales*' jeep. Manning and Hoffman respected her order to shut up. The two vehicles were so close their side mirrors scraped together as she passed.

Inside the jeep, a pair of uniformed officers sat in the front seat, giving them a close inspection.

Just as Gene was wondering if he should speak, Celia leaned over him and delivered a few sentences in rapid-fire Spanish. The closest officer gave her a wolfish look, totally ignoring Hoffman. Then he tipped his cap, said something to the driver, and the jeep started inching forward.

Celia, Floyd, and Gene all tensed involuntarily, waiting to see if it was a trick.

"What'd you say to them?" Hoffman whispered.

"Three thieves are tied up at the Plantation and this fat *gringo* asshole wants me to take him to a whorehouse."

Hoffman gave a laudatory nod, hardly willing to believe that would work.

The *federales* stopped again. Then, for an interminable moment, nothing happened.

"Hit the gas gently," Gene said. She did and the van squeezed by the jeep's rear fender, then continued on the path.

"No need to rush," he cautioned. "Just nice and slow."

"*Sé que*," she said with annoyance at his back seat driving.

As they made their way down the hill, Hoffman's eyes stayed locked on the review mirror. The jeep was just idling there in the same spot with the brakes on. Waiting to see a sudden movement in reverse, he was ready to tell Celia to floor it whether she wanted to hear more from him right now or not.

Then the jeep's brake lights died and the *federales* continued onward up the path. Only when it was completely out of sight did the three people inside Rodrigo's van allow themselves to breathe again.

34.

A little more than an hour later, they entered Tijuana's city limits. The experience of suddenly being surrounded by multi-directional urban commotion came as a shock to both Gene and Floyd. Their overnight visit to the Plantation somehow felt like it had consumed at least a week.

As Celia drove closer to the city center, they discussed what the safest move at their disposal might be. An immediate return to the Hotel Caesar seemed unwise. Manning's plan was to slip back there sometime after nightfall to retrieve his Eldorado. In the meantime, they had to get rid of the van. Celia suggested driving over to the sprawling Mercado Hidalgo on Avenida Independencia, where she and Floyd first met. Both men endorsed this idea.

They could ditch the van in the crowded lot directly behind the marketplace. It would probably sit there among hundreds of other vehicles for weeks, gathering a thick layer of dust, until someone decided to strip it for parts or steal it outright. Dumping a vehicle in the midst of Tijuana did not exactly call for a master criminal mindset, but they all agreed it was a solid proposal nonetheless.

She parked in the middle of a crowded row of cars and they got out to walk towards the massive hub of human activity. Gene held the paper sack to his chest like a mother swaddling a newborn. The Mercado was bustling at full midday capacity. With more than eighty open air stalls selling food and crafts of every conceivable stripe, it was an ideal environment to blend in and get lost. So much color and movement, such a widespread ongoing collision of bodies, the uneasy threesome surfed the crowd in search of a quiet area to take a more thorough look at the sack's contents.

They decided upon El Rincon del Oro, a snug restaurant that faced the central plaza. Gene and Celia grabbed a secluded table on the shady rear patio while Floyd ordered three glasses of alcohol-free lemonade from the bar. Without going to the effort of checking into a hotel, which none of them had an inclination to do, this was about as private a spot as they could wish for to break up the money.

Hoffman separated the bills by denomination in a silent, businesslike manner. As he'd thought, most were hundreds with a few fifties and twenties mixed in. Once they were divided he began laying out three piles on the table, one bill at a time like a blackjack dealer issuing cards on a green felt.

Celia grabbed the bill he laid to start the third pile and put it on top of the second, indicating with a cold shake of the head she had no interest in collecting a thirty-three percent portion of the stash.

"I don't want all that, just what I took on my own. I couldn't get to it before we left."

"How much was it?"

"About five hundred dollars," she said in a subdued voice, obviously ashamed to admit her theft regardless of where the money had come from.

Hoffman returned the bill squarely to its original spot.

"You earned a full cut," he replied. "We'd never have found this without you, or found our way back to the city for that matter."

"I said I don't want it."

"Take it anyway," Floyd said. "Gene's right, you earned it. And you'll need it to relocate your mother and Rita. That has to happen right away, *chica*."

"I know," she said, sounding less than convinced. "I think I'll have enough to do that."

"Come on. You can stand on principle once they're safe. How long do you think it'll be till Henry comes looking? He'll use the *federales*, and where do you think they'll start?"

"The Caesar, probably," Hoffman said.

"Well, yeah," Floyd answered dismissively. "And straight to your Mama's house at the same time."

"We can move to another place with the five hundred. There will still be some left after that," she said stubbornly.

Hoffman smacked a heavy palm on the table, making it shimmy.

"Let me be plain here, Celia. Personally, I could care less what you do with the bread. Give it to the church or flush it down the crapper, it's all the same to me. But we're splitting this up three ways and that's that."

She recognized his tone would not allow for disagreement. And a new expression on her face seemed to convey some acceptance of the idea she was entitled to an equal share. So she quit arguing and sat back in her chair to watch him count it out.

Divvying up the money took less than ten minutes. At one point a waiter started to approach the table curiously but Hoffman scared him off with an aggressive wave of the arm.

In total, it came out pretty close to an even three-way split: $22,000 each, with some of the smaller bills left over.

Floyd didn't need to be instructed to fold his pile into a few tight rolls and stuff them in his pockets. Hoffman did the same, then pushed the third stack in front of Celia.

Both men watched as she gathered it with some reluctance. Holding that much money was clearly freaking her out.

"Alright then," Gene said. "I think our dealings with one another are complete."

All three rose in unison and made a hasty retreat from the patio. Celia said she had to use the *baño* and the two men stepped outside. The chaotic whirl of the marketplace swept garishly past as they emerged into the sunlight.

He really didn't want to know, but Gene still found himself nudging Floyd with a question:

"Headed back over the border?"

"Why? You want a ride?"

"Absolutely not, I'll cab it. Just curious, I guess."

"I suppose I'll stay with her for a little bit, if she'll let me. At least long enough to make sure she gets her people moved out safely and set up somewhere else. I'd like to help her arrange the money in a way that'll do them the most benefit."

"Well, good luck. But I don't think you're winning her back, no matter what you do."

"I know that, Gene."

Celia stepped out of the restaurant and stood in place by the entrance, as if mulling whether to bolt.

"See you in the funny papers," Manning said, giving Hoffman a chuck on the shoulder. He'd taken a few steps toward the girl when he heard his name called.

Floyd turned.

"What is it, big man?"

"Just thinking. If our paths cross again, no need to pretend we know each other. *Comprende, amigo*?"

It took a moment for the comment to register. The two men traded a smile that lasted barely a second. Floyd moved closer to Celia. Another three paces and he'd disappeared from Gene's sight into the throngs of humanity spiraling around the Mercado.

35.

Hoffman sat on a hard wooden bench in the main terminal of the Greyhound station at 120 West Broadway in downtown San Diego. His body was stiff in so many places it was impossible to keep track of them all. It was an odd kind of blessing. With such a multitude of small agonies he really couldn't concentrate on any particular one for more than a few moments at a time.

Walking across the U.S. border with twenty-two large in American bills was a surreal sensation. He'd decided at the last minute to do it on foot. If he hadn't been in such a hyper state as a result of everything that happened over the last forty-eight hours, he probably would've telegraphed his unease in such a way as to invite closer interrogation from the callow border guard who questioned him.

But Gene's calm, glassy-eyed manner had worked quite well to effect a smooth entry into his home country. All four of his pants pockets stuffed with currency, he casually chatted up the guard like he had all the time in the world until the guy motioned him through. The fact that he was now sitting on this bench, a free man under an assumed name with a fat bankroll to his credit, seemed almost too much to believe.

His hand clutched a ticket for the 12:55 "Lucky Streak Express" to Las Vegas. A six hour trip with almost a dozen stops along the way. He could have bought a plane ticket but traveling via the most anonymous means possible seemed like a prudent call. Greyhound didn't require passengers to offer any photo identification. And Gene didn't feel quite up to beguiling his way past an airline counter with a dead man's driver's license, on the remote chance the Hollywood police had somehow made an accurate ID of the heart attack victim in room 219 of the Mark Twain Hotel.

After purchasing his ticket with more than an hour to spare until departure, Gene decided to handle one last errand. Inquiring about the nearest post office, he learned it was only four blocks south. So he ambled down there, ignoring the tightness in his knees and lower back, and filled an 8 x 10 manila envelope with as much money as it could hold without looking too suspicious. Then he scribbled Stella's name and address, attached a sufficient number of stamps, and dropped it in the slot.

Sending cash in the mail was obviously a risky proposition, especially a fat sum of almost $6,000, but he really didn't have any other choice. Wiring the money with a signature from Randolph Faulks was out of the question, and he sure as hell wasn't going to deliver it in person. Much as he might be tempted to knock on her door, Gene wouldn't allow himself that. He had enough self-awareness to realize what he owed Stella, far more than money, was to remain resolutely out of her life. Even if keeping that distance caused him a bit of heartache.

So he just had to rely on the old fashioned post and cross his fingers that the envelope arrived at its destination unmolested. In order not to attract attention from the postal inspector, he jotted a bogus name with a fictional San Diego return address on the back. It hardly mattered. She'd know where the envelope came from. What use she might find for its contents, Gene would never know. He only hoped she'd draw some solace from it, some way to forget or at least distance herself from the awful things she'd seen in that hotel room.

Feeling the envelope fall from his fingertips into the mail slot, Hoffman felt a brief sting of self-reproach for ripping up the letter he started composing last night at the Plantation. Even if it was incomplete and rambling, failing to express the things he really wanted to tell her, he still wished he'd held onto it. She'd probably appreciate finding some small personal note along with the cash.

Well, it was too late to worry about now. Just another small regret to add to the top of the heap, assuming there was still room for any more up there.

As for what lay in his immediate future, he really couldn't say. Truth was, he had no clue. But such matters could be considered in due time. Right now, the top item on his priority list was retrieving his Plymouth from the parking lot of the Four Queens. Hell if he was going to abandon a trusty ride like that, and besides he couldn't afford to leave any loose ends that might suggest Gene Hoffman still walked among the living.

So back to Vegas it was. And maybe he'd linger for a day or two. The roulette wheel might be a little kinder this time. As this train of thought started to accelerate, Gene quickly vowed a silent oath to take no more than a few hundred to the casino. He wasn't about the blow his entire wad, not this time. There could be no excuse for that kind of self-destructive stupidity. Hoffman knew you only got so many lucky breaks in the course of a lifetime, and he'd surely expended all of his by now.

Checking the clock on the wall, he rose from the bench with a small wince. His bus was due in about five minutes and he wanted to meet it early to grab an aisle seat. Lumbering across the dirty tiles of the terminal floor, it occurred to him he hadn't felt any angina pains for a full day. Then he dismissed that notion, not wanting to jinx any possibility, however remote, that cardiac arrest did not lie in his foreseeable future.

Actually, Gene didn't want to spend much time thinking about *anything* that had occurred since he crossed paths with Floyd Manning. He felt pretty confident he wasn't the villain in this tale, for whatever that was worth. Some people lost their lives, sure, but he hadn't killed anyone. And removing that girl from Henry Prewett's orbit meant at least one person had been helped by the whole sordid affair.

In truth, of all the things that went down since stepping into Binion's Horseshoe, only one caused Hoffman any true remorse: he would never have a chance to see what might have happened with Stella if circumstances conspired a bit differently. Maybe there were no real legs in that relationship, but it would have been fun to find out. Gene wished they'd had a little longer to get to know each other, maybe a lot longer. Remembering how he'd rebuffed her half-kidding question about marriage, he now felt a total fool. Given a chance to reshuffle the deck, he'd marry her in a heartbeat.

Well, it wasn't to be. But that didn't mean he'd never see her again. As the rumble of the bus's approach cut through the clear morning air, Gene's right hand patted the three-inch circular lump in his coat pocket. He had to smile knowing that if his yearning for Stella should ever grew intolerable, he wouldn't be totally without relief. Though it might be a pale substitute for having her with him in the flesh, he could always treat himself to a glimpse, at eighteen frames per second, on The Platinum Loop.

EPILOGUE

Eighty-two-year-old Scarlett Cheston waited in the grim, sterile silence of her Alabama retirement community for almost two weeks following her last conversation with Ben Malton before she contacted the Los Angeles Police Department. She couldn't hold off any longer. Each day that passed without confirmation of the deed she'd hired him to perform was more torturous than the last. The notion that Malton had taken her money and run only grew more likely in her mind until it appeared as nothing less than a monstrous certainty.

Three difficult telephone calls were required to gather the information Scarlett sought. Once all the jails in both Hollywood and Greater Los Angeles had been scoured without turning up a trace of the missing private detective, she was directed to the city morgue. The old woman almost dropped the phone when she learned Ben Malton's body was found in a hotel on the dark side of Hollywood, the victim of a single gunshot wound to the chest. Voice quaking, she managed to ask the morgue attendant if any other bodies had been retrieved from the same location, and chewed the nail of her right index finger nearly to the bone as she waited for an answer.

Then, against all hope, words of salvation came through the long distance circuit. Three other men had been delivered in the same meat wagon with Malton. Two of the names meant nothing to her. The third was Eugene F. Hoffman, age forty-three.

Overcome with emotion mistaken by the morgue attendant for grief, Scarlett quickly terminated the call. Then she sat very still in an antique chair in the living room of her rear court apartment. A feeling of calm she'd long considered permanently beyond her reach descended in an almost dreamy wave.

Her granddaughter Barbara could rest in peace at last.

ACKNOWLEDGMENTS

Many people deserve thanks for their contributions to the existence of this book. Foremost, my mother, father, and brother for their consistent love and support. Erik Quisling, creative visionary and co-founder of a bold new media venture. My agent Svetlana Katz for her insight and dedication. Richard Amadril, who has a real knack for titles. Scott Kosar, Jace Anderson & Adam Gierasch for helping to bridge the gap from page to screen. And others, for many reasons: Dorothy, James & Lucile Williams, Russ Meyer, Michael Caulder, Drew Bourneuf, Daniel Peacock, Shura Dvorine, Debra Joy & Mark Schwartz, Eric Fulford, Jacqueline Dial, Todd Hallberg, Jeff Gilbert, Jensen & Andrea Rufe, James Otto Stack, Art & Jamie Strawbridge, Stu Toben, and Stefanie Vishab.

The background image in the cover artwork comes from an illustration by the great Earle K. Bergey for the Fall 1952 issue of *Thrilling Detective*. Cover design and author photo by Le Baron.